THE LAST DWEMHAR

J. T. WILLIAMS

DWEMHAR REALMS

The Last Dwemhar
The Rogue Elf #6

©2021 J.T. Williams

1
ICE

IT WASN'T the stark cold that struck his face or the jarring motions of Tulasiro jerking back and forth through what just a few moments before was calm ocean. It was a sudden heaviness in the air. A suffocating feeling Kealin didn't expect, and one that forced him to sit up in his boat. Debris bobbed in the rolling waves, and many seagulls flapped above them but just out of sight in the hazy sky. The only reason he knew they were there were their caws yet there was nothing peaceful about them.

They were in the northern Vindas Sea, near the straits not too far from the cove where he had first landed before he'd met Orolo. Before the memories he was trying to force from his mind. They had been traveling for several days since Eh-Rin. His sister's ashes were in a bag next to him. He reached down and pulled the strings of the bag. He wasn't sure what to do with the ashes but he had made a point to put the one bag with the ashes into another bag considering he didn't want them to get wet. Tulasiro continued pushing them through debris. He glanced up, not sure if he saw what he thought he did. He drew his sword and stood up.

Bodies floated ahead of them, and the flaming skeletons of broken ships littered the shoreline.

"Tulasiro, take us back out to deeper waters!"

They were headed toward a rocky cove. It was difficult to see if anyone was on shore, but the narwhal refused to turn even when Kealin lay on the bow of the boat and attempted to coerce the creature.

"We need to stay away from shore. We must get to the Glacial Seas."

But in a sudden motion, Tulasiro managed to roll the boat, forcing Kealin into the water. He rolled and found his footing, jumping up. He was nearly on shore.

"What are you doing?!"

Tulasiro disappeared under the surface just as horns sounded over the ocean. Kealin stared into the fogs, making out massive ships moving through the passageway.

"Grand Protectorate fools!" Kealin said aloud. As the ships went past, he tapped his silver hammer on the stones of the shoreline. A few moments later, Tulasiro emerged. Before he could get to her, she shook her horn as if telling him "no" and then began back north along the shore.

"Do you want me to walk to the northern cape?"

The narwhal stopped, turned in a circle, and then took off at a rapid pace, cutting through the water.

He had his answer.

Kealin made his way onto a rocky shore with high cliffs. Pulling himself up over several large boulders and then up a sandy hill, he soon realized he was much closer to the northern cape than he'd thought. He was near the fishing village and not too far from the home of Marr, the woman that was a Dwemhar descendant he had met before.

As he began into the stone hut fishing village, he saw the signs of recent destruction. Broken structures, skeletal forms on the rocks, and at least three people hanging on some gallows were like friendly reminders that nothing was as it was before. A truth he would learn more of soon.

As he walked past broken fish-drying racks and noticed the house he knew to be Marr's, his desire to go north was pushed down by his curiosity. He felt drawn to it.

As he touched the door, a vision came to his mind.

He saw a pathway beyond the house and a triangular stone.

Dwemhar warrior, come to us. Come to us now. The voice was frantic but direct.

He looked around the edge of the house and followed the path as if his vision was literally just what he was about to do. As he crested over the top of a small hill, he came to a rocky outcropping and a small stream running toward the sea. He glanced around, kicking aside blue flowers growing over the many large rocks, and eventually saw the triangular stone he was looking for. As he touched the stone, the ground transformed to that of a glowing prism, and in a flash, he was in darkness.

Before he could even attempt to move forward, a single flame appeared.

"Kealin of the North." the voice said.

"Yes."

The voice wasn't female, so he was not sure who he was speaking to.

"You do not remember me, friend, I am sure, but you helped me once. You and two other men."

As the flame moved to the right, suddenly a torch was lit and the narrow passage they were standing in became alight. Kealin saw the man who spoke. It was Eurna, Marr's brother and the captain of the *Dismal Rain* of the Highland Navy.

"Much has changed in the world," he said with a careful embrace to Kealin.

Kealin pushed his hand from him. "I feel a bit tricked. I am heading north; frankly, I didn't need to hide in here. I thought Marr needed something. A moment of weakness on my own account."

"Marr is well. I was thankful we were able to hide before the raids became too much. I was able to get my father to this place, but his ailment has worsened." Eurna motioned to Kealin to follow him. "We have all been meditating since my father spoke that a stranger was coming this way. When Marr saw your face in her vision, we knew some things were making sense. Father wishes to go north; he says it is our duty."

"There is nothing in the North but death," Kealin said.

"Some would say that of the South. I would say that of here. So, in truth, there is death everywhere."

Kealin had little he could say to that.

Eurna led him down a large chasm to an eventual open cavern with a small structure overgrown with mushrooms.

"This place is Dwemhar; at least, part of it."

"Our father has learned much of our ancestry in his worsening days. It is fate that Marr had a house so close to such a place, and even more fate that you have arrived. He will be excited to know one of your power is here."

Eurna led him to a door made of a white wood. As they approached, the door opened on its own.

As they both entered, the door sealed behind them, and the ceiling of the cave suddenly shifted to that of a night sky. Kealin paused, looking up.

"It is what is comforting to him," Eurna said. "Within this place, he could see so many things across the lands and project what gave him comfort to the ceiling above, if you could call it that. Marr thinks we are in a protective realm."

Proceeding forward, Kealin looked around and saw the simplest places. This was not like the Dwemhar ruin he'd found during the war against the orcs, nor was it like the place his sister had taken him to before their attack on Fadabrin. This was a hideout in almost the purest of senses. Aside from random supplies, there were a few food stores, including a half-eaten loaf of bread. Just a few paces from there, he saw Marr on her knees beneath an elevated platform where a man lay covered in gray blankets.

"My sister," Eurna said, "the stranger we were waiting for has arrived."

Marr turned. Catching Kealin's eyes, she suddenly smiled and jumped to her feet. She bowed and then looked up, continuing to smile.

"I saw your coming. But I also saw much sadness. Standing in your presence, I can feel that you see all of this as a roadblock to what you truly wish to do now."

Kealin could not deny that what she said was correct. He went to speak, to say what his mind wanted him to. It was what he would normally have no issue doing, but the old man, the father of both Eurna and Marr, suddenly turned his head and looked out at him before he could say a word.

"Half-elf?"

Marr looked down to her father before hurrying to his side. Eurna moved past Kealin to join his sister.

Though his children were there ready to serve him at a moment's need, he looked past them and to Kealin again.

"Come to me, boy."

Kealin walked forward and bowed in respect of the elder before him, not that he was technically elder to an elf. He sensed the power of his ancestors surrounding all who stood there.

"My daughter tells me you came from the Far North, the Glacial Seas? You're one spoken of well before now, protected by the Stormborn, the inheritors of our people's vast knowledge and technologies."

"Father, you're not making any sense," Eurna said.

"I make sense to those who actually know, my son. You have done well as a captain within the Highland Navy, but you know not our embraced ancestry. Your sister embraced it before you, and then after we were pushed into hiding, your eyes began to slowly open. But this man," he said, reaching out a shaky finger and pointing at Kealin, "this man has moved beyond all. I cannot say for sure if he even cares about my words. I can see into his mind the fact that beyond heartbreak, he has more anger than I felt a single being hold for some time."

"My anger is rightful. My zeal against the cause of my anger is the purest that it has ever been."

The old man shook his head. "No, anger is a contrived emotion of one's own mind. None can force you to feel and to think that which you are thinking. But I think you already know this. The loom of death is over your heart and mind. Very few can make proper decisions when their vision is clouded. Your powers were awakened well before this day slumped, but how often have you worked to restore the mental energies, to meditate and truly release the pain? I would gather that you've only pushed to increase the physical adaptations of our ancestors. That is not enough, my friend. But since you're here, we can begin to make things as they should be. There is a calling upon the air, a sweet music from the North, and now with you here, we shall proceed together as ancestors of the lost race and finally complete the awakening prophesies of before."

The man suddenly sunk back down. His body

seemed to relax, and unlike before, he was now snoring loudly.

As Marr rubbed his forehead and placed some kind of balm upon his chest, she bowed her head. Eurna turned to Kealin and simply smirked.

"Please tell me some of this makes more sense to you than it does me. My sister has always kept to herself. Our father was ill for as long as I can remember, and that couldn't be a concern I had time for. Most of my crew was killed in an engagement with the Grand Protectorate navies a few months ago. It was a massive fleet, larger than I had ever seen. I knew many of my men simply deserted to protect their families at home. It is only a matter of time before even I myself would be forced to hide. She told me, my sister, she told me you were headed south. That you had the blood of our ancestors within you, but not much else."

"I didn't tell her much else. It was not pertinent to the small amount of interaction I had with her."

"I see." Eurna nodded, making a point to stare his armor up and down. "You have seen battle? You have armor unlike any I've ever seen, and I have sailed many seas. It is untruthful to say that you are who I expected my father kept going on about when he mentioned a prophesied person. I remember you. I remember you with your friends when you boarded my ship." He paused. There was a change in his tone as if he already knew what his answer was to the question he about to ask. "Is everyone dead?"

"Many. Many more from a senseless war, or that's how it is in my mind now."

Marr tucked blankets around her father and then joined Eurna and Kealin. "You must be thirsty, yes? Like last time?" she asked him.

Kealin shook his head before Eurna tapped him on the back. "The new wine, if you prefer. Some washed ashore a few weeks back."

Eurna went over to an overturned barrel and pulled out half a bottle of dark wine. As Kealin and Marr took seats on a stone pillar that had likely fallen over many thousands of years ago, Eurna poured them each a glass and sighed as he set the empty bottle down.

"Our father has worsened. There were many fairies here when we came, and while they helped prolong his life, he has actually been in a deep sleep for many days now. He only regained consciousness upon your presence."

"I cannot help people," Kealin said. "I feel the powers of this room, yes, and I am much more than I was, but soon I do fear death comes for him. The organ of the god called Vankou takes place in my own mind as if it is almost a constant ringing. You do not understand the death that has followed me. My brothers, my sister—" Kealin closed his eyes, feeling a burning pain in the center of his chest and straight through to his back. Tears squeezed outside his clenched eyes, and he quickly moved his hand to wipe them. "I am cursed. When I first left my home, I was so desperate to save those I love that I awakened something. I released death itself, a creature isolated on a barren island in an old tower. A skeletal form playing an organ that even now I can hear. Death is still there. Death seeks me, so I will seek Death. It started with a captain like yourself," he said, looking at Eurna. "We tried to get to Valrin, but I should have known then that our path was cursed."

"No path is a curse; no curse can hold you as you're claiming," Marr told him. "You are Dwemhar, you have the blood of our people, those that mastered their powers and ascended."

Marr stood up and went over to the corner of the ruined room and picked up a tattered book. She returned to move her barely drank cup of wine to open the book.

"There were several books in this place. This place once had a grand tower upon these rocks. Back when I understand that there were not seas in the north as there is now. This place became a hideout and sanctum for someone of the lost race. Someone of power. These were his journals."

She flipped through several pages, scanning them with her finger and mouthing words Kealin could not understand.

"Here, he writes of the great flood and even well before, and then a sign of future events and a return of those that left or were to leave. I am afraid... I am not sure what he wrote. The page is ruined. He then writes of a prophecy, a Stormborn, a man or woman meant to play a part in awakening the great race but he writes it as if it was dream of his and not a set event. He also mentioned a false belief but then there is nothing."

"But this is one of many problems with this lore,"

Eurna said, pointing with his finger at her. "You just said the lost race ascended."

"I did, and they did, but there's more elsewhere in this book." She grabbed another book that was sitting nearby, "Many ascended, some fell away, and the civilization as a whole was fractured. The Stormborn was supposed to come for another. Another that would awaken and start a chain of events that would play a massive part in the renewal of the world. The gods sealed away death, and we do not know why, but it was necessary that Kealin release the god. It is part of the cycle; everything is the cycle in our world. Birth and death are the most natural acts within these realms that we can partake in. There is an awakening, an awakening of those sensitive to it. We are being called north, and we must go. Our father has become more and more ill through the years, but I think his entire condition is prophesying something more."

She stood up and began to pace. "While in deep states of meditation, I've seen something coming. The race of men was never meant to gain the power they have in this world. I say that knowing very well, Eurna, that our mother was human and our father is mostly human, but there is a great evil, and it involves the weak minds of men. They do not value knowledge like this; they value wealth, lust, and all forms and potential forms of power. I fear what comes but we must act before it is too late."

"Men cannot be stopped. I tried," Kealin said. "Old prejudices and rivalries destroyed the elves in the Western lands. It was not the work of their sworn enemy that did so, but men. This world is tearing itself apart, and in the ruins, all the races of magical power will be destroyed."

"But that is what I wish to tell you," Marr said. "There is something we can do. We must go. You consider it your luck that you ended up back here?"

"No, I consider it the fact that my narwhal dumped me out to the water here and I just happened to find Eurna. I was headed north; I am still headed north. But I will not take any with me. As you continuously say that I must understand and believe what you claim, believe me when I tell you that those around me will die. I can stop this. I will stop this, and I will not partake in any action except that which destroys the one I seek to kill. There is nothing that we must do together. You do not know my story."

Kealin stood up, finishing his wine before placing the cup back down.

"So, you're just going to leave? You're going to flee from what you know must be done?"

"I know what must be done, and I intend to do it. Just stay with your father. Enjoy what time you have with him. If he is hearing the sweet songs of the North, then soon, he will depart this world."

Kealin began to walk out of the hideout, when he felt a tinge of energy in his mind. He turned to see their father standing. At first, neither Marr nor Eurna noticed, but upon Kealin staring in that direction, they both turned, and Marr jumped to her feet.

"Father!"

Kealin turned to see their father standing up and pointing at him.

"Kealin of Urlas, you must go north to complete what you seek. But you do not know what you truly seek yet. All of this has been constructed beyond the understanding of those within the living realm. Let not the Stormborn's death be in vain. Let not the sacrifice of your siblings be in vain. It is I who sent you along this path, not death, but death will claim you, and you must know that the seas you left are not the seas you return to. That which was so strong has fallen weak. That which was of light has darkened. Many roads converge in the path ahead, and to continue upon the path you choose within your own mind even as I speak is folly."

Their father stumbled backward, striking the back of his head on the stone he was before lying on before. As Eurna and Marr ran to pick him up and check for any injuries, Kealin stood there, staring toward them but deep in his own mind. He could see another path, and in the strangest of sights, he could see his old home, the hut where the shaman was, and two white eyes within a smoke-filled chamber staring at him in a most uncomfortable way. This was who truly spoke to him. It was not their father but yet through their father, he had received words of the shaman of Urlas.

For a moment, he had a spark of clarity, and a feeling came over his body, a peculiar tingling from his fingertips down to his toes. A binding energy brimmed through the very room he stood within, and he could see a link between Eurna, Marr, their father, and himself. He closed his eyes and witnessed vast energies spinning within the North, drawing in power from the rest of the world. But then, a sudden blast of cold struck him center chest, and his ears filled with the organ of Vankou. A shrill sound tore into his mind, and he fell to his knees, grasping his head, crying out.

His eyes blackened. All that he could see before him was twisting icy winds of snow and a barren island, with the lone tower of Vankou suddenly before him. He saw himself ascend to the pinnacle of the tower, and there upon his organ sat the god of death, laughing. To his horror, he looked around the god and saw the hanging bodies of his siblings. He suddenly saw Alri's face as she reached out to him.

"Brother, why did you forsake me?"

"I didn't," Kealin said, almost begging for her to believe him.

Vankou began to laugh, and then Kealin's vision began to clear. He could see a bloodied face staring at him, and at first, he thought another vision was upon him, but it was Eurna and Marr's father.

"Perhaps I was incorrect?" the elder man said. "There is a mark upon you, and I do not mean the marks of death magic on your arm. Kealin, I know that I was speaking to you before, but that was not me as myself speaking to you. It was another. Another like us, perhaps. I am sick with a sickness that I do not think has a physical cause. My body is alive, but my mind is even more alive. We are going north. Perhaps not as my children and I would prefer with you by our side. But all is as it should be.

"I have faith that our paths, regardless of our next meeting, will cross and continue together. You've seen events beyond us and spoken to those beyond our world. Do what you must, Kealin. You must do what you must. Our will is the only true freedom we have. Be it for light or dark, life or death, for selfishness or for benevolence, true freedom is within your own mind. I have seen the future"—he looked over to Marr and Eurna—"and I am overtaken with fear. I cannot say for sure that my path is the absolute path to what small chance of true victory any of us have. But I will trust in the workings of the Great Poet. I feel as if in my sickness, in a near eternal slumber, I have embraced the mindfulness akin to the great Creator." The elder man chuckled. "My children once thought I was crazy. But now they see." He smiled, and Kealin looked over to Marr's smile at her father. Eurna seemed baffled and almost angry at the interchange, but was not angry at Kealin or anyone else but his own confusion.

"Son, you are a skilled captain in one of many to go up on the Glacial Seas. In my visions, I also saw another skilled captain, and that captain Kealin can tell you of. He was called Stormborn, as Marr has discovered in the journals of a once Lord of the Dwemhar, all paths are truly converging. You must grasp what we are being led to, or I fear the ever-growing darkness upon all of us will overtake the world. This place we hide in was truly the last hideout of a Dwemhar Lord, I do not wish it to be the place I leave this life."

Their father suddenly began to rock back and

forth. His face was white and he was sweating, struggling to take a breath. Eurna and Marr helped him to lie back down, and began tending to his wounds. Kealin still stood in a state of unsureness. Now he felt as if his path made some form of sense beyond simple vengeance.

A few moments later, both Marr and Eurna began packing supplies, wishing to head north as their father had desired. As he wondered of his own direct path, Kealin questioned as to how they planned to go that direction, too. He had seen no ship outside.

Kealin followed Eurna away from the area where Marr was gathering supplies. They went straight down a narrow stairwell further into the ground. As they descended, Kealin noticed that there were several panels of writing that he could not understand. As he slowly passed his hand over the engraved marks, Eurna turned and laughed.

"Now I understand," he said, "Marr and you do have some kind of connection. She's been wasting away every night going over all the possible meanings behind every single rune in this ruin. It boggles my mind. Sailing is perfect. It is something unlike anything else. It's just you and the ocean. Sure, I have had men under me and I've been in battle, obviously. But there is a simplicity I so thoroughly enjoy. The wind blowing over the bow of the ship, the salty surf blowing up as a red sunrise meets you after a hard night of sailing through a storm. I just can't explain it. My sister doesn't like stuff like that. She has always been different. Aside from being a fisher and never taking a man, she's always had interest in the history of the ancient writings of our bloodline. We were always secretive about our origins. The Dwemhar were not exactly welcome, or more so, they were welcome, but no one believes you when you say who you are, and immediately they have distrust."

They came to the end of the long stairwell, but it immediately turned into a large open cavern. There seemed to be no way out of this cavern, but as they approached a large round rock, crystal lights across the expanse of the cave came to life and splashed a golden glow upon everything.

At this moment, Kealin noticed a ship at moor in what appeared to be a large underground lake. On the far side of the room was a single slab of stone that looked as solid as a rock around them, but that was the first object Eurna pointed at.

"Those rocks can split and allow a ship in or out. This place once housed many ships, or so I assume. While I'm not into whatever writing my sister looks up, I found quite a few descriptions of massive ships that once sailed the sea. And this," he said as they came to the water's edge.

Kealin noticed that there was a small boat locked into the dock. The vessel was not of elven, dwarven, or of the race of men in design. It was something else. It actually reminded him of the *Aela Sunrise*.

"I have not figured out how I can release this vessel

from the locks that hold it," Eurna told him with a bit of frustration in his voice.

Kealin noticed that the small craft was secured down with stone blocks.

"There wasn't much information about this or any of the other vessels once housed here, but there are so many miraculous drawings in some of the books we found. Ships that could even fly! Can you believe such crafts actually existed?"

Kealin smiled and stared down. He thought of Valrin. The captain had given his life for them back in the Glacial Seas. He remembered that ship, the *Aela Sunrise*. He then looked up at Eurna. "I can because I've seen it."

"What?"

"I have seen a ship like that you describe. When my journey began, I met a man who sailed the seas for his entire life. I did not know then, and I don't know if he knew what he had, but the ship he had was capable of doing exactly what you describe. I guess he did have a Dwemhar ship but just didn't know it. He was like you." Kealin noticed the man's demeanor perked up as he said that. "Like you because he was alone without a crew. His crew had died sometime before I met him."

"So, this man, this captain like myself, did he go down with his vessel?"

Kealin shook his head. "No, he did not. His vessel was sealed up in the North by some power of magic or technology. He was killed by a dwarf. Rugag, a pirate of the Far North."

The two of them stared at the water. His ship, the

Truest Bliss, seemed to have earned a few more scars before was brought into the secret cove. A large section of the deck had been upturned and only hastily patched. One of the sails was quite tattered but still looked capable of catching the wind. Eurna went to the bow of the ship and seemed to be examining the keel itself.

"Working to reinforce the ship to be able to break through the ice. The ocean in the North is not so forgiving."

"You should do well for some time," Kealin said. "There is not much ice until you get much farther north than this."

"Much ice." He laughed. "Yes, I think you've been gone for too long. The seas of the North have changed. The winds are colder, and the snowfall, once you are a few hours' sail from the cape, comes so quickly, you think it will fill your ship and sink you, though I only saw that once before I turned back. It seems not even the Grand Protectorate will chase you in that direction. Not anymore, at least. For a while, they were sailing north fairly often."

"Perhaps it was a winter storm?"

"No, the Glacial Seas have changed. And I don't know what has caused the change. I know you do not believe everything my father said, or perhaps you do, but there's something wrong."

Marr joined them, carrying a large box of supplies. From what Kealin could tell, it looked like mostly blankets and other supplies to keep warm. As Kealin assisted her in getting onto the ship, he noticed that there were already many supplies stowed away.

"You were already planning on going north?" Kealin asked.

"Yes," Marr answered. "We have to. I was hearing a calling myself before my father ever mentioned it. But when Eurna here dreamed of the Glacial Seas, then we knew. Your arrival today has just spurred on our knowledge. Will you come with us?"

Kealin walked away from them. He began to pace along the water's edge, already knowing his answer, seeing that both of them strongly wished company. He closed his eyes and saw flashes of his sister's face as she fought the inner demon of the fallen god. It haunted him. He began to hear the organ of Vankou play in his mind, and his eyes flipped open.

"I can't. I must . . . I must end this. It will be a journey beyond what either of you or your father can partake in."

"It's not like we actually know where we are going in the North," Eurna pointed out. "We can go with you to this place. We can help you do what you need to do. I'm as good as a sailor as I am with the sword. You have no one with you. Let us help you."

Kealin reached back and gripped the hilt of *Vrikralok*.

"The only aid I need at this moment is for those who value their life to stay away from me."

His words were harsh and to the point but conveyed perfectly how he felt. The time for soft conversation and hidden meanings was done. He looked at Eurna and Marr, seeing that his words had brought them further grief.

"I'm going to go. If our paths cross again, and if I survive what I must do, perhaps there can be more to this," he said, raising his hands toward them. "But for now, the only hope any of us have is for me to depart this place alone and do what must be done."

Kealin did not expect for them to say anything, and as he turned and began back toward the stairwell, they remained silent. He hurried back upstairs but, he felt a pulling to go back down to them. To join them going north and to combine their effort to do whatever it was their father wished for them. To answer the calling that he could not deny he felt. In the past few years, he acted with what he believed to be a rational thought, and everyone around him was gone. Though he did not know the fate of all his friends, and especially Jesia, he knew the action he was taking was not rational. He was going north for one purpose, and he found serene comfort in knowing just how irrational his actions were. Perhaps, for once, he would succeed in his goals.

As he reached the hideaway, leaving the stairwell behind, he looked over to see the old man still sleeping upon the stone. He walked toward the exit that would eventually lead him out of what he felt was a separate realm of protection, when just as he began to walk faster, his eyes went black and he could see only the image of the face staring at him. He could not distinguish the face at all. He attempted to speak but found his mouth would not move.

. . .

These are the footsteps of doom. You have been awakened and you must not ignore that within you. Have you not seen that you have avoided and ran from your purpose? How many more must die before you give in? There is not serenity in what you seek. There is no balance in such a short-sighted goal. You do have a choice, but will the decision before you result in a fate any different from that which is the desire of those you call your enemy?

He could suddenly see again. He looked over at the old man but noticed that he was still as he was before. Kealin looked behind him and found that he was indeed alone. He had had many experiences in his years since leaving Urlas, but never so many as he had while standing near the presence of this old man. It was time for him to go. Frankly, he could not deal with any more visions today or any day.

He now stood on the North Cape. Looking out at the ocean, he remembered this moment so many, many months ago. When he'd first come to this place, he'd had such hope. He was looking for a seer and the key to finding his sister. But when he found her, she was nothing as she was before. He reached into his pocket and took the small hammer, tapping it on the stone just as the surf rolled over it. Some of the water splashed up to his hand, and he felt an icy chill. A few moments passed, and his narwhal appeared with his boat in tow.

He wiped the tears from his eyes as he stepped off the rock and to his vessel.

"North," he said aloud to Tulasiro.

As the narwhal pulled him away from shore, he thought back to when he awoke beaten and bruised after his battle with the Itsu Priest. Back when the only thing he could see around him was sand, volcanic rock, and the small crab that fed him berries to keep him alive. As he lay back in his boat, he gave no thought to his lack of supplies or preparation. If any of the gods still desired him to live, he would be provided for. But he didn't expect their help.

Little time passed at all before he began to see the flows of ice like what he expected to see only in the furthest reaches of the Glacial Seas. Is was clear to him that something had changed since he had left these regions. The air was colder. Though, he had not been inundated with tons of snow as Eurna had mentioned. With the falling of night and the coming of the polar lights, he noticed the brightness and intensity to their undulating form was more incredible than before.

Master blesses us.

"What?"

He didn't expect Tulasiro to say anything, and her words were even stranger.

But Tulasiro was silent now, and Kealin could feel a slight pry into his own mind from his narwhal friend.

"Careful. If you keep trying to do that, I might accuse you of being Dwemhar."

No, not the ancient people. Mammal of the ocean. But more intelligent than most.

"Well, then, I am glad you know what you are. I would prefer if you did not drop me off in the next cove we come across. Aside from the water being quite cold, I would like to avoid any further distractions. It is only us now. We go to a place where you and I have never gone, but I know where it is."

To the sounds of the god? The pipes that vibrate the oceans?

"You can hear that as well?"

I can. The sounds are everywhere. I fear the place they come from. Master blesses us in time. You are not alone, friend. I and my kind are with you. They have missed us.

Kealin was not too sure what Tulasiro meant, but as the thunder of its tail underneath the boat propelled them further at an even quicker pace, he pulled his traveling hood over his face and attempted to sleep.

Kealin found himself standing upon polished floors. He was looking down.

"You have done well."

He could not look up, and his hands were gripping something. He looked down and trembled, attempting to force from his hands what they grasped. It was the head of his siblings.

"You have done well," the voice said again.

Still, he could not look up, and he could not release the heads. He glanced to his left and right but was limited by what his eyes would allow him to gaze at, and he saw only swirling red and black. He suddenly heard howling winds. There was a flash of gold light and another voice spoke:

"Do not fear the deep darkness and frigid cold, for it brings you closer to fate."

2
NOT AS BEFORE

Kealin's eyes sprung open. It was now morning, or perhaps later. Tulasiro had slowed her pace and seemed to be jerking back and forth. He looked around and noticed glaciers. He did not know how far they had traveled while he'd slept. He thought of the dream, but it faded from his mind as the sights around him became clear. There were tons of large standing stones and small beaches of white sand. The wind was blowing a snowdrift across the sands. The shore was bordered with thick ice. A bright blue hue just under the surface revealed that this part of the ocean was shallower than the waters he had been in; at least, in this area. As he moved to look around and try to gauge where the sun was, he noticed movement to his right. He moved his hand to his blade and drew the Dwemhar sword halfway.

Friends, the narwhal said.

Kealin trusted Tulasiro, but the sudden sight of many females walking upon random stones in the middle of the dark Glacial Seas was not a comforting sight. As they came to stop upon a large black stone island, Kealin was hesitant to leave his boat. Tulasiro released her grip on the bite ring and disappeared under the surface.

"I swear," Kealin said in a hushed voice, "I am done with your crazy antics, narwhal."

"Do not blame the creature," a strangely seducing voice said. "She follows the will of our god Meredaas."

Kealin looked toward where the voice came from and noticed another female emerging from the icy depths. She was like the mermaid he had seen many years before when they had just begun an adventure, as simple as they could have called it then.

"Do not leave me to walk alone, my elf friend. Come this way."

Kealin kept his hand on his blade as he began up the surface that crested before him. As he walked with a strange creature of Meredaas, he suddenly heard music, but not of the rancid organ that had haunted him for so long, but a sweeter sound. He noticed there were many of the other female figures singing in unison as they walked. It was at this exact moment he realized what was before him.

"You're a siren."

The female smiled. "Yes, and enjoy the sounds of the lovely voices of those around me, but you will not be entranced today. We do miss the many ships that would come to this region. It is no more now."

"What do you mean?"

"I do not know how to explain this in a way that your race can understand. But I can say it is just as if the temperature changes too much in one region and not enough in another, or if the earth will quake, creatures like myself know ahead of time. Just as if we can hide if we wish when someone nears our waters. But it is not my place or purpose to explain such mysteries to you. I am to offer you further passage on your journey ahead."

The siren walked into a small pool surrounded by shiny black stones that had a sliver of glowing blue in their center. She reached out her hand and brought it up toward the sky as if she were lifting an invisible chain. The water in the small pool began to bubble and roll, and a large oyster appeared floating before her. She moved her hand over the shell, and it opened, revealing at least ten white shells. Kealin remembered shells of this kind. The shells had the power to do many actions, but he did not remember white shells in the ones he'd had before.

"I know you are familiar with these," she said. "You will find that these are much simpler to use. If ever you find yourself in waters too frozen to move forward, throw this before your boat, and wherever in your mind eye you believe you are needed, a swirling portal within the water will take you forward. But beware, one such as yourself, haunted with that which is beyond yourself, must know that these waters will take you upon paths to reveal your true path."

"Oh? That seems quite a strange object to give me. Your god tells you to do this?"

"I do not pretend to know the will of my god or even why he would do something such as this. The shells were used by the Dwemhar long ago. Long before their great vessels were upon the seas, and frankly, I would keep them myself. But as the world changes and the seas become less habitable, I look forward to a time when I am safe. There is a protected place that I and many of my fellow kind are going to. You can just take my word that I do not trust any but my own. I do as Meredaas commands me."

She sighed. "Take your shells. Begone from my island. I need not another to take care of. If you desire to tell others of our location in order to hunt us for game, know that we will not be here much longer."

She pushed the shells to his hand and immediately turned away again. She stepped back into the water, and the others around joined her.

"Farewell, half-elf. Though I do not care for your kind, I do respect one who would try what you are attempting. I, too, have sought of taking paths of suicide."

The siren disappeared with the others of her kind. Kealin looked down at the shells in his hand and clenched his fingers around them. He put them into a small pouch and turned back to where his boat was. Tulasiro had already returned and was waiting for him.

"One more time, Tulasiro! You do not need to leave me. Just simply wait for me!"

As he sat down into his boat, the narwhal pulled him away from shore and began snaking through the shallow waters near the glaciers, taking a path he already had discovered to get back up and going along the open sea to the north.

The sirens were leaving the Glacial Seas. The thought of creatures choosing to leave a place already so desolate for safety truly boggled his mind. It didn't make any sense. This place had always been so cold and remote that few except those used to this environment would even come this way.

"What does your master say of these times, Tulasiro?"

But the narwhal did not respond. In fact, it seemed to try to dive deeper under the depths almost as if to avoid his question.

"Listen, your master's influence is not absolute over you. If you know something, it would probably be of benefit for you to tell me as well."

Master has spoken nothing. Much death within these waters. Much death comes for us.

The narwhal's words were haunting. He did not know what to make of his current situation, but he knew only that he must continue north.

The seas were tumultuous. The waves were growing, and large chunks of ice cracked against the shell of his vessel. Tulasiro was increasing their pace, pulling away from the larger chunks of ice and breaking through the spots where the sea was beginning to solidify using the enchantment on her head.

The clouds stirred above them. To say the sea was simply angry would not do the sea justice. As they crested over another wave, Kealin began to see what looked like mountains in the distance. But these were no simple mountains of stone. They were walls of ice, glaciers stretching as far as the eye could see, almost as if they were impassable walls literally frozen into the waters. Kealin looked in either direction, hoping to see a path or way around. But there was no path; at least, not here.

Ocean shifts. Ice shifts. One moon, the way is blocked. The next moon, it shifts and moves. One path disappears while another appears. That is the songs sung beneath the surface.

"So, there is no way around this wall?" Kealin said.

At first, Tulasiro swam in a circle, sending clicks under the surface. Kealin looked around, not knowing how else to help at the moment. The narwhal stopped swimming. It seemed to shake its head but not simply in protest. The creature could not tell a path ahead.

The path is not open to us. We must find another way.

Kealin stood up and pulled out one of the white shells. He expected to use these, but maybe not this quickly.

"How do I use these? Think of my destination, and I will be taken to it? Well, I will see if the siren's gift is of use to us."

At first, he thought to his immediate destination. He envisioned the tower of Vankou. But the shell didn't do anything. He tossed it in the water. Nothing. He thought instead of simply open water beyond the wall of ice before him. This time, the shell began to glow and vibrate violently, nearly bouncing out of his hand.

He tossed the shell into the waters before him, and there was a flash before the waters began to swirl in place. A moment later, a bright shining light appeared on the surface. Without any command, Tulasiro pulled them forward, and they entered the portal. After a single flash, Kealin could see the ocean again. He turned and looked behind him to see that they were on the other side of the massive mountains of ice. It was almost just as he had imagined. The shells worked.

It was strange to Kealin being now on the other side of the icy wall. This side was sheer as if it were carved and shaped to form a literal wall. They had made it to the other side, but the downside to this was there was nothing before them. Where before there were storm clouds high above, twisting and turning, there was now only silence and steel-gray clouds. The air seemed heavier and colder. Every few minutes, Kealin heard something like a howl on the wind. On several occasions, he thought he even saw something flying out of the corner of his eye, but then he'd look and see nothing there.

Though he could not have any idea where he actually was, the oceans here were eerily calm. The further they traveled as a waning moon dipped below the horizon again, the further away from the memories of his last few years he felt he was. His worries, fears, and anger seemed to be floating off from his mind. His focus returned. He could hear the organ of Vankou playing, but it did not drive him to near insanity as it did before. Instead of simply staring at the surroundings or dwelling on his memories, he closed his eyes and began taking deep breaths. He had not meditated in some time. As he took deeper and longer breaths, holding each one before exhaling nearly as slow as he had taken in air; the cold fled from his body. He could feel a burning warmness within himself. What remained of his armor had not been broken in the battle before Eh-Rin, seemed to come alive. From the tips of his fingers, up his arms, through his chest, and down to the rest of his body, he could feel the tiniest of vibrations. Then, at the pinnacle of what felt like a sudden building peace with him, he felt a sudden grip upon his skull from afar.

It was like before but yet different. His eyes were open, and he only saw blackness. He again saw polished stone before him. He looked down, and now his hands were covered in blood as the heads of his siblings that he grasped began to turn and look at him.

You have done well.

It was the same voice. It was the same place he had seen before in the vision. Again, he tried to look around. But his head would not move. He then heard the sounds of battle. Swords clinging upon swords. Warriors shouting. His vision shifted, and he suddenly was standing in knee-deep snow with a long Urlas blade in his hands.

"Advance, elves. Do not let them break our lines. The Hammersong have them flanked."

It was an army of elves. He looked up, and all he could see were white shrouds with glowing red eyes in the dark clouds above his brothers. There were thousands of them. He suddenly felt himself pulled forward and a flash of white crossed his eyes. He was still in the same area just a different point in time.

He looked as if from afar. Many elven archons were within an inner circle with their staves up high. In an outer circle were blade-wielding elves. The archons blotted outs flashes of arcane fire falling from the heavens, their wards flashing and shattering as fogs rolled over them. Screaming split the air, and he could no longer see his elven brothers. He saw a dwarf fall to his knees only a few paces from him. He was grasping his throat, but he had no obvious injuries. He had not been struck by any weapon.

The ground quaked, and a sound as if from a broken horn caused him to fall to his knees, driving his blades into the ground.

Around him, his kin retreated.

"We must fall back to Urlas!" a familiar voice shouted out.

He turned to see his old master Rukes, the one who had taught him so much of blade work in the Urlas woodlands.

He then saw his master, his blade brimming with energy as he spun in place, striking down multiple shadowy creatures. Two more elves fell beside him, and he grabbed one of them by their armor, dragging them toward a shoreline. Here, there were other elves and many boats.

"It has come!" one of the archons shouted. "The beast that freezes the sea! We must destroy it."

"No, my brother," Rukes said. "This is all folly. This was meant to destroy us. The visions were wrong. We will find only more death. We must retreat to Urlas and hope that we can reseal our realm."

Fire and fogs rolled over Master Rukes and the others. A piercing wail tore through the air, and Kealin jumped to look behind him. In the shroud of fog, all he could see now were massive burning red eyes. A mouth, or where a mouth should have been, opened and was like a fiery furnace, but the growing massive entity was larger than the Dagarok beasts of the undead army, larger than even the king dragon he had slain. This was something else. His eyes flashed again. He was again in the hall of polished stone, holding heads of his siblings. He tried to look up, and just as he thought he might be able to look at whatever spoke to him before, he was struck in the head.

He opened his eyes and found that he was not only struck in the vision but also the waking life. Tulasiro had beached him again. But unlike before, she had not fled and left him alone but yet was rolling in the water and was struggling to swim. He looked up and saw that they had come across a barren rocky beach. The snow here was thick on the rocks, but there did not seem to be anyone or anything of note around them.

Kealin pushed himself up and attempted to figure out where Tulasiro had been struck. The narwhal began to roll onto the rocks, and Kealin noticed a large spike of some sort in her underbelly.

"Hold on, hold on. Be still!" He grasped what appeared to be a piece of wood and pulled it from her hide. It was no mere shard of wood but a spearhead. He looked at his friend and noticed that Tulasiro had calmed down greatly. He pushed against the narwhal back into the frigid waters. Tulasiro swam around and came back up to greet him.

"Are you good? What happened?"

I am okay. Cruel fisher spear.

Kealin looked around and noticed a heavy fog on the water and assumed it likely had affected Tulasiro, and while trying to navigate the actual fogs, she happened to run upon a spear.

As he looked at the spear, he noticed that the head itself was etched with elven ruins, but he did not know of any battles that had taken place in the Glacial Seas. The fog before him was struck by a gust of wind. He looked upon something that he did not expect in the desolate oceans he found himself in. He had stumbled upon a battlefield, and the true horror of this place he would never guess.

He proceeded forward, curious what awaited him on the shoreline. There was a strange feeling about this place, a feeling he didn't know. With all the dead he had seen in his and his sister's war, he'd never felt an eerie presence such as this. As he went forward, he looked around at frozen hands reaching up. There were hundreds of elves and even a few dwarves who had all died seemingly together and from no obvious cause. Most of them had their swords in their sheaths or their axes to their sides. For a moment, he thought of the dragon of this region, the same dragon he and his siblings had released. It made sense at first but the further he got away from the shoreline the more he saw signs of a prolonged battle.

Then, after ascending a small hill a found an expanse of tents, mostly skeletal frames and covered in a thick coat of ice. Many supplies were simply untouched. Whatever death had struck this place, it was no simple attacking army. He looked back to shore and could see Tulasiro, but he was here for a reason, and he proceeded. The landscape was barren.

There were no trees, no high mountains, not even a tower or other sign of life. This place appeared to be a literal plain where, as he began across hills of snow, he realized he walked upon the bodies of his kin frozen atop one another.

He drew his Dwemhar blade and hacked away at the snow and ice, finding more of his kin beneath it. He did not know what he expected to find but he did it anyway. He took a few more steps and did the same, and it was here he found the hilt of a familiar blade. Though it was wedged in ice and not able to be lifted, he knew of these blades. He had had one until it was recently shattered. Urlas elves were at this battle.

Proceeding forward, he thought of his vision and realized that the events of the vision he'd had must've happened at some point long ago, or perhaps the winter snow was just that severe. But then again, he thought of Master Rukes. In all his years, Kealin had never known the seal upon the lands of Urlas to have fallen. Either this was indeed a long time ago, or Urlas elves and dwarven Hammersongs had come together to face an evil that Kealin did not know in the many years he had been away from this region.

He continued a fairly northern trek until at last, he could see the sea again; at least, a piece of it. To his left and right, all he could see was barren tundra. He worried risking himself to meditate again. He found no peace in the practice here. But he had to see more than what ice had covered. He sat down in the snow. Crossing his legs, he put his hands on his knees and inhaled the frigid airs.

With the severe loss of life and the trapped souls beneath the ice, it did not take him long before he began to feel what travesty had happened here. At first, his eyes flashed over with simply darkness, but then he saw a bright star in the night sky. The star came directly above him, and as the light of the star shined down upon the field, he could see a large assembled army of elves and dwarves. The dwarves were not of the orderly types from the South. There were far too few of the dwarves, and it was not a uniformed army but a ragtag group of widely random pirates akin to Rugag and his crew. But one dwarf wore adorned armor and seemed to lead the others. This was a Hammersong of the dwarven race. He spun his axe above his head, and the other dwarves shouted, lifting their weapons. There were many elves here, too. Their banners he recognized, for they were the same banners that his parents left under. Urlas had gone to war, and this place was where their war stopped. He could not see the enemy, for the snow came down too heavy in his vision. But he could hear the screams and then a distinct coughing. His mind immediately shifted to memory, and he thought of Fadabrin. He thought of the attack that came where those of magic were affected. He questioned if that same type of attack had came to those here. He lost focus, and the vision simply ended.

He opened his eyes to a sudden wail upon the air. He looked up at the clouds and could see a massively long creature of some kind. It was ethereal at best, with several specks of glowing orange crystal going down its back. At first, he thought it was turning to attack him, but instead, it just hovered above the battlefield. It seemed to be searching for something beneath it, and then it swooped down, sliding across the ice and up, turning metals and bones and ice as he grasped it with its body, and in a flash of fire, it seemed it was somehow fed by the wastes of the battlefield and took back to the skies over the ocean.

A deafening wind struck Kealin, and the stench of the dead filled his nostrils.

Kealin had felt enough. He had seen enough death, and this was like a punch to his throat. He wasted no time returning to Tulasiro. The narwhal was once again restless. As he boarded his boat, he took out a shell and thought of Vankou's tower. This time, the shell began to glow and shake. He must have needed to be beyond the icy wall before. Perhaps it was enchanted, but it didn't matter now. He paused for a moment and took a deep breath. He threw it into the surf, and in an explosion of light, the portal appeared.

The narwhal pulled them in, and they emerged again upon the open water. He saw the lone tower he had imagined for so many nights now. He did not know how far he'd been transported through the portal or how much time had passed, but a deep night was upon them. The stars were innumerable above him, and the polar lights lit up the ocean with a deep-red hue. As Tulasiro began pulling them toward the tower, a vibration shook the seas. The narwhal squealed. A shrill sound was on the air as the loud songs of the organ of Vankou began to play, reaching Kealin's ears. He looked at the single structure ahead of them as Tulasiro warily approached, obviously agonized by the sounds but not wishing to let Kealin down. The sounds were near deafening, and this time, it was not in his mind he heard it, but with his own ears. They had reached the place Kealin sought. Though he could not believe he had reached this place so quickly, he knew this would likely be the end of his journey to the north.

Approaching the island itself, Kealin noticed a large purple orb atop the pinnacle of the tower. Waves of energy rippled out from it, creating a swirling effect of clouds with periodic violet lightning that upturned the snow in flashes of strange luminescent fire.

Kealin closed his eyes as he moved his hand in the pouch that contained his sister's ashes. His mind immediately jumped from Alri's memory to Taslun and his undead form and the loss of the brother he once had in sacrifice now forced to return to this life that at this moment he didn't know if it was a good or tragic occurrence. Thinking further now, he saw the sight of

Calak as he was murdered at Dimn's palace by the Itsu Priest. He then thought of his youngest brother, the infant now lost to him. He imagined that he had been captured and very quickly carried off and ran through with a sword. He saw the faces of Ruak, Brethor, and then, Jesia. The images wrapped his mind in a haunting shadow and his breath was heavy in his chest.

Tulasiro halted the boat upon the shore of the island. Kealin stood up and smelled the air, which had a stench that he could not fathom being any worse. As he stepped off onto the snow, he turned to Tulasiro.

"My friend, I beg you to depart the shores and go with your kind. If I return, I will call you, but if fate would have me take another path and join my siblings, then it will be done."

He knelt into the water, and Tulasiro came to him. He rubbed the crown given to her by her master and placed his forehead against the narwhal's snout. "We've had many adventures, my friend. Perhaps, we'll have more, but if not, remember our time."

The narwhal squealed, tossing her head back and forth, scraping her horn on the ice. She did not wish to leave his side. She then stopped and made a long and sad sound. A wave of coldness unlike any of the frigid regions of the Glacial Seas had come over them both. Tulasiro sank into depths and slowly swam away.

Kealin stood motionless, staring at the tower in the distance. He closed his eyes, feeling the air around him, sensing the wraith-like ethereal beasts that haunted the air above the road, their forms bouncing across his path in the direction of the tower.

This will be done. These voices... I will not be tormented anymore, nor will the taker of life torment any others I call friend. The balance of life and death is not being upheld by the one who reigns over it. I released you. I will give to you what you have earned.

He reached for the sword on his back, drawing *Vrikralok*, the god-killing blade, the sword given to him by the dark god of the Itsu. Thinking of the twists of the allegiances of the gods of both the North and the South, he focused his thoughts on one form alone. He pointed the edge of the sword toward the tower.

I am here for you, Vankou.

He waited a moment for some type of answer, perhaps a jeer like what had happened when he'd departed from Brethor, but the god was silent.

Focusing his thoughts, feeling his energies surging from his Dwemhar powers, he exhaled a final time.

He ran, moving faster than he ever had, and as he came upon the icy beasts that guarded the lower ground of the tower, he swung his blade. These were the ice wraiths or, so they were called. They shrieked, swinging down to bite him as they did on his first journey here, but he spun mid-run, cracking into them with *Vrikralok*. Their bodies burst into the blue flames and fell to the ground. He did not lose momentum in his charge. He passed through the columns on the way to the doorway, the snow melting from the pure energy overtaking his body, further invigorating the fury he felt within.

As he came to the door, he did not knock. He did not wait for it to be opened. He slid to a stop, closing his eyes and lifting his left hand toward the door while his right hand held *Vrikralok* behind him. He summoned his powers, and with all the energies that he could focus at once, he lunged forward, sending a blast of raw magic directly at the tower, throwing the doors in and sending them against the opposing wall.

Immediately, he was met by the guardians of the tower. The skeletons that before had ignored him and his siblings came at him with cackling shrills, brandishing weapons of blue fire. *Vrikralok* sang into the base of the tower as Kealin smashed into each form, tearing their forms apart as he jumped from each of the creatures to the next.

"You defile our master's tower!" Kealin heard from afar.

Looking to the far side of the lowest level of the tower, he saw a massive skeleton constructed from a hodgepodge of random bones from animals and creatures that Kealin could wonder of what beast they were pulled from. In its right hand was a long staff burning with green flames that it thrust toward the ground, upturning the stone and ice with several summonings of dog-like creatures that were long dead. They appeared as if mostly dust clinging to the cold bones, yet still having all the fury of a pack of angry wolves, they charged Kealin. He flipped his sword down, stabbing into the ground, sending a ripple of energy out at the creatures that returned them to their rightful dusty forms. Kealin wasted no time with this greater adversary. He focused his energies, leaping up and then imagining himself just upon the creature's back. His Dwemhar energies shot him behind the creature, leaving it baffled. He brought *Vrikralok* down on his foe, thrusting the blade into its head and sliding down into the back of its ribcage. The creature crumbled into a burning white form, erupting with black blood as it fell to the ground in defeat.

The organ began playing louder and louder.

Are you ready to see her fate? Do you wish to see the death of yet another you loved?

Kealin growled, digging into the ground as he sprinted again toward the stairwell.

This was it. This was the last step.

He circled up the stairwell higher and higher, his sword now burning with a bright white light as his Dwemhar energies engorged the blade with power. For the first time in his entire life, he was doing exactly as he was trained back in the Urlas woodlands.

His blade master had always said to pick out the one of most importance upon the battlefield and drive his blade into his throat. In this ethereal battle encompassing his mind and physical form, he only had one opponent.

Finally, the voice of the organ played a crescendo as Kealin reached the top level, spotting the skeletal form of his enemy meticulously moving his hands above the white bone keys of the organ. He did not pause; he did not yell words of gloat or curse. Kealin Half-Elf of Urlas, brother to the fallen siblings he'd left with so many years ago, inheritor of a power beyond his understanding, accepted his fate as he hoped this bastard god was ready to accept his own.

He brought his blade down upon the head of Vankou. A white flash overtook the top of the tower, and Kealin saw through the white fires as Vankou screamed in agony, his bony form melting from *Vrikralok* and his skeletal form shattering into dust.

The white fire that was burning so brightly extinguished and became as black dust before erupting in a blue fire and dissipating.

The organ was silent.

Kealin exhaled. For a moment, he felt peace, but then, by some power unknown to him, the organ began to play once again.

He screamed, lifting his blade with both hands above his head.

He forced *Vrikralok* down upon the keys, shattering the instrument. But the songs of the god of death continued.

Not so simple will I be to destroy, you fool. You have only destroyed a part of me. You give me acclaim for that which I do not deserve the credit. You mere mortal are nothing to ones such as I. You bring about destruction with every step you take, but I know how to destroy one such as you.

Kealin was suddenly sucked back and pulled from the tower. Flying through the air, he watched the tower explode in a violent violet fire. The orb above the tower flashed, and suddenly, all the ground beneath him turned to ocean. He tried to focus, bringing about his energies to attempt to soften a landing that would at best likely knock him unconscious. He summoned his strength as he closed his eyes.

Nothing he had seen had been real, or if it had, it

was taken from this world into the realm of Vankou. The bite of the ocean was like a million spears piercing him at once. He could no longer focus. His energy was spent. He saw what he thought was Tulasiro in the far distance, and then he saw nothing else.

3
ENSNARED

Kealin was suddenly aware of himself. The very last image in his own mind was the pale sky above him with a cold embrace of the sea.

He tried to open his eyes but could not. He could breathe, and in breathing, he noticed the sweet smell of herbs. He forced his eyes open and saw only a faint light ahead of him, or perhaps he was only seeing mirages of something else. No, there was some kind of light.

He became aware of his entire body and a numbness that went from his fingertips down to his toes. He then felt soft hands moving up and down his chest and stomach, and it was then he could hear what sounded to him like a soft singing, but then he could not actually make out the words. His eyes began to see more, and he spotted the outline of a female. His first thought, his first wish, was that somehow everything had been a nightmare. He hoped to open his eyes fully and see Jesia and be back in Fadabrin.

But it was not to be. That time was gone.

"Kealin, you've been gone for such a time I had feared you'd died."

Kealin could still not see the female who spoke to him, but her voice was familiar.

"Tulasiro brought you to me on the brink of death. I was told of what transpired at the lone tower of darkness. I don't know if I can believe my friend, but as close as your body was to death, I'm inclined to believe so."

Kealin could see a figure coming to focus, and as he looked around, he could see the ocean, but he could not feel the cold of the air. There was a large red stone emanating heat directly to his left, and the female who had been obviously caring for him moved her hands over his body. He knew this person. It was a mermaid, the mermaid who had originally directed them to seek the shells of Meredaas during his first voyage across the Glacial Seas.

"I was brought here?" Kealin asked.

"Yes," she said, smiling. "Before you sit up and wonder what I have done with your weapons, know that all is here except for your sword."

Kealin immediately sat up, nearly striking his head on a low overhanging piece of driftwood in the home of the mermaid.

"Where?"

She pointed, and he noticed that his Dwemhar blade and clothing was sitting just a few paces away.

He went to stand up, and he suddenly stumbled, just caught by the mermaid and thankful that in her human form, she was nearly as strong as her mermaid form.

"What do you worry for? You jump up, nearly causing yourself more injury? I have already told you that all your items are safe."

"There was another sword, a larger one."

"A blade capable of killing gods?"

Kealin nodded slowly, surprised that she knew its purpose.

"It is safe. Tulasiro was able to retrieve it from the depths of the Glacial Seas, as it still floated down to what would've been an eternal resting place. The blade remains with Tulasiro and is waiting for you to grasp it once again. But know that though I understand what you seek, I do feel it is an ill-sought goal."

He lay back in the bed and pulled a blanket around his nude body.

"I have little to offer you in food, but you will find the broth here to serve all needs to nutrition you require." She spooned a strange red liquid from a rather small cauldron sitting on the other side of the glowing red stone. Kealin took it by the mouthfuls. His body was weakened and beaten; plus, he had not eaten in some time. The salty broth went down easily.

"Tulasiro tells me you came across a battlefield. So much has changed in the years since I last saw you. I had wondered what had shifted in the ways of the world, or at least, why the evil that was once enslaved to its tower had been freed. There was always such power there, but it left. It went somewhere else, like it was dormant, kept strong until a time. Now, myself and my kin, the sirens, are forced to flee the seas. But in truth, it is nothing you have done. Men from the South have used the magic of the dwarves. A magic once whispered in the seas, quelled by the one you know as Valrin."

"Valrin?"

She grinned. "There is much you do not know, half-elf. Much you were not told. Many who once lived upon the seas were subjected to horrid deaths as the forces of men tested what will eventually become the bane of so many. But it is beyond the simple weapon it once was. Men have found a way to the powers of the old Southern gods to poison all magic. I know what has come into our world in the deserts to the south. I fear what this means.

"So many paths are converging. The stars cross the sky in a way I cannot understand and interpret. I take only peace in knowing that my god has provided a place for me. In time, I fear the gods of the North will be the only hope for all magic. Elves, dwarves, and every person who uses magic in any form will only find safety together and as a unifying force."

"What do you mean?" Kealin asked. "You know of what was awoken in the South, the Itsu Priest, but the army of the Grand Protectorate has been fractured. I was there. That which destroyed so many of the elves of the Vumark Woodlands and the city of men of Vueric, and Eh-Rin, now are mere corpses in the dunes of the desert. I know for a fact that there is still an undead army, and many of the undead will fight to protect those of magic."

"So confident? So sure? I know little beyond the seas, but I know something that is brought back will care very little for those of the living."

"You do not understand." He pointed at tattoos on his arm given to him by his sister. "I controlled the undead, yes, but they became sentient. They are released from servitude to a necromancer."

"But you cannot say that they will guard anyone or anything. They have allegiances to themselves and perhaps you, at least for a time. Kealin, I'm not here to argue over the alliances and what is at risk. I am telling you that the Grand Protectorate came here. They raided, they pillaged, they killed. Something drove them to this. They were seeking to eliminate someone or something. The sacred realms that you knew, the ancient trees that you grew up beneath, are likely no more."

Kealin immediately thought of the Urlas woodlands and the shaman.

"Are you telling me they are all dead?"

"I do not know. The battlefield you came across is now known as the Weeping Stars of the North. Creatures of the ethereal now harvest that land for the bones and further increase the powers of magic in the world. But I cannot sense why.

"The elves and dwarves who fought the armies of the dragon, the creature you released, that which became as a mere pet of Vankou, has ravaged the land, seeking to destroy any who come within these waters. Most of the impure forms are dead, but there are greater beasts now. Creatures that have slept since the time of the Dwemhar have awoken as if hearing their master's call. The god Vankou never cared so much about such life forms, but nothing is as it was. All that no longer remains haunts those that do and the seas where my kind and I once found peace.

"Almost every place I once knew has been either destroyed or frozen. A deep freeze has taken over most of the waters, and while there are few survivors who flee, their lives dim, and I no longer feel any who once were."

The mermaid went to the door and opened it. A sudden icy gust sapped the warmth from the room.

"I have saved you," she said without looking back, "but I hope by being saved and understanding the world you are now in, you will abandon the stupidity of a narrow-minded pursuit and look to the greater world. I know the powers within you. I have seen that armor you have. I've seen at the bottom of the seas the armies of the Dwemhar who were destroyed in the cataclysms eons ago. I do not know what will happen, but if you started this as you claim in your own mind, I know you can end it."

Kealin stared into her eyes as they turned a sparkling dark blue. "I was once called the wife of Meredaas, and I bore all that became known as both mermaid and siren. I have formed that which became the narwhal, the whales, the Glacial sharks, and every creature within the seas. I crafted the shells you used to traverse these waters.

"I, at one time, had a palace in the Far South. I was betrayed by the Southern gods as well, and at the brink of death, I transformed myself into what you see now, but I was not always as this. You can curse the gods until your death, or you can embrace that you may not agree with their ways and what happened to your sister, knowing they are the only ones who will stand beside you when all falls to shadows."

The mermaid's eyes faded back to the strange light blue they were before. Her demeanor softened, and she grabbed his armor and belongings sitting them next to him.

"Tulasiro awaits you, Kealin. I invite you to go upon the seas once more and give thought to what truly should be your next path. The currents are moving you toward true fate, if only you let them take you. The sea itself is a living entity capable of protecting that upon it and within it. Trust these seas no matter how turbulent. They will guide you."

With that, the ground beneath the mermaid became as water, and the entire structure around him faded away, leaving only stone and his belongings. The barren rocky island gave him no shelter. He quickly got dressed, and taking his hammer in hand, he tapped the rocks on the water's edge, causing Tulasiro to emerge within moments with his boat in tow.

"My friend, thank you. That would have been the end of me."

It was, but my master saved you. My mother took care of you and restored you. I fear where we go now, but I am your friend, and I will go where you wish.

Kealin stepped into the boat and noticed *Vrikralok*. He paused as he grasped the hilt and thought of everything that had been revealed to him in what felt like just the last few moments. Was it all a dream? Was he hallucinating after striking his head? He slid his sword back into the scabbard on his back and sat in the boat as Tulasiro slowly began to swim away from the shore.

Everything was real. The world had truly changed. He thought of his home with some comfort, knowing those of his family had already departed this world, but he was shocked that a protected realm such as Urlas had already fallen victim to the evils of this region. There was a growing fear in his mind at what was spreading across the world.

For the longest time, he simply stared out to the water as Tulasiro pulled them through the seas. He closed his eyes, halfway hoping for a vision but also trying to feel what direction he should take. It reminded him of before when his sister was first missing. He could not decide one direction or the next, simply moving through the seas, hoping she'd been dropped off on some island like himself but finding very few islands and no sign of Alri. Now, that time seemed simpler.

As he continued to keep his eyes closed and attempted to open his mind to that which was around him, he felt a turbulent shift in the winds and a howl unlike any he'd heard before. Like some creature or spirit, a sudden storm slammed into them. There was something within the clouds; the titan of a storm had come out of generally peaceful clouds. Kealin saw what looked like massive icy arms spinning the storm around them. The ocean began to churn, and the wails became even louder. Tulasiro began to pull away from the storm with a hasty pace. Kealin could feel the creature's fear.

Do not fear, Tulasiro. Your mother has told me to trust the sea no matter where it leads us. I can trust that. We can trust that. We must.

Tulasiro still continued pulling them away from the storm. As they would crest upon the top of one wave, they would catapult off the other side. Kealin could see the narwhal's form emerging from the water before slamming back down in the lower parts of the wave.

Then came the rain, the sleet, and then literal pieces of ice slashing through the air, striking both him and Tulasiro. He tried to cover his head as best he could as literal hell came down upon them. He closed his eyes and did his best to form a ward of protection around both himself and Tulasiro. The continuous pain from the ice began to burn his cold skin. Now, they had to trust the Mother of the Seas. They were trusting the mermaid, and at this point, there was nothing else they could do. Tulasiro has stopped swimming. They were simply thrown in the surf. He felt the narwhal's body strike the boat, and he felt himself roll to the water. He thought of his magical shells, and now falling toward the water, he grasped and tossed one. The portal did not open, and a moment later, his boat struck him in the back of the head.

. . .

He came to again, and by some work of fate, he was not dead. He awoke on the black sand of a towering rocky island. While the rocks before him reached into the heavens, the island did not seem that large across. He looked to his left and saw the Tulasiro had beached as well, and he pushed himself, sloshing the icy water onto the back of the narwhal.

"Tulasiro!"

The narwhal had multiple bloody marks all over its body from the hail. The ward he had attempted to put around them was obviously not good enough. He had no medicine, and there was no mermaid this time. As the waters rolled over the narwhal, he looked around for something, unsure if trusting the seas even for a short time had been the folly that he feared once again. It was then he saw a single spark of light. It only caught his eye zooming past to his right. He stared and noticed it was a fairy. He knew little of actual apothecary methods or healing magic, but he knew a fairy had healing powers.

"I will return, friend. I will return."

The fairy ascended the rocky face of the mountain, and even though Kealin did everything he could to keep up with it, it vanished into a cave.

Kealin rushed to get to the cave opening. Pushing up a slight incline and climbing over several large stones, he hoped to catch the fairy before it completely disappeared. He could see the glow of the fairy further into the cave, but it fled around a corner. He drew his Dwemhar blade and stepped forward, using it as a faint source of light as he moved with one hand along the wall to keep his bearings. As he followed the path to the left, it seemed that the fairy had moved across a large open room. He felt another presence near him. He couldn't see, but he kept his hand on the wall and moved his sword around. The fairy was motionless, but it was at this moment that indeed a figure did appear, blocking the way from the cave.

"I have waited for this for such a long time that I did not expect it ever to come to pass."

"I want no trouble, stranger. I need help. My friend down on the shore is injured. I do not seek any treasure or anything that you have here. I just want the fairy."

"The fairy?" the figure asked.

Kealin could tell this was a man but nothing beyond that. It didn't appear that he had a weapon of traditional sense, but there was a slight glow just to the right of the figure, possibly a staff of some kind.

"That fairy is mine. You may not have it. This cave is mine. You may not have it. Much is mine. Much has been lost. You have taken from me before. You have taken from us."

"I do not know who you are, friend."

"I'm not your friend."

"I have little to offer you. What do you want from me? I only need help."

"Help? You need help? A friend of mine needed help, and you did not provide that. There are those of affiliation with myself who will not like this, but I have cared little about what anyone has thought for some time."

What was only a dim light before suddenly burst

into an orange flame. Kealin brought his Dwemhar blade up just as a figure struck him with something in the head. Then came a noxious fume in the air and it seemed that the figure had dispersed something like a powder in the air. Kealin swatted at the dust around his head but it was too late. He coughed and his eyes ran with sudden tears that clouded his vision.

Kealin swung his blade up just as a staff came down upon him, and the figure shoved him against the wall. Kealin reached out and grasped for the figure but then felt something slip up his arm around his neck. It was suddenly impossible to breathe. The figure's staff came back around, and after a flash of light, he saw that before him was an elf of some kind. But in what little arcane light he could see in the darkness of the cave, the figure became clearer but the constriction around his neck grew stronger, and he collapsed to the ground, unable to pull whatever it was that choked him from his throat.

He dropped his blade. He attempted to focus his powers, feeling it in his fingertips but then realizing his clarity was failing him as he was unable to take a breath.

"So simple you are defeated? This is no surprise that you are a failure. I see not why so many saw your coming. He was a much greater man than you. And you betrayed him!"

Kealin could barely see the man or elf talking to him. But it was a sudden arrival of another figure that caused this first person to step back.

"What are you doing?" a voice shouted.

This voice was much different and, in fact, was female. Her tone was harsh and quick. She shoved the first figure before reaching down and touching just above Kealin's throat.

"Get this off him."

Kealin felt whatever was wrapped around his throat loosen and slide off.

The female seemed to lift something just in front of his head, and he saw a small flash of magic, and his body felt extremely sluggish.

"What were you doing?" the female asked the other one.

"He doesn't deserve to live. He is dead because of this sorry excuse for an elf. He is dead. Do you not understand what part he played in that?"

"No, and neither do you. We know nothing of what happened beyond what is obvious to us. The master elf will return very soon, and when he sees what you have done here, he will not be pleased."

The figure made a motion in the darkness, and flames erupted in a pit directly in front of him. He could see the figures' features better now. The original figure was a male elf with extremely long ears, signifying that he was very old. But he was not an elf of Urlas or even of the southern lands; in fact, Kealin had never seen an elf such as this.

The female appeared to be of the race of men, but he could not be sure. She showed some affinity for magic but did not appear to hold any staff or enchanted item.

He did not know what she had done to him, but his hands felt extremely heavy.

The female knelt beside him. "You are safe. You are with those you should consider allies; I am sure you are who we wait for. The master elf would not expect you to know of us. We were not known to him when you left but many paths have led to this. Much has happened in the six years since your departure from Urlas. After what transpired, I knew I was going to meet you. I could feel it in the vibrations of the world. But nothing has been the same since then. Nothing."

The female picked up his Dwemhar blade. "This is an object of extreme power. I've seen armor such as this before, but it was only in books. I have studied much of the Dwemhar. I know you have questions. I can sense you are extremely confused. I've already dealt with the narwhal it will not trouble you any more."

Kealin suddenly was stricken with fear, wondering what she meant. Surely, she meant that she helped Tulasiro, but he could not be sure. He could not move but he could breathe much better now. He focused, drawing upon his power and feeling for control enough to grasp his blade.

She placed her hand onto his head. "Relax."

But he could not do as she wished. As he concentrated, he could see a similar energy around the being before him. At first, he felt relief but that feeling fled as quickly as it came. He did not know what she was or if she was friend or foe, but he would not be held here.

His eyes flashed white as his energy moved around

him, and though his physical body was stricken, his spiritual body became enraged, and he stood up, sending a single blast of energy away from himself.

The elf with the staff merely summoned an orange ward around himself as the female Kealin felt had a more potent power attempted to grasp him.

He rushed past her, seeing the entrance of the cave before him, when suddenly, he felt ripped from behind and turned slowly around. He tried to bring his hands forward, but he felt as if chains held him down. His back was bent backward. The female was holding her hands up, directing energy toward him. As she released the grip with her right hand, she then summoned a massive ball of fire as she walked toward him.

"Do not flee us in fear. It is fear that has brought about the fate which is the world we live in. Know you were not one of a kind, and know there are those who studied for much longer than you in the one thing that gave you an advantage as you went south on personal vendettas."

Kealin felt pushed down to the ground as the female walked up to his face with fire. The searing heat coming from her hand could only mean one thing. She was a Rusis, but he had never seen Jesia use power like his own.

"The master elf told us of where you went and why he could not tell us what happened to our friend other than he was killed. The one in the other part of the cave wants you dead, and I would be lying to deny that I have wished you dead as well. We lost a great friend after we risked so much to save you before."

The woman shoved her finger to his chest and turned and walked away. He could now control his body as normal, but he no longer had the same desire to flee. He did not know either of these figures and had no recollection of them in the past, though he felt as if, at least in part of his memory, there was something of them there.

"You saved me when I was younger? I do not know either of you."

Kealin heard footsteps behind him, but he could not make out the figure that approached.

"Kealin, it has been far too long, and even though I was told you were alive, I never believed I would see you again."

As a figure drew closer, Kealin realized who this was. He knew that voice. He had heard that commanding voice of guidance and instruction for well over two hundred years. It was the blade master Rukes from Urlas, his old teacher.

Kealin stared in disbelief at the arrival of his old master. The man was a shamble of what he once was. His clothing was tattered. His silver armor that adorned his chest was chipped and broken in pieces. It even seemed that in the time since he had last seen his master, his master had developed a limp. Master Rukes quickly moved toward Kealin and embraced him.

"I thought you were all dead. Everyone else is. Everyone, Kealin. I don't know how to explain to you what transpired in the years since you've departed, but then to discover by our own shaman that something haunted you, and he knew exactly why you had left, and frankly, I did not believe it. What have you been told?"

"Very little. I was attacked by the elf here and this female and her abilities raises even more questions."

Rukes nodded. "I will explain everything. At least, as best I know it."

Rukes moved into the inner part of the cave with Kealin following him. The two other figures walked to assist him to remove his cloak, and suddenly, he realized that his old master once agile and strong, had been severely weakened.

As Kealin joined him by the fire, he tried not to make it obvious he was staring at him and his injured form.

"A result of the war, I am afraid. I took a blade to the back of my leg, attempting to take down one of these beasts. The enemy is not anything like what I have fought in the many wars before. They are spiritual beings; they do not have a skeletal form that you might expect. I say that because we knew at the time it was an ethereal form that moved against us. It is the god of death. While he does have minions of smaller stature in great numbers, it was the larger ones. The larger ones that have red eyes."

Master Rukes stared into the flames.

There was silence for a while before the female stranger suddenly spoke. "We have told him nothing . . . nothing beyond that we had saved him before and that things were not as he understood. We did not know what he could be told."

Master Rukes rubbed his face. "None of it matters anymore. He needs to know the truth."

"What happened to Urlas? How did they get into the sacred realm of Urlas?" Kealin asked.

"Should you not know?" the strange elf asked. "From what I understand, you went to the realm of the god. I would think you as the great warrior Dwemhar, the one that was coming to save all of the living realm, would have the wisdom to know such happenings as that."

"Now is not the time, Evurn!" the female said.

Kealin looked up at the face beyond the glowing fire.

"Evurn and Aeveam, two companions of Valrin at a time before now. They indeed saved Urlas some time ago, as it was told by the shaman Iouir."

Kealin noticed that neither of them looked at him now, and the elf seemed distraught.

"As for Urlas," he continued, "it was the dragon. Though many within the higher ranks of the elven societies believed that this dragon was somehow tied to the god of death itself, it was a dragon that came within the realm and burned our home. But by that time, there were few of us left there. Now, the only one drawing breath still is the shaman. He has insisted to remain there until your arrival."

"Now that he is here, will we return?" Aeveam asked.

"That is what he wanted, and it is what we will do. Kealin, I know you do not know the two people before you, and it may shock you to know that they know you."

"Not too shocking, for the elf here knew more about me than I even expected, and seemed to think I was responsible for the death of someone."

"I know it is strange. These two here have had a very heavy hand in your life well before now. If I would guess based on what I do know, they saved the lives of all within Urlas."

"How? He is not an Urlas elf and she is not—I don't know what she is, but there were no strangers then."

"They were with Valrin."

"Valrin? I only met him at the beginning of the journey. His crew was killed."

"No, we are not dead. It was part of the guise," the elf said. "I am Evurn, a shadow elf from the East and a dear friend to the boy Valrin. This is Aeveam. She is like you and the shaman, but she is also a Rusis. We risked our lives to save yours. Valrin was Stormborn, a guardian of the seas. It was his fate that he would protect the way for you and, in turn, help you. But you did not help him. He is dead!"

Evurn jumped up and quickly moved away from the fire and made a sudden outburst of screaming toward the cave walls before pointing his finger at Kealin. "What was so important that you would abandon my friend? Why? What could have been so important that you would leave him? You were supposed to be some great warrior, some foretold person. Why did he die?"

Aeveam embraced Evurn, somewhat to comfort him but more to assure he did not move against Kealin. At that moment, those within the cave simply stared at Kealin. Kealin closed his eyes, seeing the dwarf and pirate Rugag and the last moments of Valrin's life.

"We tried to save them. I and my brothers. The pirate captain Rugag had him and my sister. Not only did we kill numerous dwarves and take command of the ship to sneak up on the board and fleet, but whales and sea creatures of all kinds took part as we took down multiple ships. I moved from ship to ship, searching for him. I tried to save Vals."

"You call him by that name? The name he was called as a young boy?" Aeveam asked.

"It is what he told me he preferred."

"You tell the truth, then," Evurn said with a sigh. "What was his fate? What finally took our captain?"

"Decapitation."

The words Kealin spoke were cold, and the conversation completely halted.

There was silence for some time, and Kealin dared not move, for it seemed that the shadow elf was on edge and shaking. Aeveam led Evurn to a spot away from the fire and set him down.

Master Rukes began to stare at Kealin, noticing his armor and then his sword.

"I see my blades were no longer good enough?" he said with a tease.

Kealin looked down and pulled the Dwemhar blade from its sheath and handed it to his master.

"It is of the Dwemhar, as is this armor. It was one of two blades I was using in the wars to the south. My Urlas blade was shattered by a beast." He paused. "The beast that took my sister, Alri."

Master Rukes handed back the sword. Kealin slid it back into the sheath, and then again, silence befell them.

"Where is my narwhal, Aeveam?" he asked.

"It is resting down by the shore. I saw that it was injured, and aside from healing the creature, I saw that it had a black boat nearby, a sign we were told to be watchful for by the shaman. He said to look for a 'half-elf upon a black boat pulled by a narwhal.' It was a description that could not be mistaken. My powers allowed me to heal her, so I did so. Tulasiro told me of her worry for you."

"So, you have the abilities I have? How long?"

"My entire life. My father attempted to give me the best chance to be in control of these powers, and for the most part, I've been able to. Having the focus of the will of my captain to guide me has helped. Now, Shaman Iouir tells me that these powers will hold much power, especially over my future."

Master Rukes pushed himself up to stand, waving off any assistance as he tapped Kealin on the shoulder.

"Walk with me. Let me see this narwhal." He looked to the others. "Prepare. We move to Urlas in mere moments. It is time."

As Kealin walked with Master Rukes toward the exit of the cave, it was almost soothing to see the sea expanding out before them.

"Too long, too long we of the Urlas Woodlands stayed in hiding. I can't tell you the amount of loss of life I have seen of so many I've known from over double your lifetime. I do not pretend to know the suffering that you have experienced or even the bloodshed you have witnessed. You mention a war, but I have heard very little of that."

"I saw evidence of war here. The middle of the seas, upon a barren rocky plain."

Master Rukes began to tear. "That place saw the last of countless of our kin, my friend. The Blades of Urlas sang their last song upon that icy hell. I escaped by the will of the shaman. He is much more than he appears, and frankly, I'm fearful of him, but he is the only guide we have in these dark days. He is different, Kealin. He has changed."

They reached the shoreline, and Tulasiro squealed, now in a much better condition than before. Aeveam had indeed healed his friend.

"Master Rukes, meet Tulasiro, a narwhal of the Glacial Seas. This narwhal and I have been through a lot. For many years, it was just me and her, but among many troubles, I can tell you that Tulasiro has even fought a sea monster."

"A sea monster?" Master Rukes exclaimed as he slowly moved his hand toward the narwhal.

Tulasiro squeaked as Master Rukes rubbed her snout. He then bowed. "Brave Tulasiro, warrior of Meredaas. I thank you for taking care of my friend here."

The narwhal squeaked.

"We will not travel by sea, Kealin. We take a . . . quicker and more direct path now. She will be well here, and in time, I am sure we will come back to these regions. You're far north, much further than I believe you've been thus far, though in truth, I know very little of your journey."

Kealin could tell that Master Rukes was curious of his path the past few years but was not sure if he should ask at all.

"My journey has been dark. I had come here to kill a god who has terrorized so many. I am haunted by him."

"All in time, Kealin. Your purpose will be revealed soon enough. Our path is set. You were the last we waited for. Go up to the caves when you're ready." Master Rukes turned away, and Kealin knelt beside Tulasiro.

"I must go, my friend. Please stay safe and listen for the hammer. I do not know the path I am taking, only that all our journeys have converged to this point. Or so I'm told."

Tulasiro bobbed her head up and down and then quickly descended into the depths.

Kealin stood on the shore, looking out to the Glacial Seas and then up to the many stars high above him. There was a feeling in the air, but he could not explain it. A coldness rushing over him, giving him peace. His memories were starting to feel distant from his mind; his focus was suddenly centralized and pure. He turned and began back up for the caves, and with each step, he could feel the power growing beneath his feet. As he entered the cave, he noticed that Aeveam was waiting for him. She was a particularly beautiful woman. A bit young, at least in appearance.

"They're very few who can understand what it is we can feel within us. I'm happy to have another like myself. I don't need to know your story, for I already have seen the horrors of your mind. I do wish I could tell you that they will fade, but in truth, you can only distance yourself from them and focus. This place makes it easier."

He followed her back to the main cave where a fire was burning brighter, sending flames up through the top of the opening above them. Evurn and Master Rukes were standing near the fire, and as Evurn stared at him, an albino snake slid out from his robes and moved up to the top of his glowing staff.

"Is that what was choking me?" Kealin asked.

"Rasi does not choke," Evurn said. "Rasi embraces you with death. It can be peaceful or horrible. Rasi chooses. In the case of your death, I was to do it myself. I have decided not to eat you. For now."

Kealin had never heard anyone say such a phrase as that. This elf was quite a strange sight, from his patchy skin, unlike any elf in the rest of the lands, to his longer curved ears. The exact term shadow elf did not bring to mind anything in Kealin's memory. He believed he might actually remember one such as Evurn.

"My thanks. I will get you something to eat, then," Kealin said.

Aeveam chuckled. "Oh, Evurn eats . . . things . . . that we won't."

"It has been a very long time since I had an elf. There are too few of them now," he said plainly.

"Well, that's enough of those kind of words," Master Rukes said. "Go ahead, Aeveam. Let us go beneath."

It became obvious to Kealin within just a few moments why he could sense his power so strongly here. The fire faded away as if it was enveloped by the earth, and around them, pillars of glowing stone appeared. This was another Dwemhar ruin.

It was then the floor shifted and the pathways of the cave began to rise as they twisted in place, revealing a shiny black door hidden in the ground beneath them. Aeveam reached out toward it with a glowing hand, and the door opened, revealing a hidden passage.

They began down a dimly lit hall, and from the glowing stones and a feeling now much stronger around him, Kealin knew where they were was Dwemhar in origin. At the far end was a cylindrical tower with a simple metal gate at its front.

Aeveam opened the gate, and they all filed into a strange stone cell. It was like the device he had seen in the ruins before his duel with Vakron-Tur.

"The shaman activated this passage for us. It will take us to where you once called home," Aeveam said to Kealin.

"What remains of it." Master Rukes sighed.

4

ALL THAT NO LONGER REMAINS

ONLY A FEW MOMENTS passed before Kealin was blinded and he felt his body shift sideways. By the time he could see again, he was within another cave. They couldn't see to much in their immediate area. Moving toward the light ahead, they followed through a single archway that led to a long passage leading upward, and suddenly, he was no longer cold. In fact, he was very warm. Warmer than he had felt since before when he was in the desert of Lost Sands.

Master Rukes led them up and out of the cave, taking a twist between several passages that then opened to a large and unfamiliar sky. The sky was no longer blue, but red, and on the other side of the void, he saw the strangest of contradictions. While the land before him was glassed over with ice, the sky itself appeared to burn with red flames.

"Welcome home, Kealin," Master Rukes said.

The only part of his home that he recognized was

the lake. Everything of the elven lands beyond that was gone. Upon a lone peak, the hut of the shaman somehow still remained. A single path from where they stood went to a series of large boulders at the base of the shaman's stairwell.

"How did he survive?" Kealin asked.

"He was able to unlock an old power within himself. He saved me because I was nearest to him. He had summoned me just before the dragon's attack. I cannot explain it, but he is not the same as he was."

The moved down from the cave to the base of the hill where the shaman's house was and after climbing up the boulders, proceeded up the stairwell. Kealin paused outside the hut, looking around and thinking of the last time he stood here. He pushed down the feelings of sorrow. He couldn't let that distract him. The shaman was always a source of comfort to him and his siblings. Perhaps, that truth would remain.

As they entered the hut they found the shaman meditating. As soon as Kealin walked in, Shaman Iouir's eyes sprung open. He stood, and without taking a single step, began to speak. "You have come. You, like all Dwemhar, have heard the calling. At last, you realize that you should have never left."

Kealin stared at the shaman's eyes, which seemed to be the deepest black. "You did not tell my siblings and I to stay. You did not tell me any of this. You told me that those who went to war were in extreme danger. Why did you tell us such if it was so important for us to remain?"

"Kealin!" Master Rukes said. "Respect. Please."

"I will not be told I should never have left as if I was commanded to stay. Not by you, not by any person standing beside me, not by the gods. The state of this land will not be placed upon me. I have already lost too much."

"Yet you still draw breath?" Iouir asked. "Look here at those who once called this home."

The shaman moved away from Kealin. He began to go through parts on the far side of the hut and mix various alchemical ingredients.

"I see what has happened around me, yet I wonder how you have survived."

"For I'm no mere shaman. By now, they have told you that your life is only spared because of the actions of the crew under Valrin the Stormborn? Do you not wonder why I speak to you so plainly without the slur to my speech? Darkness was coming. The workings of many moved forward upon your departure. Your brother Taslun, intoxicated that morning, was quick to take my words and depart. Your actions until now have been driven, in part, by your own desires. The time for that has fallen away."

Kealin attempted to process what was said. He did notice that the shaman's speech was not slurred. It had been so long since he had done it himself, not to mention the amount of anger he had toward the shaman building in his mind, that he hadn't realized it.

"I have managed to unlock my mind once again. I am truly one of the last of the Dwemhar. I've been hiding. This place for the longest time was safe. Here I prepared for what I knew to pass. With your birth and the birth of your siblings came to pass an ancient prophecy of the Dwemhar. None knew this except me. I did not even tell your mother though I had a heavy hand in ensuring not only that she could remain in Urlas but that her bloodline was hidden from the Urlas hierarchy.

"But now all has come to pass. The ascended will return. The Dwemhar will come again to this life to balance what the imbalance created. If you would like to place blame, you can blame the gods. The gods, all of them, fear the growing power of my race and your race. We sought immortality, and we stepped on the verge of awakening the Great Poet. They claimed it would cause the destruction of the world and attempted to strike us down, but instead, we became a part of our own realm, ascended beyond the living realm that we walk upon now."

Iouir took the concoction he was creating and threw it on the mat on the floor. There was a shimmer, as if water was before them, and suddenly, as the shaman spoke, what he spoke of appeared and formed before them.

"Here you see the world as a whole."

Kealin saw a great expanse of light and a formed globe of spherical blue. He then saw the image of mountains, rivers, and the great oceans of the worlds.

"Here, you can see the living realm, and above it, the realm of the gods,"

Kealin could see different layers of color and existence that made up the homes of the many gods though the exact image was difficult to discern before it faded away.

Iouir continued, "and below it, more of the greater realms of the gods in this circle around the slumbering light that is the Great Poet."

Kealin could only see a great light and grew so bright that he shielded his eyes for a moment.

"You see, these realms that we speak of, these places of protection and sanctuary, are simple walls. Walls that can be pierced with one's mind. All events past, present, and future can be seen and manipulated. I remember the old ways before magic. When the Rusis began to throw fire at one another, when they thought they were supreme, but it is the power of the mind that is truly supreme. The gods do not wish us to know this; they would have us remain ignorant like the foolish gods truly are. So many pray and revered the gods though I tell you right now that even the gods themselves do not know all of the workings of the Great Poet."

The ground before them became as a field of stars.

"The ascended return, but they cannot return as they once were. They will come as new souls, eventual children of life with better balance and thought. If the Dwemhar can be pointed to one problem, it is that we did indeed know too much. Some of those broke away in an attempt to save our race; those Dwemhar became the 'accursed' and were flooded from this world, but they saw this truth. They saw the future and knew that the need of the Stormborn to guard and protect our living realm would be needed. It was some of the last actions that they did. It was our folly as a race. We did not listen to them. Too long were we at war with the only other power that could contend with us. Elves in their eternal lives, clinging to trees, were almost as bad as a dwarf scraping stone, seeking the riches of this life. The most valuable of riches in life is a mind that is both strong and open to the greater powers."

He turned and stared at Kealin. "Most of this I have told the ones with you. Some are accepting," he said, looking toward Aeveam. He then looked to Evurn. "Some are more resistant. I even attempted to tell the elven lords of their own folly, hiding away for too long. When at last they went to war in the North, the time to act had passed. Vankou is all that exists within the Glacial Seas. His beasts, the ones that are so terrifying, are Dwemhar in nature, those he captured who came upon him. Those are ascended, trapped before their full ascension.

"If you want to know why the god of death was a slave to that island, it was because by conquering death, the Dwemhar had superseded the embodied power of that god, essentially destroying the balance of the world but enacting a way of eternal life and the Dwemhar could control more than some would say they should have been able. They could take that which was known as a god-form, a being of power, ascending to that of equal power to the gods by channeling the energies of Vankou. But the god of death could not kill all. Vankou could not kill other gods.

"The Dwemhar devised a way around this but only after working with Vankou. He embraced them and assisted them in their endeavors. Though he lost the ability to claim our souls, he gained many gifts in the form of promised ascended beings. But when ascension began, the gods of the North moved against Vankou before the ascended could be claimed by the god of death. In the fury of the events in those days, many were sealed upon this world, unable to seek death until events that were not even set into motion at the time of their sealing, began.

"Time itself was manipulated many times over, and that which could have been was changed to that which was. Time was twisted." He gripped his head. "I cannot explain it in a way that any here can understand. I can tell you that the Dwemhar did not seek any true alliance with the gods. Those who bound themselves and promised servitude were cut off from true ascension, trapped in the body of a beast. They were betrayed by their own kind, and I will not judge that at this moment. But now the ascended come to our world in a fragile form. Their literal souls will descend upon the Glacial Seas, and it will be at that moment they are most at risk. The many threads of twisting time converge to a single line. All the deceptions and lies of old fall away to the one truth. That truth is that all of the Dwemhar origin who still remain upon this realm are gathered in this room or coming this way. There are more of us, and you can imagine the very few will make it to the final moments of our old race. I have sent out the call; many have answered me and thought I was no more than an a spark of madness within their own minds, while others like you,

Kealin, know and feel the completeness coming upon the living realm. You know of others who have heard my call, do you not?"

"You speak of the ones on North Cape, the elderly man, the captain Eurna, and the woman Marr?"

"Yes, even now, they come to us."

"Where are we to go?" Evurn asked. "You don't have one of these portal devices to go wherever it is we must go?"

"No," the shaman responded. "We will need something that only you have the key to, my friend. There is but one way to the place of ascension—the old ruins of the Dwemhar city. It will take the realm ship."

Evurn pointed at Iouir. "I do not even know where it is, and you claimed it was hidden from you because of its creation by the accursed Dwemhar."

The shaman smiled. "I do not know, but I do have the one who does." He turned to Kealin. "You know where the vessel is hidden, that of the Stormborn?"

"Valrin's ship? The *Aela Sunrise*."

"I do not care what it called, only that you know where it is."

"I did based off the old seas, or, I had some idea. These seas are not what I sailed upon before."

"Foolish half-Dwemhar," the shaman said.

He moved his hand across a shimmering pool. Before them, the Glacial Seas appeared. Kealin attempted to trace the path they had taken six years ago, and pointed to approximately where they were when Rugag kidnapped Alri and Valrin.

"The island of the Hermit. The one with the shells

of Meredaas. It was surrounded by a golden ward of some kind."

"It was sealed by Valrin. It only requires a key. A key he made sure to leave," Evurn said.

Evurn reached into his robes and pulled out a necklace. "This device is placed into the mast of the ship. It was a key to a lock in a way. It allowed him the power to take control of the vessel when he was a young boy. He gave it to me before he went to the tavern where he was to meet you. I did not know that he would never take it back."

"It is all as had been planned. Death and life are cycles." The shaman looked at Kealin. "We do have little time. Now it's time, Kealin, for you to cease the thought of killing in vengeance. Vankou must remain alive. The gods are vile, but they play a part in allowing the ascended to return. The world was designed by the Great Poet for those of the living realm to remain there. They seek the return of this balance. This is beyond the gods of the South. They are wretched in their own lot, having desires and wishes contrary to the ways of all life. This is about the greater wholeness, which is the power of the Great Poet. If anything has been made clear to me in my meditative state, it is that the gods do not wish Vankou destroyed. That was not part of the task of the Stormborn or the foretold ones such as you and your siblings."

"You mean all of us were to be a part of this?"

"Yes, all. But you were the only one who showed true potential. Your brothers and your sister did not embrace their better half. Your sister dwelt in magics of simplicity. It was only you who showed true defiance of your own home, and this turn toward the hidden blood within yourself to defy that around you was enough to unlock the secrets of your mind."

Kealin was at a loss for words. His defiance was the reason for his powers or at least why they had awakened ahead of his siblings. The shaman was staring at him with a glare unlike any he'd ever seen.

"My words were harsh; the truth is harsh. I pray none of you ever know what it feels like to be the last of the people, to have the fates upon you so strong. Kealin, I tell you that as we draw closer to the final moments of our fates, we will stand together as our brothers and sisters return. Once the stars have aligned as I have seen, we must be in position upon the site where the first ascended fled this world, for they return to this world to bring balance, and there will be evils that intend to prohibit this.

"You will go to the realm ship of Valrin. From there, it will be as fate has decided. We will guard all Dwemhar in their return. In this last stand, we will embrace the rebirth of the supreme race into our world. I fear the times coming. We of the original races were meant to keep the travesty that is men of the South from becoming what they have become. They threaten the balance of the world further with the poisons devised upon these very oceans. I have been blinded to some actions, and that is a source of great fear to me. I know our path ahead, but I have taken the words of Master Rukes to heart. I do know that Vankou may have some workings with an Itsu Priest, a being whose, by the downfall of your sister," he said, pointing to Kealin, "presence has entered this realm. The forms of the Itsu darkness are part of the workings of this world, but those of our race will deal with such evils upon their rebirth. I must continue this path until completion. All will be as it should.

"Now leave me. Go down to the shoreline beneath the hut, and you will see the path north with the coming sunrise. You will have rest until then. You will be guided by my spirit to that which you pointed upon the map. Go and embrace the true path."

As the others began to back away, Master Rukes bowing as he did, Kealin shook his head.

"What? This was all some plan by some near-ascended beings? The sacrifices of those I care about mean nothing beyond the return of the Dwemhar?"

"It means what it should mean by your own desires."

"By my own desires? You put the value of the sacrifice of those I loved on me and what I feel they are worth?"

Master Rukes grabbed him by the shoulder and pulled him. "Come, Kealin. Now."

Kealin swatted Master Rukes' hand off him and approached the shaman. "Truly, what form of lunacy has taken control of your mind?"

The shaman glared at Kealin. "Watch yourself, half-elf. You have powers that do not come close to my level. Do not tempt me. We all have a part to play, but not all puppets get to the final act of the cosmic play."

Kealin went to say something again, when

suddenly, all within the hut and Iouir vanished before him, leaving only a bare mountainside.

"You pissed the mumbling hermit off," Evurn said. "Perhaps we can be friends. Come, everyone. We have a simple road to the shore."

Kealin was beyond upset, and he could not find any form of comfort from those around him. He turned away from the hut and followed just behind Evurn as Aeveam and Master Rukes followed behind him.

Kealin seethed with anger. His hands trembled as he tried to avert his thoughts from the shaman. The thoughts simply came again.

The sky above, with its appearance of flames, seemed to begin to ripple violently as Kealin passed Evurn and began out toward the beach. A few moments later, that which was behind him faded away, and he said he saw as if he was only sitting on a random rocky island in the Glacial Seas. They were outside the realm of Urlas now. As the others left the realm, he took the bag containing Alri's ashes and the broken shards of his Urlas blades and threw it on the ground.

"Their sacrifices mean nothing? Are we all simply playing into the loyal game of the shaman? We cannot seriously be considering actually doing what that mad Dwemhar proposes?"

"I do believe we are," Evurn said. "I would rather return to the evils of the Shadowlands than protect ascended beings returning to our realm of existence. Why in all the realms would they want to return? I've thought about going east again. I would do it, but Aeveam would be angry."

"Yes, I would be. We have a purpose. We honor our captain and we will see this out."

Kealin lay on the beach as Master Rukes knelt and opened the bag.

"Who?" he asked.

Kealin opened his eyes for a moment and glanced over before closing them tight. "Alri," he whispered.

"For the time I knew her, she did embrace the elven way. I feel her spirit can live in a better way than within the confines of this sackcloth bag. With your permission, I would like to take this. I feel . . . I know I can give this better meaning to you."

Kealin shook his head. "I don't care. Take it. Toss what remains of her into the ocean. She was nothing of value, or so I've been told."

"Kealin, the shaman thinks beyond us. We put a value on that which he does not. We can't understand his ways, and we don't have to agree with them, but this is as he believes. What we believe and what we hold to be important is what is important. His folly is that he is alone as he attempts to live this life as some great completion of a grand plan. It will be us who are truly defending the souls of the ancient race. I would not risk my life, Kealin, for something I did not believe in. All that I had was done. If I did not care about you and your sacrifice, I would've made sure that I did not draw breath any longer. It is by that focus that I ignore my injury, that I still lift my blade, and by that which I stand with you now."

Kealin was silent. He felt Aeveam step near him and heard her take a deep breath.

"I sense an approach of something far off. We have much time before the sunrise, but it is going to come this way, or so my foresight sees. We should try to rest," Aeveam said.

"Rest is good. It prepares one for battle," Evurn said.

The shadow elf lay not too far from Kealin as Master Rukes stood with the bag of Alri's ashes in hand.

Kealin only glanced at the others and then forced himself to sleep. He had nothing else to say.

It was sometime later, and Kealin was not too sure exactly how much time had passed, when Aeveam shook him awake. He sat up and looked out, seeing an all-too-familiar ship before them.

"The *Truest Bliss*? How did that ship make it all the way here?"

"What do you mean?" Evurn asked, stretching his arms up into the air. "The ocean goes all the way south. I presume they sailed here."

"There was a wall of ice through the sea," Kealin said. "It took me using magic shells to get this way."

Aeveam snickered. "Some things just happen to be working to our favor. These seas are shifting. The ice that blocks one path will free up another. We should probably start to formulate a story as to why we are standing on a bare island in the middle of the ocean."

Kealin glanced around for Master Rukes but did not see him. The *Truest Bliss* was drawing closer, and as it did, he noticed Eurna was waving toward him.

"Friends of yours?" Evurn asked.

"Acquaintances. We do not need to formulate a story. They already know of the Dwemhar. They are Dwemhar. They tried to get me to come this way with them before, but I had . . . other ideas."

"You cannot run from fate," Master Rukes said from behind him. "Such is the way fate works."

As Kealin turned around, he saw in the short time he had been sleeping, Master Rukes had been busy. In his arms was a brown cloth, and he walked slowly toward Kealin.

"I'd have you know that normally Ruinite ore takes a significant amount of time to refine what I needed. Though much was destroyed, my old forge was built well before most of these trees had grown to the size that we know them as. It was ruined, but by some luck, the fires within still glowed even with a coating of ice around it. It took some time and a bit of blessing by the gods of the North, but I have re-forged what was broken and believe you will find it useful."

Master Rukes walked to Kealin and revealed two red-bladed daggers. Their hilts had the crest of the ocean, made of some type of shell.

"I would have forged you two new swords, but I did not even have the ore to put together the one that was broken. Too much of the actual material is lost in the refining process. Within these blades, I infused that which remained of your sister." His voice quieted as Kealin's hand touched the blade.

"Thank you, Master."

Master Rukes smiled. "I loved each of my students. I loved the families they came from. I do not know what you went through in the South, Kealin, but I know the power of your family. Now, you can carry part of them with you. It is said that when we die, that which remains of us holds nothing. In most cases, an elf returns to the trees. But in these days, a tree is simply not worth what it should be. With these blades, you will do great things. Strike down those who come against you and threaten that which you held dear and will hold dear."

Kealin took both blades and the simple leather scabbards setting underneath them. He took one of the blades in hand, twisting his wrist. Making a point to set down the scabbards and wield both blades, he spun them, feeling them slice through the air almost silently. They were shorter than what he was used to, but he felt they fit him. He focused on the feeling of the hilt on his bare hands and closed his eyes. He saw Alri smiling in his mind.

"Thank you, thank you," he said as he embraced Master Rukes.

About that moment, a shout came from the ship that was nearly upon the shore.

"It seems our paths have crossed once again. We know you've been waiting for us, or so my sister claims. If you'll come on board, we have hot tea, a bit of coffee, and an overeager father who has suddenly regained quite a bit of vigor. And . . . something else." Kealin noticed Eurna nodded strangely. "Come now, I will let down the ramp."

As they boarded the ship, Kealin shook hands with Captain Eurna.

"It seems we are to venture together. I warn you, if you think what your sister says and does is strange, you might want to sit down for what we have to say," Kealin told him. "I think you'll find it rather unbelievable."

Eurna patted Kealin on the shoulder. "We will see. There is a lot I did not think possible, but recent encounters have challenged that."

"We shall follow the spirit of the shaman, an ancient Dwemhar who has hidden within a protected ground for some time," Master Rukes told them.

Marr smiled. "So, it is as my father foresaw. We would have passed this place up had he not told us to move opposite of the rising sun. What few maps we could find of this region showed nothing here, save an old abandoned fisher's island. There did not appear to be anyone there."

"That was Corson," Evurn said, "one of many small towns frozen over by the great dragon of ice."

At this point, they all seemed to notice that Kealin was getting directed by Eurna to the back of the ship. Kealin himself assumed it was here that he would find their father, who was supposedly at much better health. As they approached, the door opened, and he did not see the old man who before appeared to be on the verge of death. The man looked a bit younger now.

His eyes had a greater light, and he was walking with some amount of excitement. But it was what was beyond him that suddenly took Kealin's attention. He thought it was a strange flame, like an arcane light, emanating from behind the old man. But then emerging upon the deck of the vessel to ferry them north into the Glacial Seas, stepped Taslun.

"Brother! What are you doing here? Are you not with the others?"

To Kealin's side, both Master Rukes and Evurn had drew weapons and held them to either flank of Kealin. Kealin turned and held his hands up. "Stop, he is fine."

"I can see his skull" Evurn said. "He is not fine. I know fine. He is dead."

"The term is undead," Marr said. "He is of the Dwemhar."

"Taslun, my student. Taslun, how has this come to be?" Master Rukes asked. "He did not have the affinity for your mother's powers. I do not understand what has happened to the warrior I once knew."

"Dragon fire," Taslun said. "Dragon fire and death magic. My elven form did not survive, but somehow, what was in my blood of the ancestors came to life and, in truth, engorged me with a power I do not understand."

Taslun raised his arm as blue flames started at the tip of his fingers and engulfed his entire limb. "I am me, but I am also who my sister created."

"A necromancer? That is what became of Alri?" Master Rukes asked.

"Yes," confirmed Kealin. "But why, Taslun? Why have you come here?"

"I heard the calling. Already, your friend Brethor departed, and I saw no others, save the undead. I spoke with Suvasel, and he deemed that I should go. It is amazing; the undead seek a new life within the deserts. They move into a place of hiding deep underground. But that is not for me. Not yet. My brother needed me. I could feel the presence of a change in the air. We both lost all, my brother. Calak, Alri, and the one I never met."

"Another?" Master Rukes asked. "Your parents had another child?"

Before anyone could answer, Eurna made a point to break up the conversation. "I enjoy the revelry of meeting once again as much as the next person, but perhaps we should get moving."

"The sign comes," their father said.

In the light of early dawn, a single bright burning white orb appeared in front of the bow of the ship.

"That is our sign?" Eurna asked.

"It is the presence of the shaman," Aeveam said.

Eurna went to the wheel of the ship and directed Marr and their father to tighten the sails.

Evurn made a point to help, and soon, they were following the spirit of the shaman as it led them across the oceans in a northernmost direction.

The ocean itself was calm. Once they had a steady heading and good winds, Marr made a point to brew coffee. As each of the companions did their own thing, Kealin and Taslun stood at the bow of the ship. Kealin was still not getting used to seeing his brother in such a form. Taslun could sense his brother was uncomfortable, but remained silent.

"So, Brethor left?"

"Yes, he said he had to go to the others. He did not tell me where. After he told me you were going north, I just noticed how upset he was. I guess he is a true friend, the closest to a living brother I could say you have. But I heard the calling in my mind. I thought of seeking them out first, but no, this is our battle, and what little Marr told me of the ascended Dwemhar and what has been revealed to her within the past night, confirmed that I made the right decision."

"Jesia, did you, um, hear if she was okay?"

Taslun shook his head. "I did not. Brethor was not quite up to talking to me. I am sorry. I know nothing of the fates of your friends."

Kealin stared off across the ocean. He bowed his head into his hands and wiped away a tear.

"You care for her. You . . . you loved her, even?"

Kealin said nothing because he knew he didn't need to. His brother put his hand on his shoulder and remained silent.

They continued north for a prolonged period. The short time of the day and night cycle where it was not completely dark seemed to pass quickly. As stars shined above, Kealin noticed that none of the consolations appeared the same as before. He could see no seahorse or penguin or any sign that he'd been taught on his original voyage. Though it seemed at this point, they were not going north as before. The spirit of the shaman was tracing to the west.

"I'm leaving these waters," Evurn said. "If I survive this, I've decided I'm going home."

"Such a strange and random decision," Aeveam said.

"Why? I have been here longer than I care to say. I have been here longer than you've been alive. In fact, I came here to be left alone, and it was your father who dragged me off on an adventure. Chasing after some magical staff . . . Fighting monsters." Evurn slurped his coffee. By now, it was not only old but partially frozen, and he crunched the ice and spit just to the side of Kealin.

"So where exactly is home?"

Evurn made a sarcastic snicker. "It is where I say it is. But if you're asking where I'm from before I came to this desolate icy hell, then I can say the East. The Shadowlands is what some call them. A place of blood magic, shadow elves, horsemen in the western plains, and to the further south, you'll find dragons and swamps. Oh, a very lovely place. I don't know why I left. Oh, it was the shadow elves themselves and their affinity for blood, blood magic, bloody gypsies. It is a place I have grown to hate. There are many reasons why I left. But I was thinking that this would be some form of retirement, but that damn gypsy mother told me I would *'find my truth,'* and all I have done since I left is edge closer and closer to some level of power I do not understand. Now I've been wondering around these oceans with this one," he said, motioning toward Aeveam, "for what? Forty years? I still do not understand these Dwemhar energies and powers and stuff. I miss poisons. Nothing grows here anymore—it is too cold. No one lives here; I can't even get a good snack, for no dwarf or elf comes this way anymore."

Both Kealin and Taslun stared at him with confused looks.

"You eat your own kind?" Taslun asked.

"Yes, why is that so strange? Have you tried elf? Or in your case," he said, pointing at the undead form before him, "other undead?"

"I do not need food," Taslun said.

"Well, why even be alive, then?"

"I am not alive. I am undead."

Evurn stared blankly at Kealin. "I already had issues with you, and now your brother here who died and came back gives me all kinds of feelings, and none of them are good. Yes, to return to my first statement, I am going home. If we all survive this, you people can enjoy these icy waters on your own."

Dawn was approaching again, and at the moment, the only companions awake were Taslun, Marr, and Kealin. Eurna had gone to lie down for a few hours, and Kealin agreed to take the helm. It felt good to be sailing again, but Kealin could not stop thinking of Vals. Standing next to two of Dwemhar power did not fare well for him, for more than once, the conversation was brought up by Taslun of their original voyage, to which Marr was more than happy to ask questions about.

Kealin did his best to keep his thoughts far from being involved in interchange. As he stared upward at the glowing light of the shaman leading them to wherever it was they were needed, he noticed that to the sky to the right, the polar lights suddenly erupted across the sky. At that moment, the essence of the shaman halted. Kealin did not move or lower the sails or otherwise adjust his path until it seemed that suddenly, the essence of the shaman began trekking east. Kealin came about and redirected their path. Something had changed.

5
SANCTUM OF MEREDAAS

KEALIN WAS curious of the signs in the heavens and the shift in path. Eurna came to the helm. It must've been obvious to him that they were traveling in a different direction.

"This is strange," he said. "I see you are still following the strange form of the shaman, but we are going in a very different direction."

"Yes, shifted some time ago. I'm not sure where we are headed at the moment, but I still see nothing but open sea."

As the others began to awaken and Marr chose to begin meditating, it became very clear to even Kealin who was not concentrating on it that a familiar presence surrounded them.

It seemed that Evurn and Aeveam both had become much more somber, as if they were smothered in lost memories quite suddenly. He wasn't sure what to say to them.

As Marr struggled to get a small fire lit to boil some water, Taslun took the vessel containing the water and, using his own power, the water quickly heated up to a rolling boil.

"That is amazing," Marr said.

"Some would say that. Some would call it strange. I would call it strange if you'd asked me a few years ago. But, even the undead enjoy some pleasures of living."

It seemed that Kealin's brother gave a strange look to Marr, to which Marr did not feel as comfortable as his brother assumed. Though it was not like she was not socially awkward to start with, Kealin could imagine how a dead or undead person confessing primal thoughts toward her would be difficult to accept or even explain.

Kealin gave up the helm to Eurna and began to pace along the deck of the ship, moving his hands through the grooves of the railings as he walked.

"Such strange icy seas we are upon," his brother told him. "Now I can sense thoughts on the air, the wanderings and memories. You, too, can still feel this?"

"Brother, you know what I feel. My own feelings are part of the reason why we've had so much struggle. Now, I try to seek some form of truth or intelligence to my actions."

"Intelligence can be hard to find, and I don't mean just simply in the world in general." He laughed. "You went across the lands to take action you believed in. That is more than many do in many lives. You made the choice, you acted, and though it did not work out, you've pressed on. I made a choice back when I was still alive that doomed my old form. But I had seen a brother who had pulled me from the darkness at sword point. At the time, I could not fathom your inner strength, yes, but now I understand. It was not some blood lust that led me to charge toward my death and attempt to kill the general of the Grand Protectorate. It was love. It is a motivation greater than any habit, creed, or anything else that we claim binds us and controls us. It is what led you to take such a small force and attempt to relieve the siege of Eh-Rin, which in the end, would've claimed your life."

"It was a degree of luck. The point I see is I took my final actions mere moments before the arrival of the better swordsman," Kealin said. "That is why I am alive today."

"No, in fact, it is not. I believe there is more to it. Oh, and I wouldn't call myself a swordsman anymore. The term is too simple, too elven. Please, do not insult that which I have become!"

As he said this, Kealin noticed that he reached into his robes and pulled out a large black staff. He flicked his wrist, and the staff grew, and its length almost tripled. As he placed a hand that typically was made of fire onto the actual pole, the edges began to glow green, and in a sizzling explosion of a strange magic, a massive blade emerged.

"You're a dwarf now, wielding an axe?"

"It is not a bastard axe. It is a weapon I saw in my visions. It was something that, using some random objects I found around the great city where you left me,

I was able to construct. I guess at best I can say it is a true weapon of my own design."

He offered it to Kealin, and as he touched the blade, the fiery form it held solidified into what appeared to be a green glass.

"Strange." Kealin reached out to touch the reformed blade and noticed that his fingers actually passed through the material as if it was not even there. He stood up, gripping the weapon, intending to make a small mark in the actual deck of the ship to see if this weapon could even be used by someone other than his brother. As he very slowly tapped the wooden railing, the head of the weapon pierced through the wood as if cutting through silk.

"Come now!" Eurna shouted. "I'm already not charging a fee to go gallivanting to the northern oceans, but don't cut up my ship."

"Here, Brother," Taslun said. The blade immediately burst into flames again.

"Your connection to our ancestors is not strong enough for the blade to take full form, but in your hands, it is still a deadly weapon. I can change its form at will. From axe to spear to sword. I can channel both death magic with green fire or Dwemhar energies with blue. I do pray that such an object will be useful against whatever we face in the coming days."

"The coming days are of shadow," Evurn suddenly said.

The shadow elf stood up from a seated position, and Marr joined him. He walked to the deck and pointed just as Aeveam gasped.

"The city of Muera is gone," she said.

Kealin was not sure what she meant, for while he did see a large mountainous land in the distance, he could see no ruins of a city. But it was clear that the site of this place was distressing to them.

They drew closer, and Kealin could see the earth itself had been upturned and broken. A large outcropping of crystals were upturned to the sky, glowing in the dim light of the North.

"You know this place?" Eurna asked.

"It is a place we went to many times," Evurn explained. "The Stormborn conversed with a water spirit here on several occasions. It was only recently that I was privy to such experiences. Just before he went with you half-elves, it was the spirit who told him to give me the key to the ship. He had believed it was just to fall upon the deck of the ship but it wasn't that simple. He did not know how to pull it from the actual wood but she was able to provide the incantation through the power of Meredaas."

The image of the shaman sped away from them and hovered high above the top of the ruined island.

"It is here we must go," Marr said. "For some reason, it has been deemed we return to this place you and Aeveam know."

Eurna guided the ship as close to the island itself as he could get. As he went to drop anchors, Evurn shook his head.

"No, we must get closer."

Aeveam outstretched her hand and sent a stream

of bright fire into the icy field for them. The path that had been blocked by ice quickly melted, revealing a narrow channel for them to follow. Eurna once again pushed it forward, following the path directly into an icy ravine. There was little light here, and the torches they had on the ship did not help too much.

"I do hope you know where you're going," Eurna said to Evurn.

"I am looking at ruins of what was once a large city. I don't know for sure where we're going, and I don't even know why we're actually here, but trying to set the anchor so far away from anything recognizable would most definitely be ill-advised."

Kealin noticed that as they went deeper into this ravine, it became much darker. They were now surrounded by ice on all sides, save the one they came from. In time, they came to a large stone platform with a lone torch burning.

"Someone must be here," Eurna said.

About that moment, Eurna and Marr's father emerged from his room and looked around. "I do not see this place in my visions. Why have we come to this place? Do you still follow the will of the shaman?"

"Yes, Father," Marr said. "This is a place known to Evurn and Aeveam. I believe it may play a part in our tasks ahead."

As the ship came to rest at the makeshift dock, Marr and Eurna threw out several large spikes to help anchor them to the actual surface.

"I'll go," Evurn said.

"But where do you go?" Kealin asked.

"I go to talk to the spirit. I was the only one of anyone standing here who was deemed worthy to go, and so that will continue. I shall serve the Stormborn with my actions. It is what he trusted me with."

"You're not Dwemhar," Marr said. "This journey is of the Dwemhar, and they must be part of it."

"This journey is for whoever is insane enough to go on it. Currently, that includes me, a shadow elf. Hello, it is great to be a part of the experience with you. I need no mind-reading Dwemhar with me. I will seek out the spirit I have spoken to before, and I'll return with whatever information we need. You do not need to watch me like some child."

Evurn, a voice said.

It was a strange tone. The voice came as if speaking from far above and echoing over them. Kealin was suddenly struck with sadness, and it seemed the wind which was before not present suddenly tore through the narrow gorge in icy gusts, but then, the air became warmer. A sudden peace overtook him.

Evurn. Aeveam. Followers of a precarious path.

Kealin suddenly understood who this voice was. But even if he did not know who it was by the voice, he would soon go by sight. A light suddenly sparked directly before Evurn, and from the growing shimmering fire emerged a figure. It was Valrin with flames around his body.

"Stormborn!" Aeveam shouted out.

Evurn bowed but looked up. "You return to this life to give counsel?"

"Very little. And what I know is that if you are typical of yourself, Evurn, you are attempting to forbid my friend here from following you. Take Kealin to meet with the spirit. There is little time, my friend. I do wish that I was there to fight beside you."

Evurn, who was suddenly weeping, looked up to Valrin.

"I know your memories and the vile thoughts you had at the one you put responsible for my death. The one responsible for my death is dead. Kealin and his siblings did everything possible to save me, and it was not enough. But I daresay this is not as if it was supposed to be. You, one of the originals of my crew, have much more to do in your life. I was born but for a purpose, and I have served that. I am content with that. I have seen a potential future. A dark future, where all is burned away by the light of the Dwemhar energies for good, and yet, I see it also as evil. But I also know this is only one way that the future may come to pass. Embrace the half-elf. A prevailing wind came about when he came upon the Glacial Seas, but now there are even more shadows moving from place to place within the world. What was meant to be of his foretold actions has escalated with the events he came from before he returned to us. It is not my place to explain the mysteries, only to give charge to you, Evurn. Take Kealin forward and show him what I showed you. Have him meet the one of the temple."

Valrin began to fade away, and both Evurn and Aeveam reached out to him.

"Wait, please!" Evurn said.

"Serve the sea," he said to them. At just the last moment, when the presence of Valrin had all but faded, Kealin heard the voice of Vals speak to him.

"Aye, friend, you have come so far. No matter the cost that should be levied in the coming days, know that many of the ascended will stand beside you."

With that, the light of Valrin faded.

Evurn turned to Kealin. "Come, let us go. You heard his wishes. Oh, and keep the ship ready. I do not know what else may await us here."

"Where will you go?" Taslun asked. "I see nothing here but ice and rock."

"We'll proceed north from here and figure out our path as we go. The island is not very big, and if we are looking for the tower that once was here, I have to imagine I'll see some sign of it."

As Kealin and Evurn departed the ship, Evurn's snake uncoiled from his staff and jumped to the ground.

"Rasi will lead us. She knows the way better than any."

Kealin looked back to the ship, and those who were looking on as they departed. Though he knew each of them had significant feelings toward their actions, these were not his companions like before. He did not feel the same loyalty as he did when around Veora, Ruak, Brethor, and Jesia. In fact, the mere thought of them made him feel as if he should not even be here at all. But this was the path he was on, and for once, he liked not directing his own steps and instead relying on another, be that a good feeling or not.

Evurn kept a fast pace, and his snake was even faster. Moving north from the ship, they began through a series of narrow ice passageways and then came upon several interlocking stone walls.

"Up we go, half-elf," Evurn said. They began to climb up each of the steps, pulling themselves higher and higher. Evurn became more confident as they finally reached the upper region of the old island.

"So, half-elf? How the hell did your elven father end up with your mother? That's quite a strange combination."

"I can't actually tell if you're being serious right now. You expect me to know the answer to that question?"

"Well, you have these 'mind powers' as the Dwemhar. I just assumed that would be something you would know, considering your strange lineage. Perhaps not."

Kealin still wasn't sure what to make of the shadow elf. He seemed dedicated to their path, but he asked the most peculiar questions and made comments that others would not make.

"It took a while for our mutual friend Valrin to get used to me as well. I will say I have little respect for many of the other races, for all things can change. A long time ago, there was a Rusis in our crew, and I had little respect for her kind. She grew on me rather quickly. One of many of the old crew. Life seemed simpler back then."

They pulled themselves around several other large rocks jutting up into the sky. Kealin noticed that the top of the island was essentially just many large crystals. As Rasi snaked around and found the path that led toward the other side of the island, Kealin, in fact, noticed what appeared to be a structure on the very edge of the land.

"So, what happened to the Rusis in the crew?"

"I'd rather not say."

"Dead?"

"Did I not just specify that I would rather not say? You are a daft elf to have survived this long. You're like the elves who whine so much before you kill them. I once found myself with a plentiful reserve of dwarf meat and simply released an annoying elf because frankly, I was afraid I would catch something from his meat. The elf literally did not stop talking for eight days. Eight days! I even paralyzed him, but come to discover, he had been poisoned by some beasts and some type of herbal medicine he'd consumed had made him resistant to my spell. The strangest turn of events."

Kealin had known this elf for less than a full day and night, and in all his travels, he had never known an elf to talk about eating elves and dwarves in such a nonchalant manner. He wondered now if the captain of the *Aela Sunrise* knew how crazy his companion was.

Evurn led them directly to a large tower, coming to a strange walkway that seemed to be built upon shattered rock and pieces of crystal.

"You must think I'm crazy."

"I don't know," Kealin said. "You do talk about

things I cannot imagine, but perhaps that's just because you're trying to scare me. I do not scare easily."

"I would not expect you to be scared. Fear can be a healthy weakness, but you're not weak, and I know this. But like I once was, you seek to veil your inner emotions and become trapped by your own desire for grander actions.

"When I was younger, much younger, the sense of adventure and the chance to do something crazy was enough to get me to do essentially anything. Then I had some strange individuals show up on my beach. That somehow resulted in me being here and I would not change that now. But I have unfinished business in the world, or so it seems. When I think I should have just stayed out of it and not become a part of some travesty in the world, I think of hiding, but every time I tried just to let go, even when I first came north, I could not. I tell you, even simply having a drink and planning to keep to yourself means someone will absolutely need you. I once spent quite a bit of time with an elf who had quite a few young ones, and that's what he said. *'If you have children and try to do something for yourself, they will be right there with you no matter what they will essentially destroy anything you're trying to do.'*"

"I've never had kids, nor have I really been around them," Kealin said.

"Well," Evurn began, "I have not, either. But frankly, most everyone I have been around have been so much younger than me that they could count as children. I have watched after the one back on the ship called Aeveam for many years now. Her father and I were good friends and shared in a bit of an unfortunate adventure, but I guess it was useful in some way. Never trust the gods, my friend."

"Do not worry," Kealin said. "I trust little of any god, be they of the Northern gods or the Southern."

"I still don't like you, but your words make sense. Now, we go to where nothing makes sense. This here is just a strange place of lunacy."

They had reached the door, and like he was visiting a simple merchant, Evurn quickly knocked on the door.

"Damn, I forgot to bring a fish. This damn woman likes her fish."

But to their surprise, the door simply opened, and they walked forward.

"So, you don't require fish this time? Valrin had said you wanted fish. Is there something about your island getting torn apart that quelled your appetite?"

They proceeded deeper into the darkness until Kealin heard rushing water around him. He felt for his sword blades and glanced to his left and right but could see nothing in the dark room. Ahead of them, a single candle lit, and a female's voice filled the air.

"My island has been destroyed, and you make jokes of it. I knew upon our first meeting that I would be dealing with you again, and with one of more appropriate power, but in truth, so much has changed in the way we first saw it, I am simply surprised you have actually returned."

Evurn laughed. "Well, I assure you if it was completely up to me, I would not be meeting. You know my feelings toward the gods and the gods' patrons and the gods of the patrons and basically any form of religion."

"You made your point the last time you were here. I am well aware of your disdain of us, of all of us related to religion. But you have brought the one I had only felt upon our realm. A rare feat considering the gods."

"What of the gods?" Kealin asked.

"What of them? I will tell you."

Suddenly, the dark room with a single candle became alight with several large candles on the walls. Kealin could hear the rushing water again, and it seemed then that in the lower region of the room was a strange appearance of a watery form crowned in light.

"Down here." Evurn motioned for him as he began to walk. "She doesn't like having to yell. I learned that last time."

Kealin followed Evurn down to the actual spot where the strange watery apparition had taken form. The figure was made of flowing water, alight with a slight glow, and moving almost as if dancing in the pool he stood before.

"You've come here, Kealin and Evurn, but yet you do not know the full path. The gods themselves can no longer converse near these realms, and I speak by proxy to what I've observed and what I know of the gods before. You seek the realm ship, and while it is an important factor in all that comes, the imbalance of the region of the Glacial Seas is the work of something greater, something evil an ancient one stripped of its power by the ancient Dwemhar. It is an icy form, a true demigod. It has gained powers to resist magic and to move with great speed. This creature is a threat to the path of all who are not aligned with that of the god of death, Vankou, and those who would appear as such."

"No," Evurn said. "I already know what you are doing." He pointed at the spirit. "If you think I'm going to go after any creature, then you should go speak with the one called Wura. I do not go fight creatures anymore. I did that once long before now, and once, I thought it might be fun to go back and do it again. It was not."

Kealin stared at Evurn, not sure what he was talking about.

Evurn turned to him. "When I have time, I will tell you of what I am talking about. But the last time I went against beasts of any particular power, as I'm fairly sure this one is, both I and my companion were nearly killed."

The spirit smiled at them. "You must defeat this creature. This creature is known by the half-elf, set free by the half-elf. The gods of the North decree it must be destroyed."

"The dragon. The dragon that opened up the path to Dimn's Temple?"

Evurn laughed slightly. "What did you not do on your first trip out of Urlas?"

The water spirit splashed Evurn and then began again. "That is the beast I speak of. A fortnight ago, the polar lights were alight just above the ruins of the city. The god Wura gave me the knowledge that you, Evurn, know better than any of how to kill creatures such as this."

"You can tell that god to fuck off. The most powerful wizard I knew struggled to fight the creatures of that god, and those of us here are not exactly the greatest group of warriors."

"Do you not know who stands next to you? Do you not know that he defended the realm of the wind god with his siblings with little access to his Dwemhar powers? That in his journey, he was able to secure a weapon capable of killing the gods, something that not even the gods could find in all their searching? He defeated the leviathan of the southern seas! Surely you do not need another warrior? The dragon has caused a severe imbalance in the region. It can go from place to place with rapid haste, doing the will of its god or something else. This creature is a threat to all, and its defeat will secure the needed alteration that will bring the world closer to balance. It is a true demigod. At one time, it was said it walked the realm as a man, but its ability to transform like that was stripped from it by the Dwemhar. This creature, if allowed to live, will stop all that you and your companion seek, Kealin."

"You keep referring to something else, the will of the god or something, and before referring to Vankou and those who would appear as such. What is beyond our sight?"

The water spirit, which rippled with energy, seemed to pause before again rippling as normal.

"There is much twisted within the memories of the gods; time has been manipulated. The gods dealt once with the god-form of a great evil, stopped before by the Dwemhar. This form exists still. It is a divergence in the balance of the world made worse by this beast I speak of. When the Dwemhar return, it will be the work of such to bring true restoration to the world, left unfinished since their ascension. But this dragon will inhibit any who attempt to go between realms. The demigod will seek retribution on the Dwemhar, and it must be destroyed before more of the living realm is affected."

Kealin guessed the answer he'd received was enough. "Where is it?"

"You do not need to know where it is. You only need to know how to call it, and by calling it, you can set a trap."

Evurn shook his head. "That is the wisdom of the gods? Shall we set a trap for a dragon? And not just a dragon, but a dragon that is somehow a bound demigod? Somehow, this will work because of the presence of my friend here who has defeated other creatures? Am I understanding all of this correctly, or am I just so famished, tired, and cold that I cannot think straight?"

"Shadow elf, I will not entertain any more extraneous words from you. The god of death knows of the arrival of Kealin within the seas. If you seek to use the ship of the Stormborn at the time of the return of the ascended before defeating the dragon, it will tear that ship apart and your fates will be the same as the ones who seek to return. You must defeat this beast by any means necessary. Kealin," she said, reaching out with a parchment in her hand, "this is a very old map. I do not believe it has but one more use within it, but if you only speak the name of what you seek, it will direct you to it. You must seek a Dwemhar device known as the Dragon Scream. It is a sacred item of your people, and with it, you must only think of an image of the beast itself as you blow this horn, and it will have no choice but to come to you. It is then that you must be ready."

With that, the spirit faded away, returning to the water of the fountain as the candles within the room went dark.

Evurn sighed. "When I first came to the Glacial Seas, I went on an adventure, if you could call it that. I fought many strange and powerful creatures, but I swore I would never do such a thing again. Then, I may have caused destruction of an entire island of people in my failure to again face a monster." Evurn turned and stared at Kealin. "You know this creature. We will do as the spirit commands, for that is what the Stormborn wanted. I will honor him in that."

As they exited the shrine and stood atop the wrecked island with pale light above them, Kealin unfolded the parchment that was given to him and stared at the blank image.

"I'm happy that you see things as I. Trust me when

I tell you that doing anything but striking down the god of death is extremely difficult for me. I know you still are angry at me regarding Vals. I cannot bring him back. We were all brought to the Glacial Seas for one purpose. We will find this horn, we will seek out the *Aela Sunrise*, and we will defeat the dragon because we do not need our fight to be any more difficult than I can already sense it will be."

He wasn't sure how this map actually worked, or if it would work as the spirit had said in any form that they could discern. He lifted the parchment to his mouth. "Reveal to me the path to the Dragon Scream."

Through some work of magic, the parchment suddenly began to draw a set of symbols, followed by what could be unmistakably noted as a constellation. The runes of the constellation formed the lower portion of the map, and it seemed to be a set of islands east of this position.

"I know this place," Evurn said. "We must go a great distance east, beyond most known islands. This constellation is not a constellation of the stars but a marking of an old observatory, one of many in these regions. A place beyond this is a chain of islands that I saw but once on a drawing of my old friend Lorlaam."

"Lorlaam?" Kealin asked.

"Aeveam's father and the wizard I fought the many monsters with in my younger years. He told me then that it was one of the places that he went searching for rare treasure. It is a strange place, he told me. There is untold wealth to be had there, but also danger. He would not elaborate on this, and frankly, I never intended to go there. But I do know this place."

They departed the shrine and began back down to the ship.

"I wonder if we even need this map?" Kealin asked. "Surely we could tell the shaman what we seek and he can determine where it is."

"I've heard you call him a shaman, but what worth was that when he could not tell that your siblings would face death. What act did he do for the elves of Urlas so that he wasn't questioned? I asked Rukes of this, and he only silenced me and stated he would not speak of it. Who is this shaman?"

"You know nearly what I know of. He dwelt within in my realm since before I was born. The elders went to him for advice on future progressions of the Urlas elves, but by the time I was born, it was deemed he was partially mad. Still, he was like a window to the outside realms. When I was younger, he told me stories of faraway places and the grand happenings in the world."

Evurn snickered. "Grand happenings? How grand were they once you were a part of them?"

Kealin said nothing.

"A window he may have been, but perhaps his glass was murky. It seems to an old shadow elf there is much to worry about someone like him. I trust very few people; right now I barely trust you, but I trust you more than I trust that thing."

"He is of my people. I have to believe he aligns

himself with us as he claims, to help those of the ascended."

"Why didn't he ascend, then?"

Evurn's question definitely made Kealin think of the shaman. He hadn't thought of many questions, but at this point, he really had not thought too much at all. As they came around a large upturned piece of ruin, they caught sight of the *Truest Bliss* at anchor ahead.

Those aboard jumped up upon seeing them, and Taslun was the first to go to Kealin. "So, have you discovered why we are here?"

"A map," Kealin said, holding up the parchment. Aside from the realm ship, we need something else. A dragon, an ice dragon that terrorizes these regions, and we must destroy it."

Taslun's eyes got large, and he smiled. The flames of his blade suddenly sprang to life. "I would much indeed like to deal with that dragon. This map leads us to the lair of this beast?"

"No, not his lair, but to a device that can call it toward us. Pursuing the beast will do no good. His ability to bend the space between realms and distances allows him to appear and disappear nearly as quickly as he arrives. Somehow, between the dragon and whatever magic the god of death is spreading within these regions, the gods are cut off from us. We must be diligent."

Eurna and his sister, along with their father, joined Aeveam as they gathered around Evurn and Kealin.

"We must retrieve this horn?" Eurna asked.

"What is it supposed to do?" Marr interrupted.

"It brings the beast to us when we want," Evurn said. "I have fought many beasts, but none of them were deemed demigods, yet this one is."

"I remember this creature. I remember him tearing into some type of monster outside some ruins when Kealin and I came through the seas the first time," Taslun said. "The beast was cunning. Not only did he attack the lower level of the gods' mountain and attempt to cut us off from returning to the gods' realm, he also pierced the portal between the living realm in the realm of Dimn. But I am confident." Taslun smiled.

"Confidence may not be enough," Marr said.

Eurna nodded. "I know for a fact that my catapults came off a dragon-hunting ship when it was first retrofitted onto my vessel. I still have the projectiles. While the lines themselves might need to be greased, I'm confident I can take down this creature, demigod or not."

"What about the *Aela Sunrise?*" Aeveam asked. "I know that vessel has weapons capable of dealing damage to creatures of the sea."

Evurn nodded. "Yes, it can."

About that time, the image of the shaman appeared on the bow of the ship.

"I can hear the calling of this place to our vessel and directed you here. I know the Stormborn contacted you from the realm of the dead, an interesting feat considering normally those from beyond cannot easily contact such as that. The realm of the afterlife and the realm of the living blends together in these darkening days. I do ask, though, what did the spirit of Valrin speak of?"

Kealin already knew of Evurn's mistrust, and he caught the shadow elf staring at him but then looking down before turning, looking the opposite way of the shaman.

Kealin cleared his throat. "We are to seek out a device, a horn. It is said that there is a great dragon causing issues between the gods in this realm. They said it is folly to take the ship of the Stormborn to the place of ascension while the dragon still flies."

The shaman stared without saying anything and seemed to be scanning each of them. "Well, I did not know that this dragon that I have felt moving within realms would actually be such an issue for us. I am afraid I do not know of this horn you speak of, but I sense a name upon your mind. *Dragon Scream?* I do not know its purpose, yet you say it is of our race?"

Kealin had not said that, but of course, it was on his mind and something accessible to the shaman.

"I-"

The shaman suddenly walked toward Kealin. "Do not doubt your path. Do not let the words of others steer you away from your path. I say nothing else at this but that. Now, follow the parchment. You will be without my guidance for now. I will meditate deeper into the realms in an attempt to assure we have no further disturbances. I fear even I may not see the full path. Trust in yourselves and your companions. Those aboard this vessel are the key to a greater future." He looked to Marr and then to Aeveam. "You two are capable of meditative communication. I will keep my mind from your affairs as of now. I have my own work that needs to be done in preparation for the return of the ascended, but once you have this horn, we will proceed to retrieve the realm ship and continue with our work. "

In a flash of white, he was gone.

6
LESSONS OF OLD

"That was strange," Rukes said. "What was that about?"

"He is grumpy," Evurn said. "We should set sail and begin our journey east. We are far from where we must be. I wish to go and meditate myself. Aeveam, perhaps you can work with Kealin. If he can see where we must go, he can use his shells to move us there quicker. Being on the open ocean with a demigod, especially an angry one, for longer than necessary is something I prefer to avoid."

The crew dispersed. Eurna went to the helm and began to move the ship away from the ruins of the island. Aeveam went to Kealin, who was standing with Taslun near the railings.

"Those are strange shells you have," she told him. "If it is true that you must only see our destination within your mind's eye for us to traverse there, we should get to work right away."

Kealin looked to Taslun, who shook his head. "I am not for meditation any longer. My energies are focused to battle, as were my mental energies at the time of my death, I am of no use at this moment. Sometimes, I can touch the mental aspects of our powers. Currently, I just need to kill something."

Taslun walked away, and Aeveam watched him with a raised eyebrow. "You know, I'd find him strange if I hadn't spent so much time with Evurn."

"He was always strange," Kealin said. "The perfect elf of Urlas."

"All those are dead now. He should be happy he was not there."

Kealin smiled. "He'd have died proudly."

Aeveam turned and looked toward the open ocean as they made their way to the east.

"You and he were prepared back then. When Valrin led us to Urlas to stop the dwarven Bard King from poisoning the entire realm, your parents and you and your brother attacked us. I believe you nearly killed Valrin but stopped at the last moment."

Kealin shook his head. "It is strange to hear that, because I literally have no memory of those events."

Aeveam smiled. "I believe that was the point. But when I discovered what your fate was following the events in the Glacial Seas, it did not surprise me. You were ready, just as your brother was, to die defending your realm. It was only when your father told you to go protect your siblings that you willingly left. You cared deeply for them. Now I know the sorrow that haunts you."

Kealin leaned over the railing. "You only know what you think you can see in my mind."

"That's enough. What was her name?"

"Who?"

"The woman, the Rusis whom you keep imagining by the sea?"

Kealin had tried hard to force the images from his mind. In fact, he didn't even know he was thinking of her at the moment. Over and over, he had seen a vision of Jesia in his mind that was just as Aeveam described.

"Someone I loved. She died. I think."

Aeveam sighed. "You do not feel her within the living realm?"

"I don't feel much anymore."

The conversation faded and they stood in silence.

Eurna came over and tapped Kealin on the shoulder. "I'm headed east, but where?"

Kealin pulled out the parchment and handed it to Eurna. "I do not know any of the symbols, but it seems there's a small mark on the map that is moving."

Kealin took back the parchment. It looked strangely similar to the map aboard the *Aela Sunrise*. He could see a small mark that appeared to be their ship upon the sea.

"I have never seen something like that!" Eurna said. "What kind of magic is this? Elven?"

Aeveam laughed. "No, no, not elven. This is Dwemhar, by some stretch. If this amazes you, you will not believe what you see when we reach the *Aela Sunrise!*"

"May I take the parchment?" Eurna asked.

"Sure, you're the captain," Kealin said.

Eurna nodded. "A captain with the best map in all the oceans, no doubt!"

Kealin didn't care to tell him that this parchment would likely not work after this journey. He'd hate to ruin the excitement.

Both he and Aeveam looked at one another, but she did not bring up the subject, either.

"I sense distrust toward the shaman. Why?"

"You are not like Evurn? You trust him?"

"I am asking you. I have my feelings toward the events of my foresight, and my powers are very foggy. I am careful to not make assumptions or claims, unlike Evurn."

"I trust him. For now. But I am careful with many of my thoughts. I can tell there is something meddling the very edge of my consciousness. I'm like you. Before, there was a clarity that I felt when my mind would take a surge of energy for my Dwemhar blood, but now . . . I just do not know."

"Then I will work with you," she said. "There is a way to ensure those on the outside cannot come within your mind. It is an advanced skill, but it is something I can teach you even upon the deck of the ship. Come, let us meditate on where we go, and within a protective realm of our own minds, we can discuss this further."

Considering they were on a ship with very few options for actual privacy and Evurn likely taking the only good private spot there was within the ship itself, Aeveam and Kealin went to the front of the ship. Marr and her father moved away from them as they set down. Marr wished to give them privacy.

Aeveam sat across from him, and their knees touched.

"I know you have some experience with meditation."

"I do, but I had no real teacher for the process. My sister and one of her acolytes used to meditate quite a lot. I know when I've been extremely stressed and conflicted upon my next path or actions, it has been a helpful tool."

Aeveam smiled. "It is. I have been meditating since I've been able to speak. There was some fear I've learned now, some fear that I would become like my mother. She was a horrible person, and there was worry that I would follow the path she did. I don't know if I agree with them, near-blaming a child for the actions of their parent, but I've had little choice in that matter. Evurn knew the story. In fact, I believe he was part of it at some point. I don't know why he will not tell me. But most people who practice meditation only see a small amount of the actual benefit. As Dwemhar, even not full-blooded, we can go deeper. I have a feeling you already know of the battle skills that you may gain from using Dwemhar powers."

Kealin nodded. "Yes. I have moved to where my mind's eye could imagine, jumping through the air and appearing just before my enemies to deliver a killing blow. I have caused the vessels of my enemies' brains to burst, bringing instant death. But I've never traversed a greater distance without some aid such as the shells of Meredaas, at least, of course, any great distance."

"You have actually used a hodgepodge of skills. I would assume, considering your last few years, that combat has been your primary focus mentally. The transport side of the Dwemhar magics you know is what we need to focus on."

She closed her eyes, and Kealin did the same. As he attempted to get the first stage of meditation, he forced all thoughts from his mind and concentrated on taking a deep breath.

"A novice."

"What do you mean?" Kealin said, keeping his eyes closed.

"I mean, you still meditate as anyone else would. When you close your eyes, you must have a place that you go to every instance of meditation. I am already there."

"As you said, I have had no actual teacher in the art of the skill."

"You do now."

Kealin stopped concentrating so much on his breathing and instead saw himself on a high cliff. As he focused his mind's eye, he could see a single image of the lake with the moon glistening on the water surface. The longer he focused on this image, the more appeared to him. There were vast woods surrounding him, and it was then he noticed he was somewhere in his childhood. As he looked around within his mind, he could see no one else, but then there was a small spark of energy next to him. A moment later, he felt the sudden presence of another within his own mind. Then, as if she were sitting within his mind, he saw Aeveam.

He spoke within his own mind, and she was able to answer. "How is this possible?"

"I have joined you within the realm of your mind. It is ironic; I had to set up a high place within my meditative realm. I would guess that this place holds the same significance as my own. It is a place of your childhood?"

Kealin nodded and stood up, looking off the grand cliff toward the great Lake of Urlas. "It is. I came up here many times by myself just to get away. I wasn't necessarily angry or sad or happy. It was just a place of peace."

She smiled. "The ocean gives me that feeling."

They sat staring for a good while, and Kealin looked over at her. "Shouldn't we be worried about what is around us in the waking world?"

"That is the beauty of this. Time has slowed around us. It would allow us to converse as long as we need, though I do not feel we need that long. There are times when in particular circumstance, you might need more time. I will be frank, you are worried that someone is trying to get within your mind to learn something that you yourself do not even know, or to influence you in some way."

"I do not know. Many times, I've had a vision within a vision. I see death. I see a place familiar to me yet completely different than any place I've ever been, and there's a figure there, but I can never actually see the figure's face."

"Like a dream where you cannot control what is around you but something that happens while you are awake yet not a vision?"

"Maybe that explains it. I feel like it is something sent to me, someone that is intentionally sending me these images. Is there a way to stop it?"

Aeveam stared away from him and then closed her eyes, gripping him. His vision suddenly went black, and when he opened his eyes, he could see a rising sun and a grand sea before them. He looked behind him and noticed they were in some type of tower or castle upon a lone island.

"This is where I grew up. The Wind Temple of Swia. This is where Valrin came with Evurn and told me my father had fallen helping them. I have not been back to this place in some time, yet I come here so often, it's like I've never left. The best way I can answer your question is to say that if you feel someone is dwelling within your mind, you must envision them within it, but at that moment, destroy them. It will knock them from their state of clairvoyance, but it's not a skill you can necessarily practice; at least, with me. We can attempt it once but that is all we can do."

"So, I just imagine within my mind? Like, within the realm before?"

She nodded. "Yes, it is impossible for them, whoever it is attempting to get within your mind, to know that place. They are focusing on their direct assault upon your mind, trying to grab you in this situation you are in. That is why only beginners use breathing techniques to enter a state of meditation. When the Dwemhar close their eyes to see themselves within their meditative state, they gain instant access to a whole flurry of their powers. Once you're able to master this skill, you can actually access nearly unlimited power. It is the skill of the Dwemhar, and one that proves we as a race can walk very close to godhood."

"But that is actually the fear, right? We have a Dwemhar leading as the last; at least, we can guess. He knows this information."

"I cannot think that someone like him would remain in hiding for so long to betray those around him. He is who called us together to support the return of the ascended. I would worry of the hold this has upon your own mind and the risk that if you or I are susceptible, any one of our companions can be misled by the enemy. That is what we must remember at this moment. Do not fall into the trap the enemy set. Do not doubt just because of a few words. I admit that I might be wrong, but we have few friends left in this world. But," she said, reaching out and embracing him, "if he turns out to not be our friend, this method of keeping him from your mind will work. I believe we should keep our own minds open to the chance that perhaps, for once, those within our group are true to one another. We must have hope. When the Dwemhar return, I know you and I can learn much from them even though their form may not be a form that can teach us yet. The world is quaking, Kealin. The gods of the South grow in power, and I have lost so much sight. Where before I could see upon the lands south of the Glacial Seas, now I just see fogs."

"I think it is because of who has entered the living realm."

"Who?"

"The Itsu Priest, the being that I and my siblings fought when we protected the realm of the god in our first trip within the Glacial Seas. When it came that time, he brought angels of the Itsu. He used the very dragon we intend to fight now. It did not matter what we did at that moment, the endless waves of enemies we threw back down into the clouds returned even stronger. I have to wonder if that priest will come to the North, if somehow, he works with the god of death like before. He was looking for a way to the living realm back then. Now that he is here, I can only imagine the power he has."

"He is a priest, not one of the gods. I know you do not know much of our race, but the Dwemhar can protect us. We must protect them on their return. We will not be alone. But we must keep our sanity until then. It is time for our next lesson."

Suddenly, they were no longer within her meditative realm. They stood surrounded by white light.

"This is the transverse realm. I have brought you here myself so that we may concentrate your powers. It is a learned process to come here by yourself, so I will guide you for now."

Kealin wasn't sure what he felt within this place. It was like he could only stare out of his body, but his body had no material to it. He attempted to walk forward but could not.

"You do not need to move your physical body in this place. It's the mind that gives us true freedom here. Let's imagine the ship we are on within the living realm. See it with your mind's eye. Do you see it?"

Kealin closed his eyes and attempted to focus his mind on what she told him. He thought it to be more of a struggle, but suddenly he no longer saw white at all but was floating high above the ship. He could see Evurn standing just to the side of him, and he could see Eurna at the wheel of the ship. Even stranger, if he stared at himself, it was like he was suddenly right over his own shoulder. It was the strangest feeling to see himself and to see Aeveam just as she was when they'd first started meditating.

"How long will they be like that?" Marr asked from behind Evurn.

Evurn turned to her. "We must not rush this. Aeveam is with him and will guide him as she needs."

"Now," Aeveam said, "you must imagine everything that you were told of the place that we go to. Imagine whatever your mind can fathom for what the Dragon Scream is."

"It's a horn."

"But think of it."

Kealin saw himself floating back above the ship. He then focused his mind, knowing that what he saw was within the cave. He suddenly saw rock, and then moving through the rock, he could see a small glimmer of light. He thought of what this object could possibly be that they sought, and he saw what appeared to be a gold ribbon leading out from the ship and across the actual ocean far to the east to an island.

"I see something. It's like a ribbon guiding us from the ship to a random mountain."

"Is the ribbon solid?" she asked.

"Yes, it is like a rope or something. Is this what I'm supposed to see?"

Aeveam suddenly was directly next to him. He felt a sharp pain in his head, and the entire image of the ship surrounded him. He was on his back, nearly flying off the ship itself, with the roar of the wind so loud, his entire body began to shake.

He opened his eyes, and he was back within his own body. He was shivering and trying to catch his breath.

"Are we here? He did it?" Evurn asked.

Aeveam stood above Kealin for a moment and then reached down. Kealin saw her just above his face and then felt Taslun's presence.

"Kealin!" Aeveam yelled.

He could not speak, but he tried.

"What is wrong with him!" Taslun shouted.

"He's stunned. I took control of him for a moment to activate the region of his mind that is needed for us to move the entire ship, but he is unpracticed. He is okay but just . . . give him a moment to recover."

Kealin could feel himself a bit more. His hands and feet were tingling, and his face felt heavy. He then was able to force himself to sit up.

"Are you okay, my brother?" Taslun asked.

"I am okay. Dis, dis." He could not say it correctly.
"Dis is strange. I have not talked like dis in some time."

"It's an effect of the powers," Aeveam said. "You no doubt felt this way and spoke this way before?"

"It is how the shaman always spoke," Taslun said.

"It's how I speak when I've had too many ales," Eurna said.

Evurn laughed. "But this is not alcohol. This is a damaged mind."

"Damaged?" Taslun asked.

"Yes, this can happen once the brain is injured. I have seen it in my study of medicine back when I was younger. But in the case of the Dwemhar, be them full-blooded or half or only partial, it accesses powers beyond themselves beyond what they're trained for. This can happen. It can also happen when the realm you are within does not have access to Dwemhar energies. This is likely why the shaman spoke for so long with a slur in his speech that our captain here so accurately described as how a drunk might sound. The third reason you hear this type of speech from a Dwemhar-blooded individual is they have been cut off from the Dwemhar and have been given access to said powers for a time. That is a rare happening overall. But he will recover."

Kealin was still trying to process everything that had been said to him. He almost did not make sense of it, and now he was wondering if the shaman was actually cut off from the Dwemhar. But he remembered what he was told and attempted to keep his focus on the actual truth. He stood up. Taslun grabbed his arm, but he shook him off.

"I'm fine. Evidently, I was pushed a bit too far," he said, staring at Aeveam.

He could see a massive chain of islands with rigid spikes almost like bones sticking out of the top of the rock. The very tips glistened with a blue ice.

"This is it? This is where we are supposed to be?" he asked.

Evurn tapped Kealin's side. "Check your map."

Kealin pulled out the parchment and immediately saw a trace of their journey from where they had begun, but now the mark identifying the ship was upon the mark of their destination. He looked up, noticing the strange formation of islands, and then looked at everyone else on board, including Eurna and Marr's father emerging from below deck.

"We're here. Now we need to figure out the rest."

The parchment he was holding suddenly caught flame. He dropped it as it fizzled into nothing.

"Why did you do that?" Eurna asked.

"The magics within the map were done," Evurn said. "I rather like the fact that the map is gone. It keeps us from getting distracted, and it eliminates the chance of this map falling into the wrong hands."

"I was just going to take a nice tropical destination in the South. Somewhere warmer," the captain joked.

"I've been to the South," Kealin said. "I prefer the North."

. . .

They gathered supplies not to mention their own weapons; none of them knew what to expect, what they would find, or how far they would need to journey from the ship. As Eurna brought the ship up as close as he could to the island, Aeveam used her powers to bring the ship alongside an opening in the sheer rock that they guessed was the entrance to the island chain itself. These were not islands like other places, but more like large spires rising out of the ocean.

"Who will stay with the ship?" Marr asked.

"You will," Evurn said.

"What? We are part of this crew!"

"Yes," Evurn said, "but you have no experience in combat. I do not know where we are going or what we're going to do here, but if this place is anything like any of the other desolate troves of treasure within the Glacial Seas, I would prefer not to have you here. You would just get in the way."

Master Rukes and Taslun jumped from the ship on to white rocks. Taslun moved into the shadows with his glowing axe at his side.

"There's a path this way," he said.

Aeveam and Kealin joined them, and Evurn stood staring at Marr and her father.

"You will have time to fight in the future. Listen to someone who has seen plenty unskilled in warfare killed. If you value life, you will let those skilled in acts of physical violence take care of this bit of a quest. Besides, it shouldn't be that much fun. We're just grabbing a horn."

Rasi jumped from Evurn, sliding out of his sleeve, and hissed at him.

"What? Really? You're not going?"

The snake seemed to change its hiss, and Evurn shook his head. Kealin walked up to try to see exactly what Evurn was doing.

"Fine, you stay here. Make sure they don't leave us. Don't bring up the crystal cave. Aeveam doesn't need a reminder of the last Glacial Sea cave we were in while on a grand adventure such as this."

"No, I do not."

Kealin looked to Aeveam. "What?"

"A saga of a tale for another time. I think it was Valrin who actually defeated that titan, though."

"He defeated a titan?"

"Oh, Kealin. You did not know the Valrin we knew."

As Evurn exited the ship, leaving the slightly angry Marr and the perfectly happy Rasi behind, Kealin pointed to the snake.

"You can actually talk to and understand the snake? I thought it just followed basic commands."

"And can't you talk to your narwhal?"

"Well, yes. But I thought that was my Dwemhar—"

"Don't. Don't say it. Dwemhar powers? You are a sad excuse for an elf. Any creature can be tamed and conversed with if one has the patience and the creature actually likes you."

"Don't waste your time." Rukes laughed. "We could never get Kealin to embrace the way of the Urlas

Blades. He was too busy doing his own thing his own way."

"Well, I cannot deny that it is preferable to do that. But no one can ever leave me alone. If it isn't a wizard coming after me in a tavern, or a ship nearly running over Rasi on my private beach, it's my Dwemhar companion claiming we 'must seek Urlas; we have been called,'" he said, mocking Aeveam. "I swear to each of you quest-mongering types, eventually, I will stop going about the world to help everyone else!"

Taslun laughed. "You can join the undead!"

"Keep your bony fingers from my life force, Taslun. I prefer not. Let's get moving."

The small group of them began moving away from the water, following the passage, with Taslun's weapon giving them light. Evurn summoned light with his own staff, taking the back of the line as his own position.

Kealin noticed that as they began to descend, they quickly were coming to an open area. This was a strange place. While he expected some form of Dwemhar architecture or something of that nature, he instead was met by the sight of what could only be described as a graveyard surrounding and reaching over their heads forming the very ceiling above them.

"I am beginning to feel like my new home in the South has come to the North," Taslun said.

Kealin looked closer and noticed that these bones were not actually human or animal; in fact, they appeared to be, of all things, small dragons.

Moving forward, they noticed that there were several glowing stones slightly covered with ice but still visible in the darkness. Aeveam went to them and used her powers to melt the ice. She pressed the stones, and a long line of torches lit before them, leading a great distance out from them. It didn't produce that much light, but it was more than they had.

"I was wondering if there would be a Dwemhar device in here. But I've never heard of Dwemhar decorations such as these," Evurn said, looking around at the many multiple massive skeletons of dragons."

Rukes scratched his head. "Didn't the Dwemhar hunt dragons?"

"If they did, they did not write of it, or we do not have text showing it," Aeveam said. "I have studied almost every book I could get my hands on from this region, even some of the southern regions for the time I was there. There is not too much said of dragons this far north.

"It could've been strangers to these lands," Kealin said. "Or dwarves or elves, it doesn't really matter."

"It does matter," Aeveam said. "Knowing our history will help us in the future."

"No, he is right," Evurn said. "We can discuss history at another time. We need to get to the horn, get back to the ship, and get moving. I cannot believe that we made it here without being harassed. I also cannot trust that we will continue to have the favor of good luck that we've had thus far."

7
DRAGON SCREAM

It was obvious to them this path was not simply a broken road or ruined structure. Kealin looked around, realizing that this cave was dug and crafted from the literal stone they were walking upon. The internal structure where they walked was in a state of near perfection to its original form as if it had been left untouched since its abandonment. But the number of bones both put into the structure itself and scattered around the paths were quite strange.

"I've seen a place like this before," Evurn said. "They exist in my homeland. I try to avoid them."

"I would have to assume it is because of dragons?" Aeveam said.

"Of course. I am a hunter of said dragons, or more so their riders. I have dealt with dragon riders, and you do not want to. They're a merciless lot."

"I have reason to believe there are very few dragon riders in their lands, shadow elf."

"Oh? You have heard they have fallen in some 'battle, or perhaps lost a bet? Assassins do not need to kill dragons, and we only kill the rider. Has death taken those I called enemy?"

"Death, and the second death. There are many who are now of the undead. Like Taslun."

Taslun looked back to Kealin. "The dragon riders are working to help create the new necropolis beneath the surface of the deserts."

"They work with the undead?" Evurn asked.

"They are the undead."

"A necropolis? A city of the dead?" Aeveam asked.

"Yes," Taslun explained, "a necropolis for all undead. The beacon of the goddess Mortua is still burning brightly high upon the cliffs in the sea. The dead go to the calling. It seems the great Dread Lord has determined the way to reconstruct the way undead come upon the world. We construct a new place, a place of the dead where all dead are safe."

"I daresay it was easier when the dead remained dead, but I do feel that might be rude with the present company," Master Rukes said.

"I do not take offense to that," Taslun said. "I know what I am. We all do what we must to save our own worlds."

They came to a flat area with many strewn-about tables and chairs, as if this place had been hastily abandoned. Kealin turned to look back up the way they had come and saw literally a series of bony structures rising high into the sky back the way they had come. He looked back to where they were and noticed that as they began to approach a large open expanse, massive torches before them burst to life with dark red flames.

"This place awakens before us," Aeveam said.

"It does. But as to why, we really have to question."

A bridge was before them. It was not a simple bridge of wood or even one carved of stone, but in fact, it appeared to be the skull of a dragon. "I have never read of dragons in the Glacial Seas," Aeveam said.

"But you have read of the time before the Glacial Seas. Of the Dwemhar in the mountain structures that were once here. How the deep seas were once valleys and grasslands? That is what you must concentrate on now when you think of this place," Evurn said. "At one time, this place was likely high on a mountain. A place of pilgrimage, perhaps? As much as we know of the vast histories of elves and dwarves, there is too much that we simply do not know and understand. Perhaps, in time, the full story will be revealed to us, but not yet. For now, it does not matter."

They began across the bridge to look down the chasm beneath them. A slender ribbon of burning green flames like a river was under the bridge.

"An arcane fountain?" Evurn said. "Or at least signs of one"

"A what?" Taslun asked.

"An arcane fountain. It is a place of significant power for people such as myself. The substance can be used for any number of potions, acting as a much stronger strengthening agent and elixir base. One could also leave their sword or axe or really any metallic object that they wished to enhance in the substance itself, making enchantments more powerful and more likely to grab hold. If we weren't all pressed for time to retrieve this object we seek, I would absolutely love to find this fountain."

"We are pressed for time," Aeveam said.

"Oh, how I know. We must hurry," Evurn said in a sarcastic tone. "Let's get to the point where we can fight the beast. Defeat the beast, and then we will have our answers. I've heard this before."

Crossing the bridge, they came to multiple hallways with large rooms jetting off to the sides. Kealin stopped at one and looked in, noticing that the chamber itself was relatively unadorned. There were bones here, and not just bones of dragons. Massive chains were attached to the walls, and even stranger were large weapons two to three times the normal size that one would expect a weapon to be.

"We shouldn't linger," Aeveam said

"I'm not lingering. Looking," Kealin said. "I befriended one of these dragon riders of the Shadowlands. He was killed and brought back as an undead servant. I do wonder of his culture, for they were proud warriors to fly into near-certain death in my solemn opinion.

"These people are likely nothing like those of the Shadowlands. Though perhaps they are descendants, I feel there is very little of the past that we can embrace. Besides, we both must keep our minds focused upon what is ahead of us," Aeveam said.

Kealin agreed but the further he went into this place, the closer he felt the feelings he'd had back with his old companions in the southern seas, at the place where he had been bestowed Vrikralok. A feeling of dread fell upon him and suddenly was stricken with the angst that all amongst them would be dead soon.

It was then he began to hear the organ of Vankou in his mind, but it was very soft. Strangely, it was somewhat of a relief to him. As he pushed those thoughts from his mind, he closed his eyes and tried to focus.

"I do not see many paths ahead, but I daresay I see our prize!" Evurn said.

Kealin jolted himself from the focus he was trying to obtain and opened his eyes. In the distance, he could see something glowing ahead of them in the far distance. It was still quite a distance ahead.

They hastened their pace, coming to a narrowing gateway that led to a narrow hallway. It was there that Evurn stopped and looked up at the runes along the door.

"Halls of Desires and Histories."

"A strange name," Master Rukes said.

"I did not name it; I only read what name was given to it," Evurn said. "It seems this place knows what we seek."

"We know this will not be as simple as picking up a trinket left in a cave," Aeveam said.

"It never is. You must be on guard," Kealin said.

Aside from the strange name of this chamber, as they first went into the passageway it did not seem to be anything special. But as they began to walk down a barren path in a narrow hallway with cavernous walls, there was a sudden shift in the light. What was dark suddenly became light, and the bare ground became as a red carpet. The walls were suddenly much taller and closer to them, causing Kealin and his companions to stop. On either side of them were massive murals. It was impossible to know the exact time period they were staring at. It was a land none of them recognized. From the tall mountains and strange structures painted atop the hills, to many large obelisks made of crystal. If it was a progressive time line, the massive image of a sun on the far-left side, in fact, behind them, was the creation of the world. They began walking forward and saw many unknown events in writing that none of them could read, not even Aeveam.

"I recognize some of the letters, but it's like we're staring at a language that doesn't exist."

"Anymore," Taslun said. "This is clearly a record of events, and I know from my journey to the Glacial Seas that many places are iced over. Many secrets are still waiting to be discovered."

As they reached about halfway down the long hall, Evurn stopped and pointed at the painting. There were massive dragons descending from the sky breathing fire down upon the valleys beneath. He had seen this breed before. In one particular image, there were actually realm ships high in the sky blasting electricity at the beast attacking them. A bit further down, the many massive crystal obelisks were being devoured by a great dragon.

"Is that our beast?" Evurn said.

"No, but I have fought a dragon like that before," Kealin said.

The dragon had the form of the massive dragon he'd fought above the city of Fadabrin.

"You fought this, Brother?" Taslun asked.

"Yes, me and Alri," he told him.

Taslun smiled and nodded. "Good work."

As they continued, Rukes took note of the series of panels nearing the end of the hall.

"It seems from these drawings that they destroyed the large dragon, but that it destroyed nearly all of these strange settlements. There seems to have been a meeting between the dragons and the people. One dragon was made into a holy creature by the people."

"That's our enemy," Kealin said. "That is what we fought. What we unknowingly released."

"So, this dragon was given power by the Dwemhar? It was made into a god?"

"Can they do that?" Taslun asked.

"The gods do what they want. Both for good and for bad," Evurn said.

They reached into the chamber and came to another opening and a much larger room. It was here they saw multiple large ruby lamps casting the chamber in a strange red hue. As each walked in, the room around them shifted, greatly expanding in size in all directions as upon the floor, several more of the ruby formations appeared engorged in light. The light was only enough to see the floor, and above them, they could see nothing but blackness. But in the center of the room appeared something that was unmistakable to all of them. A dragon skull. The head was massive. Its open jaws were at least three times the distance Taslun stood in height, and he was the tallest of them all.

"I don't like this," Taslun said. He spun his weapon in his hand and the flame grew brighter.

"Come now, no premature assumptions. It is just a skull, after all," Rukes said.

Evurn shifted his staff in his hands. "Except that I have seen the shifting of rooms like this before. This is almost like a test. We should be aware of all things, both what makes sense and what does not. But I think I see what we have come for." Evurn pointed ahead directly at the skull.

Kealin walked faster than the rest of them, coming to the edge of the skull and scanning it with his eyes, looking for some sign of arcane life or a trap. At the very center of the bony structure there was a small white pedestal. Sitting on the pedestal itself was a glowing object covered in several jewels. The object was a sheen black, like onyx, and with smaller rubies that made a spiraling pattern from the mouthpiece to a large open horn. This was the Dragon Scream. As he reached the pedestal, he stopped, looking behind to see both Taslun and Evurn staring up into the shadows. Aeveam walked into the skull with him, looking from a different angle at the horn itself.

"These are some form of Dwemhar ruins. I would be very surprised if something so barbaric as a pressure switch was on this treasure."

"You do realize this is entirely too simple?"

"It is. But no matter the beast," she said, turning around and looking toward Evurn, "we have a beast lying among us."

Evurn shook his head. "I hope you are referring to Kealin's brother. I will not deal with any beast. I have told you that for more years than I care to admit. I do not like dealing with large creatures."

Rukes gave a nervous laugh. "You do know we're trying to hunt a dragon, right?"

"Unfortunately."

Kealin reached down and grasped the horn. It was very cold to touch, but as he lifted it off the pedestal, it seemed to become warm in his hands. He paused for a moment, looking around, expecting to hear something. But there was nothing.

Kealin and Aeveam stepped over the teeth of the skull and walked toward the others.

"Simple," Rukes said. Kealin noticed the horn had a strap of its own. As he put the strap on his back, he pointed for them to leave.

"We should not test our luck in this place anymore."

The mutual agreeance between the companions didn't require them to talk. As Kealin and his companions began a rather hasty walk toward the door, the random sounds that Kealin had expected started.

First, he heard simply a scraping sound in one direction. Then, he began to hear it more and from different spots. Looking up, they could see flashes of white all headed back toward where they had taken the horn from.

"Damn monsters," Evurn said. "Run toward the door. Let's go."

They were no more than beginning a sprint when a massive stone form dropped between them and the door. Behind them, they hissing filled the air.

Kealin turned around and saw that the dragon's eyes were burning with a red fire. The stone form blocking their way out ran toward them, and they dove in opposite directions from each other, attempting to clear a path as the strange enchantment of sorts ran directly between them. It was not something of stone but bone. A skeletal form seeking to reunite with its head.

Evurn and Aeveam both cast spells almost simultaneously. Evurn sent vines growing up from the earth twisting into the ribcage of the creature and forcing it down just as several blasts of the white fire shot out from Aeveam's fingertips, leaving burn marks on its ancient form.

The creature rolled on that side, attempting to break the vine that had caught it. Just as its claws began to tear at Evurn's spell, Taslun jumped upon its back with his burning blade slashing into the bones, taking off multiple pieces. But the creature had gotten free. With a rolling kick, it knocked Taslun across the chamber.

Evurn attempted to cast several more spells to entangle the creature, but it was now running too fast. It was attempting to get to its head. To become whole once again.

"I don't believe the battle is one we can win," Rukes said. "The door, it's still open."

They began to sprint again. Kealin looked over to see Taslun on his feet, running to join them. Another hiss filled the chamber, and suddenly, the air became icy cold. The light around them became blue, and an arcing spray of ice just missed them and struck the doorway, solidifying and blocking their path out.

Aeveam wasted no time in casting several bright blasts of fire at the ice. But it did not melt.

Kealin slid to a stop, drawing *Vrikralok* as the creature revealed its monstrous form.

This was a massive dragon, though not of flesh but bone. Its eyes burned red, and from its wings were glowing spikes of ice.

"I was the first, betrayed. Held to this place to guard such a device. Why have I been awoken?"

Evurn and Aeveam both shot spells at its head, but the creature simply lifted its massive claws, and the spells disintegrated.

"Brother, from either side!"

Taslun and Kealin ran to the flanks of the creature as Rukes, Evurn, and Aeveam made a forward approach.

Kealin ran and slid across the floor, striking one of the ruby lamps and launching himself into the air. He brought *Vrikralok* over his head just as Taslun sent a blast of Dwemhar energy into the dragon bone. Kealin reached the beast and swung his sword, breaking several more bones before the dragon flapped its wings, knocking all of them back.

"You fools! How could some so eager to fight find their way into this sacred place. Has the world truly become so barbaric? I thought ascension was the path to greater good, not to this."

Kealin had been thrown across the chamber and was bleeding from his mouth.

Evurn and Aeveam held spells as they looked up to the creature.

It wasn't fighting them.

"You do not wish to battle us?" Evurn asked.

"I never attacked you. You attacked me. Tell me, what is your purpose."

"Don't tell this beast a word. He will tell the demigod," Rukes said.

The once red eyes flashed blue as it rose up on its hind legs and then smashed the ground, "Tell the demigod? I am the demigod! I am Vaugar, marked by the ascended as a guardian of the regions of the North. Have the dragons of the South come to attack? Must I fight them?"

"No," said Kealin. "But if you're the demigod, then who did we fight? It was a dragon, a dragon with glowing blue eyes. My brother and I helped retrieve a necklace that allows it to move between realms."

"Well, it is true, then," the bone dragon said. "That dragon is me, but not as you'd expect. Vankou turned me to this form, claiming it was the will of the gods."

"Vankou was imprisoned by the gods."

"Then you are fortunate. The god of death has more power than he should. He managed to sever my soul from my body. He told me I should ascend like the others of the great race, but this never felt as ascension."

"It is not," Aeveam said. "Your form was split. I have heard of this, but I thought it was simply lore."

"Then we must kill you here," Taslun said.

"I cannot be killed. But I cannot feel beyond this body of bone."

"So, what is the beast above the Glacial Seas? What is the dragon?" Evurn asked.

"It is my captured form. It is my impure side, my malice. Part of ascension is separating evil from within your body and the good, not to eliminate either side but to find a true balance. The only form that is truly pure is that of the soul. Upon ascension, when the Dwemhar left their bodies, they became as near to the Great Poet as they could. In that form, there is near limitless power, a power that cannot even be summoned and used by those not yet ascended. It is that power that the one known as Vankou sought. He used avatars to attempt to gain said power for. It is why he was imprisoned. Now, I do wonder why you've come here."

"The Dwemhar are returning," Kealin said. "The ascended are coming back to our realm. There is a belief that they will come under attack, that the passage from the ascended planes to our world is fraught with peril. We must take down your other form. That is why we've come to the Dragon Scream."

"So you mean to call my form?"

"Yes," Evurn said. "That must make some sense to you considering we did claim the horn."

"And I see you have a blade capable of killing the gods," he said, looking at Kealin. "Your struggle against my malice will require more than that blade."

"We have a realm ship. Well, we will again, soon," Aeveam said.

"Then you have a chance. It will still take much to bring that form down, but now that I know what the god of death did, I can use the limited power I have to attempt to assist you. While I cannot take form in fullness, I can be the key to death. Though my body has been stripped from me, I retain some of the gift given to me. If I have appeared here within this chamber, then you saw the murals coming in.

"We dragons descended from the stars. At one time, we could all move between realms upon coming to this living realm, as it is called. We lost that ability. We enacted a war upon the first races, and it was only the Dwemhar who were able to stand against us. I tell you, when the gods intervened and set upon the realm there was peace and the world truly did flourish for a time. But I speak of times that are not of importance now. Though, seek out what you can to seek. Now that I have been awakened and am together whole again, I feel something upon the realms. I tell you, I have not felt this since my first arrival within the lands. It may be trivial to you. While many of the Dwemhar sought ascension for the purest of reasons, there were those who were not as pure. I remember the sea people's, the branch that broke off. I remember the Dwemhar wars. But there was so much of the unknown in those times. I do worry of the return of the Dwemhar, and I do not understand how this is possible. I did not believe returning to the world after ascension was possible."

The bone dragon paused, staring at Kealin who could feel a radiant cold upon him coming from the gaze of its sapphire blue eyes.

"I sense malice upon you, or as the Dwemhar—I can sense both. With all my knowledge of the vast world, I see a shadow centered around you. There is much you do not know yet of your powers. There's much of your path in the past years that were not meant to happen. You being alive was not with the plans of those who set them. I wish I knew beyond the hints of words I have within my mind. As much of a mind that the bones of a dragon can have."

Kealin smirked. "My own path has been one I have mostly carved myself."

The dragon nodded. "That is the only true path any soul can take. Go now. Be prepared for the full reveal of that which is to come, my friends."

The sealed passage of ice behind them suddenly melted, and their way was open.

The massive form of the bone dragon became still and it seemed its enchanted form was returning to a watchful slumber, though its eyes were still glowing blue. In his mind he suddenly heard the voice of the dragon.

Much horror is to befall you. Friends and enemies will become the same. You will walk a path that none of the living realm have. Your choices will solidify the world's path, much like the ascension of the Dwemhar.

The voice said nothing else.

As they exited the chamber, they were now met with the Hall of Histories again. Seemingly, the Hall of Desires was where they found the Dragon Scream. There was a single stairwell that led straight up a white glowing passage. They ascended back the way they'd come but even so it seemed the halls had shifted. Aeveam walked beside Kealin and Taslun.

"I feel like every path we take reveals a slightly different version of the history we all think we know."

"History has always been written to the advantage of the ones who survived," Taslun interjected. "I suspect men will tell great accolades of the victories they had against the elves, leaving out the great undoing of the Grand Protectorate in the West. The undead do not care for conquest yet. But I can assure you that none else within the living realm will speak of the undead until we are ready to secure our place with our blades in their throats."

"We are of the Dwemhar, my friends," Kealin said. "I have heard both good and horrible of many different races. We must be prepared for an ever-changing path. For now, you must trust that all in our company will remain along the same path. I do not know what the return of the ascended will mean, but if this all has happened and the gods are being blinded to the happenings, we are the only powers that can protect our world."

Evurn was the first of them to reach the glowing light, and he walked into it, not waiting for the others. As they appeared on the outside of the ruins, Kealin looked toward the *Truest Bliss*.

"Did you find it?" Eurna shouted out. Both Marr and their father were standing there.

Kealin held the Dragon Scream up, and Eurna clapped.

As they reached the ship, they boarded, and Kealin showed the horn to Marr and Eurna. It was then Kealin noticed a massive crossbow taking up part of the deck.

"We are ready!" Eurna smiled. "I may not have magic but this should hurt our foe!"

"Was there any more revealed, anything else of our path?" Marr asked.

"Nothing has changed," Evurn interjected. "We must keep our path as it is until more has been revealed to us. Our next path is to find the *Aela Sunrise*."

At that moment, the burning image of the shaman appeared.

"You have retrieved what we need. We must set sail to obtain the realm ship and then may enact our plan."

8
GLOWING ORB

THE PRESENCE of the shaman left the ship.

"He appears and then leaves in haste," stated Evurn. "Too bad he cannot stay to assist us."

"It requires much energy to appear as he does," said Aeveam.

Evurn shook his head and stomped away from the others.

Eurna immediately glanced at the map and nodded. "Well, we might be able to sail this way, but it will not be easy. This is literally over three days at least from us. That is if the ice is not high in these regions."

"We do not have need. I can get us to the ship," Kealin said.

He reached for one of the shells of Meredaas and walked toward the bow of the ship. With an arched throw, he hurled the shell into the water ahead of them. The seas churned upward, and the portal opened.

"Those shells could be useful for trading," Eurna joked.

"That of the gods should not be used as such," Marr said.

"I know, I know. Damn this Dwemhar holiness."

Evurn laughed. "The gods are not so holy themselves. But I would assume shells such as that to be rare. The true value is knowing when to use them."

The ship lurched forward, moving through the portal and using Kealin's mind as an anchor as they emerged to a familiar site for the two half-elves.

The golden orb of the *Aela Sunrise* was before them. The orb though was encased in ice, untouchable, or so it appeared for now. The island surrounding them was just as it was before, except for the pillars that produced magic into the heavens. There was an exceptionally bright white fog rolling over the bow of the ship.

For a moment, Evurn and Aeveam just stared at the ship that had been their home for so long. Kealin walked to edge of the ship and glanced to Evurn who avoided his eyes. The shadow elf looked instead to the island itself.

"Strange, some effect is upon those standing stones," Evurn said. "What was this place before?"

"The home of a hermit, a man cursed to live until released by Vankou. A driving spirit on our journey when we came here." Kealin paused. "It was one of the last times I spoke to Valrin before his death. Before the dwarves came."

"Bastard Rugag," Aeveam said.

As Eurna guided the *Dismal Rain* near the edge of the ice-covered ship, Aeveam tossed a ball of fire at the ice. The flame did nothing to the frigid ice.

Evurn angled his staff at the ice, sending a streaming blast of arcane fire, and again, nothing happened. Not even the frost on the ice dissipated.

"Ice that does not melt?" questioned Master Rukes.

They were now right against the ship, and Taslun drew his weapon. Taslun moved the runes along the hilt, a flaming blue sword emerged with a sizzling sound in the air. He pressed the blade against the ice, and still there was no searing steam, no cracking of the solid form. Master Rukes even struck the ice with his sword, and it seemed nothing was working.

"I believe our answer is the first riddle we saw upon our arrival," Evurn said.

Kealin looked toward the towers and the white fogs.

"That is not too far away. We can dock the ship at the shore, and I and Taslun will go there."

"Truly not!" Aeveam exclaimed. "We must all go and keep only Eurna and perhaps one other."

"That's how your captain died," Taslun said, "and back then we only worried about dwarves. My brother and I will go. The rest of you will remain. Keep an eye on the skies, seas, and coast. I think that those spires somehow affect our magic use here. Something is not as it should be, but we will deal with it."

Eurna took them away from the icy form of the *Aela Sunrise* and then brought the ship nearly to the shore.

"That is close enough," Taslun said.

They were still a distance away from the shore.

"That water is cold," Marr said.

"We will not touch it," the undead form said. "Come, Brother."

Taslun grabbed hold of Kealin and, in a feat of acrobatics, leaped toward the shoreline, landing several paces from the water's edge with an eruption of ice.

"A new skill?"

"One of many, Brother!"

Kealin looked back toward the *Truest Bliss* as Aeveam tossed two unlit torches toward them. Taslun caught them and managed to light them with his blade.

"Watch yourselves," Kealin shouted.

Evurn made a motion upward with his staff in acknowledgment, and the two brothers turned toward their destination.

Kealin shuddered to a bitterly cold wind that tore through him. It was ironic to him to be at this moment. It was a familiar feeling yet one that felt cursed all the same. They were missing one who should be with them, but that was before. The time before with the lone hovel beside the shore was years ago now.

He looked back to the *Truest Bliss* and noticed an increasing flow of snow caused his clear view of the ship to fade.

Taslun was like a massive living torch. His body was glowing, and his staff formed a large ball of fire that showed the path before them. Howling winds tore across the open fields, and down and back up, they journeyed over the frozen badlands and ancient carved-out sections that were once rivers.

As they came to a large monolithic stone, Kealin tucked himself against the stone to shield from the wind, and Taslun looked down at him.

"It is cold for you, I am sure."

Kealin shivered but shook his head. "Yes, but do not worry of it."

"I am not. Not for myself. An advantage of being dead. Here." He handed him his staff with the burning orb. As Kealin grasped it, the orb shimmered white and then became red. He could feel warmness emanating from the flames.

"There. Good," Taslun said. "Stubborn brother, even after so much, you will not admit the simplest of things! If there is one truth I can give you, it is that strength of the physical body is but one pillar holding the temple of a strong spirit. Not in your form as of now, but one day, you'll unlock that which is within you beyond flesh."

Taslun turned from him, and they began to journey toward the tall spires still quite a distance away.

Kealin noticed that as he stared at the staff in his hand, the etchings and design of the device were beginning to change, even though only so slightly. It seemed his brother's device was altered by Kealin's own powers. The warmth from the magic was much more useful than he'd expected, and as the harsh storm began to subside, the sheer black cliffs at the base of the spires greeted them with the strange sounds of melody as the winds twisted up through the spires. The white glow they had seen before was much more defined and appeared as wisps of raiment high upon the spires as if in some way, they were placed with intention, though as the wind blew, the fogs undulated like clouds.

They were now ascending the spire itself, leaving beyond the tundra before they began a climb up the narrow paths that led to the base of the spires. From the lower portions, they couldn't see an easy way up, but ascending the icy exterior of the spires, they found a way up to a slightly flat plane that then led to a slight incline that snaked up and between the spires themselves.

"I did not think, Brother," Taslun began, "that I would ever be with you as this again. But I do not deny that I praise our sister—even now that she is dead—I praise her for opening the path."

Kealin thought of Alri for a moment as he then saw Taslun reaching a hand down to him to pull him up to a flat area and a pathway further up.

"Tell me, Brother. I already know you were there for her death. Was her heart evil or was it something else?"

Kealin took his hand and ascended up to the level of his brother. "It was the evil that destroyed us before. The Itsu Priest. But the desire to save our baby brother, to destroy those who threatened him, that was her. I did not know that my strike would end her life, for I did not know she was the true evil."

Taslun smiled. "She summoned an army for you and our sibling, our sibling who I believe is still yet alive. That I am sure. Alri was not the evil in the land. She was taken. We will honor her soon, Kealin."

As they began further up the snowy, rocky pathway, Kealin looked around at their surroundings and noticed that the rocks themselves seemed to be glowing.

"This is an odd place. When we came before, I did not think too much of it."

"But now you wonder of its origin," said Taslun. "I tell you, none know the origin of magic, but the presence of something upon these spires tells me there is something of power here."

They continued up the pathway. They were soon surprised by the finding of a random torch glowing in the snowdrift. As Taslun went to touch the torch, the winds shifted, and several other torches suddenly became alight, leading up a snaking path that led further upward.

"Something or someone expects us," Taslun said. "I will not deny this is a strange presence in such a desolate place."

They could no longer see the sky as it was before. The white fog-like substance now shifted to silver and gold, moving alongside them as they began through two spires. There was a sudden apparition to their right, and in a single motion, both brothers brandished their weapons.

It appeared to be a female wearing a white dress. She stared at them and then moved through them before dancing across their path and moving further up. As she did, other apparitions appeared, more females almost just like the first, followed by a large group of men. These were backing up and held weapons, but they were no threat to Kealin or Taslun. It was as if they were seeing events that transpired before.

Kealin turned to see that the spires they'd passed through now appeared as great towers, aflame with the polar lights, and further beyond, there was a single figure brandishing a large blade. The men holding weapons simply faded away as this man was immediately amongst them. Then, in flashes of light, they saw the man come upon each woman, cutting into their forms one after another.

Taslun stopped and looked back to Kealin, "This is not happening now, it is as if we are seeing a memory."

The lights of the lone warrior suddenly darkened, and the fog rolled over them, nearly veiling the path.

Go now, your kind is not welcome here.

It was a sudden, unexpected shout, and with it, the silver bands rolled over them, causing Kealin to wince in pain and fall to his knees. Taslun ran to him and pulled him up.

"Brother, that was a spirit bane, meant to keep spirits clung to the living out, but I even felt pain from it myself. Whatever haunts this place is a strange entity. We must be watchful."

They came to one of the main spires that had purple energy undulating from its base. Though it could be seen from below, this place had a large ruined temple with several broken-down columns and shattered crystals that where partially covered in snow.

"This is not a place I have heard of. Not in any book of Urlas or elsewhere," Taslun said.

The place they were in was older than most. Perhaps older than the elves, or so Kealin thought. A sound like thunder rattled through the peaks.

Kealin and Taslun pivoted on their feet, both hearing the rapid crunching snow behind them and turning to see a spectral warrior in mid-jump. The arching swing of Taslun's spear as it ignited with a blue blade gave Kealin a moment to spin with his Dwemhar blade. Both of their weapons passed near the warrior, but as it touched the ground, it launched itself atop one of the broken columns.

This was not something Kealin had ever seen. It had white raiment flowing with the arctic winds, and a silver blade not too unlike Kealin's own. Its eyes were white, and it seemed to be out of breath. The white fogs of the spires wrapped around it, and it gained what appeared as massive tentacles for arms. The snowdrifts spun around the two brothers. From the icy earth rose creatures of ice and stone with the form of bullish beasts.

The spectral warrior pointed, and the creatures attacked.

Kealin charged forward, jumping over the first one and arching his sword underneath him. It slid along the icy beast before getting caught in the creature itself and pulling him down. He landed on his knees and attempted to force his blade from the creature, but found another creature nearly upon him. He released his sword. Closing his eyes, he focused his Dwemhar energies and slammed the ground, throwing the creatures back in a wave of force.

Taslun dealt with his own issues. His blade was not halted by the creatures, but neither did it hurt them. As his energies raged and his body burned with a blue fire, he swung and sliced into the creatures, but they simply reconstituted themselves. Kealin closed his eyes once again as the two creatures he had thrown back now charged him. He reached out, seeing their life forces within their bodies, and seized them with his mind, imagining them splitting apart. With the sounds of shattering ice, they were destroyed, freeing his blade. Taslun sensed what Kealin had done and did the same, taking out three more of the ice beasts before the spectral warrior dropped between them.

Kealin and Taslun both swung their weapons at it, but in a spinning fury, it parried both and tossed the brothers back.

Kealin brought his sword back in a guarded stance and focused his energies. Taslun engaged their foe, making repeated strikes against its white blade. Kealin shifted his feet in the ice and imagined himself just behind the warrior. In a flash, he was there, but before he could strike, the warrior did the same and was behind him.

He made a sloppy parry, catching his opponent's sword just as the tip cut into his side. Kealin recoiled and slammed the ground with his blade, sending a ripple of energy at his foe as Taslun leaped over him, stabbing his spear point into the ice just next to the warrior.

A blast of blue fire engulfed their foe.

Layers of silver flew down from the peaks of the spires, and magic erupted upward into the night sky. The streams of silver moved around the warrior, wrapping into one form, shifting and rolling off its body before it made the strangest shrill. It leaped forward, two wide arms of fog swiping at them, and began running around the ruins like some type of possessed beast. Kealin evaded it as it nearly trampled him, reminding him more of a strange bird than an agile warrior like before. It made several shriller sounds before the remaining foggy silver strands wrapped around its form, leaving a layered mass of flesh.

"What devilry is this?" Taslun asked. "I saw much of strange magics when near Vakron-Tur. This is no magic I have seen before."

An eruption of white fire shot out from the mass, sending both Kealin and Taslun behind cover as in an eruption of white, the warrior reappeared. This time, it floated high above them. It held a much larger blade but did not directly attack them.

They both slowly stepped out from where they

were hiding. Their weapons remained angled upward as they crept out into the open.

"What are you?" Kealin shouted.

The warrior slowly lowered to the ground and removed a tall white helmet.

It appeared to be a man. He had white skin and flowing white hair.

"You are not Dwemhar assassins? This is not the time I was told to prepare for?"

"You speak our language," Taslun began, "but so does our enemy. You cursed this place. What allegiance do you have?"

"I am a saint of the gods."

"A saint of the gods does not curse a place of magic."

"Perhaps I save it? Save it from the destruction to come? What are you?" the man said, staring at Taslun.

Taslun smiled with a crooked grin. "I am what this world created, a being unlike others. Unlike the living."

The man placed his blade on his back and walked away from them.

Kealin lowered his blade but did not move.

"I assumed you came to kill me, but I can sense the Dwemhar have faded away. It is true?"

Kealin looked to Taslun and then back to the warrior. "What are you?" he asked. "You claim you are a saint, but I know no saints, and you are in a desolate place. You were not here many years ago when I and my siblings came through."

"I am old. I am part of a plan that was. That is."

"What god?" Taslun asked.

The warrior turned around and stared at Kealin.

"The one who gave you the blade upon your back. The highest Itsu god, the fallen one."

Taslun's glare jerked toward Kealin, but the warrior did not move for a weapon.

"You are angry? I told you what you wished. That deemed evil and holy are dependent on the view you have of them. I am one of many to awaken. One of many to return, or so I understand. Not all our kind is good. The stories and pictures within the region talk of sea peoples and the Dwemhar, but not all Dwemhar were holy. The sea peoples understood. I was forced here by a Dwemhar, forced to sleep as others were forced to live until death was allowed. There was the one who took the form of the god Vankou, the being I was sent to kill. I could never find it."

"What took the form of the god of death?"

"I do not know anymore. That being disrupted my memories, fractured my mind. As was done to others like me. Ones I once called friend. Though, I can no longer remember their names. I remain sentient because I draw energy from you two. I have no form in this world. I remain between the realms of life and death, awakened for my purpose—to protect this source of magic—but you are not mere Dwemhar. You are half-bloods. Well, one of you is. I sense raw Dwemhar magic upon you, dead man."

"You must keep the sources of magic open here. We must take a ship encased in ice."

"The realm ship," the warrior said.

"Yes."

"Then the time does come. Soon, the master will release his plan. Something drove me to this madness. Something beyond us all."

"For someone who has a 'fractured mind,' you sure do remember much," Taslun said. "What are you not telling us?"

The warrior shook his head and floated upward.

"You defeated me as best I can describe it in a simple word. I fade from saint to guardian of the spires. I will serve my place as the path is further rocked. The undead one is what drew me from my deeds. I would have killed you," he said, looking to Kealin. "I do not know the plan of my master, but I can sense I must allow you your vessel. All has not come to pass as the old one expected. Much still will be revealed in the coming storms."

Kealin shuddered as the warrior dropped to the ground and became as dust and ice, sending a ripple across the ruins.

"Why does every bastard being we meet speak in riddles?" Taslun shouted. "Come, Brother. Let us retrieve our ship."

As they left the area of the spires, they found it extremely strange that there was no wind anymore. Looking back up, Kealin could see the magic flowing out the spires just like the first time he and his siblings came to this island.

Ahead of them, they could make out flashes of magical fire. Their friends had seen the change in the spires and hopefully were melting the ice that before was not touched by their powers. With luck, the *Aela Sunrise* would be free from the ice prison soon, and they could go about the next leg of their quest.

As they began on to the icy plains, Kealin thought he heard a scratching sound behind him. He looked back, not seeing anything out of place. The rocky face of the base spires appeared to be untouched and unmoved. The sound returned, and this time, Kealin noticed something moved high above them. He drew his blade, and Taslun realized that his brother had stopped.

"You see something?"

"Nothing, but there is another presence here. I hear something but cannot tell from exactly where."

Taslun moved several steps in front of Kealin and pulled out his staff, flicking his wrist. Its blade flashed to life, and he made several swipes in front of him, sending a blast of blue fire outward against the rock face. Several areas of snow melted and rolled down the mountainside, and small flickers of white appeared across the rocks. Kealin glanced up higher, and it seemed that upon a single ridge, there were even more of these white flashes. At first, he thought it was some type of magic or a torch or another device, but staring, he then noticed the snow was shifting around. This was no snow. In a flash of snow and blackness, the many eyes revealed themselves to be the head of some form of stone creature.

"Accursed Itsu!" shouted Taslun, "I know what

these are. There are some in the deep places of magic in the South. They cannot withstand sunlight."

"Were-beasts? Vampires?"

Taslun shook his head. "No, Brother, I'd prefer those."

One of the creatures on the highest reach of the spire made a motioning calling with its hand, pointing to the sky. Beneath this one, several of the creatures upon the cliffs outstretched massive wings and leaped down.

"Gargoyles," Taslun said. "A few of them are fine, but this is quite a bit more than a few."

The first of the creatures landed just beyond where Taslun and Kealin stood. As more of the creatures swooped down to surround them, Kealin and Taslun charged the ones in between them and their way out.

Kealin arced his blade and upward slashed, catching the left leg of the creature and moving across its fleshy but bony form, splitting up through its chest and notching just below the shoulder. The creature wailed, its pointed ears like razors as it attempted to burrow its head in Kealin's armor. He placed his hand on its throat and squeezed. Its eyes darkened, and it collapsed. In the time it had taken him to kill one, several more now blocked their path.

Taslun had been using his weapon with a single blade, but now he held it to the staff, bring about two large scythes of burning Dwemhar energies moving about the gargoyles in a spinning fashion. His blades worked exceptionally well to cut the creatures, and Kealin took the lower path to simply finish the other ones off that were not completely dead yet as they moved their way across the snowy lands.

The further they got away from the spires, the more the gargoyles took to the air, and soon, it was a massive blue flash above them. Whatever trap they had hoped to set, it seemed they had wandered into one on their own. With a roar in the air splitting through the winds off the Glacial Seas like ice shattering upon the snow, their foe, the dragon, had arrived.

"It seems there's a rift upon the lands. Old friends returned to be dealt with. I am the master of the seas."

The dragon's voice was a booming sound that brought with it crazed amounts of wind and ice. The gargoyles circled around their dragon master.

"Why the hell do we need to get the horn. The dragon is right here," Taslun shouted.

"We need to get to the others. We cannot be separated."

The portal in which the dragon had come from was still open, swirling the crackling of thunder around its edge. The gargoyles were flying into it.

"The time of true reckoning is upon us. Go, go and prepare as our master desires. I will deal with this rabble. If the blight has been removed from the spire tops, then the absolute conclusion of all things draws nigh."

Kealin and Taslun were sprinting toward the masts of the ships ahead. The ice covering the realm ship had all but melted and its golden orb surrounding its surface was shining brightly. The air around Kealin's face suddenly became colder. He glanced behind him to see the monstrous form of the dragon swinging down upon them. He sheathed his Dwemhar blade, twisting and reaching for *Vrikralok* on his back and turning just as the dragon landed within snapping distance of him and his brother.

Taslun jumped up, soaring high above the dragon before slamming his spear into the middle of its back. The timing of this could not have been more perfect for the dragon. As Kealin swung the god-killing blade Taslun's distraction caused the dragon to rear its head up in an attempt to snap his undead brother. This sudden motion caused Kealin to miss.

The brothers tried again. Taslun ran up the neck of the dragon. Lifting his fiery blue blade, he thrust the weapon into the dragon's eye. At that exact moment, Kealin thrust his sword toward the dragon's chest, piercing his ribcage for a mere moment, spilling white blood all over the snow. The dragon recoiled, flapping itself backward, sending both Taslun and Kealin rolling across the snow.

"You are not as feeble as before," the dragon Vaugar snarled.

Its gaping maw was alight with a blue cyclone of icy wind. Whatever prideful attack the dragon had thought would be successful had failed. But this next one would not be avoided so easily.

Kealin looked over to Taslun, who was stumbling to stand but was brandishing his weapon again. The dragon shot a blast of serrating icy wind.

Kealin put up his hand just as a wave of energy coming from the opposite direction shielded them from the blast. Kealin looked up to see the furling coat of Aeveam, with a ward of magic shielding the three of them.

The dragon roared, taking to the sky and ascending with full purpose to smash the ground where the three of them were.

"Come to the ship, now!" Aeveam said.

Kealin ran with the other two as the dragon went into a dive from high above.

He could see a clear view of the ships ahead. Aeveam turned, summoning a white spear above her head and sending the bolt with a crackling sound toward the beast above. The dragon screamed, somehow halted in its descent, before sending another blast of ice raining down upon them. Kealin and Taslun fell beneath the hastily crafted ward of Aeveam's magic. Aeveam and Kealin had both been struck with icy shards.

"Damn this thing," Taslun shouted.

The dragon struck the orb, and it shattered in an explosion of arcane ripples, crackling around them.

The dragon stammered back, not wishing to get too close to the blade that had already pierced his chest once.

Aeveam summoned a blast of fire, and the dragon responded with its own icy breath, the two of them fighting back and forth to push each other's attack. Taslun and Kealin fell back behind Aeveam as the icy breath of the dragon was turning the ground around them to an ever-increasingly large icy mound. The dragon stomped forward as Aeveam struggled to keep her spell strong enough to deflect the dragon.

A large iron bolt suddenly flew into the dragon, and it snarled, taking to the sky. Kealin looked to see Captain Eurna angling his ship and Rukes and Marr loading another bolt into the deck mounted crossbow. The dragon was nearly upon the ship, when the golden orb around the *Aela Sunrise* fell, and the ship sent a volley of white orbs at the dragon.

In a blinding explosion, the dragon was thrown against the snowdrifts across the bay. It said nothing else, its wings pounding as it ascended into the portal and left the island in retreat.

Kealin made a point to run toward the shoreline, seeing the *Aela Sunrise*. He noticed Evurn at the helm, who at first was happy they were okay and that the dragon had fled. He then put his head against the helm and began crying.

Captain Eurna brought his ship alongside the *Aela Sunrise*, and with a loud thump, Taslun leaped with Kealin onto the deck of the *Aela Sunrise*. Aeveam floated over the water and landed just behind them.

Kealin paused for a moment, thinking of his friend who had died many years ago. He looked up and locked eyes with the tearful Evurn just as Aeveam embraced the shadow elf.

"He told us it would work out in the coming days," Evurn cried to Aeveam. "We told him not to go alone, but he trusted the half-elves. He said it would all come to pass, and his path was one he would hold to the end."

Evurn looked up at Kealin and Taslun and then turned away, going to the rear of the ship.

At that moment, the polar lights began to dance above them, and Evurn noticed. He balled his fist and shook it at the sky.

"Is this what the gods of the North desire, Wura? I saw good within the boy, something I was lacking. A hope that my homelands had sapped from me! But fate took him away?"

"Not fate," said Taslun, "the acts of a hateful dwarf. His fate was broken. So many fates are not what they should be or at least as we feel they should be. The word fate is an excuse to help those that live on to cope. The world is full of dead souls in living bodies, while those with very much living souls are tortured in crippled bodies.

"Still others find life in death as the physical body dies; there is a place beyond. I see flashes of my journey there, before I was brought back. Your friend may have moved on from the living realm but that is not the end of existence. Take solace in that."

Aeveam smiled and embraced Evurn.

The shadow elf kept a stoic stance and then relaxed, embracing her back.

Kealin approached Evurn and bowed.

"He was my friend too, in the small amount of time we spent with one another. I cannot bring him back, but I will make sure his sacrifice was not in vain."

Evurn looked up and wiped more tears from his eyes. "He trusted you," Evurn said, "so I must. We will bring down that beast, and then we will continue toward the true purpose of our companionship. I feel my life has come to a point where it is complete. I have fought many monsters, but perhaps it is the greater monster within that is my final challenge."

Evurn embraced Kealin. "Stay aboard the ship. He would want you to fight from this deck."

"Let us depart for where we will face the dragon," Marr said, holding a large crossbow bolt. "We are ready to move forward."

"This is all great," Captain Eurna shouted, "but where the hell would we stand a chance? We need to take its wings. Keep it on the ground."

"I know the place for that," Taslun said.

Kealin looked to him. "Where we fought the beast before? Where we met the dragon?"

Taslun grinned and nodded. "It has plenty of space to maneuver, and I think it would be quite a feat to bring down that beast upon the very place where we set it free."

"You set the monster free?" Marr questioned.

"Different times," Kealin said.

At that time, Marr and Eurna's father emerged on the deck.

"Father," Marr said.

But the man did not look well. He looked toward Kealin and then to his son.

"Death draws near. I have had nightmares. Many nightmares. The realm of the ascended draws upon this world, and soon, nothing will be as we wish. There is a growing terror in my mind."

He suddenly dropped to the deck. Marr fell to

her knees as Aeveam leaped the distance between the two ships with her powers, landing beside the old man.

She placed her hand on his forehead and then looked to Kealin and the others. "His powers are waning. He has been focusing his Dwemhar energies to sustain himself, but his mind is beyond troubled. We need to get this done and get to wherever the shaman directs us next."

Kealin nodded and looked to Evurn. "There's a map on this ship, a map that appears above the deck."

Evurn nodded and moved one of the crystal switches.

The map of the Glacial Seas appeared but seemed to become shadowy instead of the typical clear view of the islands he had remembered. Ice covered all the seas on the image.

"The helm," Evurn said. "Come up here and direct us. I know the way to open a portal that the *Truest Bliss* can follow us through, but you must be at the helm to focus the way." He paused. "He taught me."

Kealin gave a half smile, as it was clear Evurn was tearful once again.

Taslun, not paying attention to them at this point, was walking around the deck. "So, this ship is a Dwemhar vessel? Looks like a common fishing vessel. Strange."

As Kealin gripped the helm of the *Aela Sunrise*, he remembered suddenly the night he had stayed up with Valrin and learned of the constellations. That felt like such a long time ago, but in the blink of time, that was his life as an elf—it was nothing.

Evurn walked back behind Kealin. "Dead one, let me show you the true vessel. What you saw and see now was a mere disguise. We have no need to blend in within this apocalyptic sea."

As he said that, he moved a crystal, and the weathered wood and scraped deck shifted to the pure-white ship that Evurn knew but Kealin had never seen. The vessel seemed to glow for a moment, and Eurna had his hands up in the air.

"Now my ship looks like a wreck! I need that kind of magic within the ship."

"It is not magic," Aeveam said. "It is the sciences of Dwemhar ingenuity! I could tell you much of this."

Eurna laughed. "Next time we make port, I'll buy you a drink and you can tell me about it!"

Kealin was in awe of the ship, not expecting what he was now standing on, and feeling for a moment that he was exactly where he was supposed to be now.

"Focus on the place we are to go," Evurn said, passing him. The shadow elf went to the center mass and placed Valrin's amulet against the wood. The amulet began to glow brightly.

Kealin closed his eyes and saw those around him of Dwemhar descent glowing in his mind's eye. He shifted his thoughts from the present to his memory, seeing the blue eyes of the dragon and then suddenly floating above the island and the volcanic mountain where the ruins of the sea people were. There was a shuddering feeling from his feet up through the wheel in his hands, and he opened his eyes to see a flashing portal of sorts appear in front of the ship.

The masts of the *Aela Sunrise* shifted, and they moved into the portal. For a moment, he saw stars in every direction, and then the ship struck water once again.

The island of the dragon stood before them, and the volcano roared with plummeting black smoke. He looked back to see the *Truest Bliss* just behind them. Now, they had to prepare to take down the beast, however they were supposed to do that.

9
RETURN TO A MEMORY

IT WAS beyond strange to Kealin being back on the island. Evurn guided the realm ship to the small docking area on the far eastern point of the island. Kealin noticed that the corpse of the creature that the dragon had fought six years ago was still encased in stone. Although, more lava was flowing around its form even at this moment. As he and Taslun exited their ship, Aeveam and Rukes tended to Marr and Eurna's father. He still was not doing well.

"Has the sickness worsened?" Evurn asked.

"I don't know," Aeveam said. "His body is already so weak. In truth, I believe he would already be dead if it was not for his drawing of Dwemhar energies."

"That is the one eventual path for all," Taslun said.

Both Marr and Eurna looked up at him.

"Well," Eurna said, "That is not something that we are ready for."

"None are ready for it. But we must be," Rukes

said. "We must plan this out. That beast is able to flee with such haste that upon its arrival we must be sure it has no way to flee at all."

"I will be our bait for the trap," Taslun said. "I do think I'm capable of drawing a dragon down to the ground, or at least distracting it long enough for a few well-placed shots for the ships to injure it. Plus," he said, pulling out a large circular black disk, "it may be time for my friend to come play with us."

"Your friend?" Kealin asked.

"My friend." Taslun smiled. "So do I just blow this horn?"

"Think of the dragon in your mind and then blow the horn. It will have no choice but to appear before you."

"If only I could control this beast like I do my friend!"

Evurn twirled his staff and looked up at the sky. "We fight some type of dragon beast demigod thing, and all you will tell us is you have a friend?"

Taslun bowed. "You think I walked from the southern Lost Sands regions all the way to the northern coast and then just swam across the Vindas Sea to the northern point just near the Glacial Seas? Do not worry about my friend. My friend is a gift from a certain undead commander to aid me in my quest to assist my brother here," he said, motioning toward Kealin. "I will beat this dragon one way or another to death, and if my brother can have a narwhal friend, I can have another kind of friend."

"Okay, so the undead will stand in the middle of

the island and wave his hand up and down to attract the dragon," Eurna said. "I suggest we keep our ships separate on either side of the island. I'll take the western portion, and you, Evurn, be on the east. We may only have one shot to hit the beast. I suggest going for its wings, obviously. We also want to try to get it on land and not let it return to the water."

"Why?" Marr asked. "Can it swim?"

"We have to kill it. You can't tell if you actually kill it while it's in the water. We must be sure of its death," Evurn pointed out. "The last dragon of any special significance I fought required following a particular set of instructions to keep it from regenerating. We have to assume this dragon will be something like that."

"So how did you kill it?" Aeveam asked.

"Your father and I worked together, and as he severed the head, we used ash to keep it from regrowing."

Taslun laughed. "Screw ash. Once the damn thing is on the ground, we strike it from all sides. Weapons, magic, whatever it takes. Something will work. Plus, my friend can kill it if we can get it down."

"It is a simple plan, but we should not complicate this," Rukes said. "We get it down, we kill it, and we end this."

Evurn nodded. "And move your father to my ship. I can protect him better than the *Truest Bliss*. No offense to your simple vessel, Eurna."

"No, no offense to the vessel that took us to your dear ship!" Eurna laughed.

"Is there not a place on the island?"

"There is," said Kealin, "but I agree. Keep him on a ship. We do not know what will happen if we are able to ground the beast. There are at least wards upon the *Aela Sunrise*."

Though they had definite intent to get going with their plan very soon, it was decided that they best try to at least eat something. The stores were limited and getting thinner. There was still quite a bit of salted meat within the bowels of the *Truest Bliss*. As an impromptu dinner upon a lone island was had, along with a pot of coffee, Kealin and Taslun stood off to the side and stared at the gathering.

Though Marr ate quickly and returned to her father's side, not too keen a warrior for such an act as was to soon be upon them, the others made small talk and laughed every so often.

Taslun kept twisting the black disk in his hand, looking to Kealin, who sipped his coffee.

"You're not going to tell me what your friend is?"

Taslun laughed. "Well, if you are wondering, my friend is not this disk. This is a portal device capable of creating a passage to where my friend is resting."

"You have a device that is a portal to your friend?"

"Yes, he wouldn't quite fit on the ship. When we got to the North Cape and I met up with these others, I figured the sight of the undead warrior standing before them to be better received without my friend standing next to me."

Kealin shook his head and raised his eyebrows as he exhaled and just stared at his brother.

"Come now, Kealin, you know I would not let you down. Besides, where is the narwhal?"

"Wherever it wants to be. It's also something that might be summoned, though I do feel mine more alive than yours."

Taslun nodded. "Indeed, good brother, indeed. Suvasel will not let us down in a time of need, and my friend is always ready."

The time had come. Captain Eurna positioned himself to the far western waters, and Evurn took to the east. Taslun stood in the dead center of the island not too far from a flow of lava that came shortly before a series of quakes rocked the island.

Kealin, Rukes, and Aeveam ran toward the area where Kealin and his siblings had spent the night, before emerging on the island's surface years ago. The shifting island and frequent lava flows had managed to open another pathway that led to the water's surface. From there, they could see the *Truest Bliss* and a portion of the island itself. Kealin crawled back up to where he could see Taslun holding the Dragon Scream.

The skies above them began to twist with a turbulent amount of wind. With some favor, the winds might help them against the dragon or protect the beast, considering the effect on the *Truest Bliss'* weapons. He knew Taslun was only waiting for them to descend, and as his brother looked down at him, Kealin sank away to the lower area, joining the other two in watching what they could from their hideaway.

The sudden horn call of the Dragon Scream slit the otherwise random sounds of wind and crashing seas upon the southern portion of the island. Taslun made several long calls and then paused. There was silence. Not just silence from the horn itself, but the wind had stilled, and as Kealin looked down toward the water at the base of the cave, he noticed that it was still striking with the same velocity that it had before.

The air had shifted. He looked to Aeveam, who was speaking, but he could not hear it. She tapped her ears, signifying the same. Kealin heard the horn call again and clamored up the passage to the outside. Taslun dropped the horn at the same time, brandishing his weapon.

A roar split the air, and Kealin investigated the sky above the western portion of the island. A massive spinning portal of clouds and white light emerged in the otherwise bleak skies.

A dazzling blue flash came before another roar rolled across the island, and the massive form of the great demigod dragon, Vaugar, made a pass just over where Taslun stood and circled around the volcano. It swooped down, landing just before Taslun, and roared at him before bowing.

"Cursed horn!" Vaugar roared. "From what rotting hole did you find that?"

Taslun laughed and jumped at the beast.

"Damn creature of the gods, you are foolish!"

The dragon recoiled back, flapping its large near

blue sapphire-esque wings, "You summon me with that which was lost. Where did you find that accursed horn?"

The dragon recoiled in surprise. At the moment, Kealin made a point to motion for the others to move upward. The dragon pounded its wings, attempting to get altitude just as Taslun jumped up midair, reaching the creature and driving his blade into its arm. The dragon roared, snapping his tail around, slapping him back down to the snowy island. As Kealin, Aeveam, and Master Rukes emerged onto the battle plain, the dragon seemed to growl with a strange cackling.

"So, this is a trap? You're not my master summoning me. You are not some dragon hunters seeking my head? This is all arranged. Dare I say I have been betrayed? My place was secure! What wretched northern god moves against me?"

The dragon's questioning was cut short as Aeveam summoned the energy of the Dwemhar before releasing a bolt of piercing white magic straight into the creature's neck. The demigod dragon seemed to simply brush off the attack and take higher into the air. Kealin ran toward his brother, sliding to where his body lay, and attempted to pull his arm out of the icy rock of the island.

"He hit you quite hard," Kealin said.

"Are you kidding me? Are you actually telling me that he hit me hard? My damn arm is stuck in the rock."

Even as he said this, his brother ripped his arm upward, shattering the rock.

"That beast is fleeing rather quickly. Perhaps we should not have given it so much berth."

The dragon was up and moving higher, making a spinning motion into the sky, no doubt attempting to summon the portal to draw itself from this world. At that moment, there were multiple flashes as the *Aela Sunrise* let loose a volley of projectiles. Like before, the dragon was struck and flung backward, landing in the ocean.

The *Truest Bliss* advanced toward the creature, firing two iron bolts into its form, striking it in the back and in its right wing. The creature roared clamoring to take to the sky, not to escape this time but to destroy the *Truest Bliss*.

"It is going for Eurna!" Aeveam said.

The group of them ran toward the edge of the island, and saw the *Truest Bliss*. The dragon was moving toward it. It made a hard left, headed toward the island, and fired another volley of bolts, striking the creature at least once more, but not slowing it.

Evurn was bringing the *Aela Sunrise* in range to support the *Truest Bliss*. Kealin ran down to the rocks. He took out his hammer and smashed the rock, summoning his narwhal to the surface.

As Taslun saw what Kealin was doing, he did the same, summoning his own little friend, as he continued to refer to whatever it was he had.

As the narwhal emerged from its portal in the water, Kealin looked back to see the black disk his brother had had now on the snow, and a large green cyclone of energy erupting from the form.

Taslun laughed. "Do not worry of this Brother. You get on your little whale. I will show you real power."

Taslun seemed to be dancing around in the strangest fashion as Kealin went down to the water's edge.

The narwhal was acting erratic, motioning toward the dragon.

That thing? Why? It is an old creature of the seas, nearly like my master.

"You question? We have to kill it, but first, it seems the captain of the *Truest Bliss* may need us quicker."

As Kealin boarded his boat and tugged the reins, moving away from the island in a quick fashion, he turned around to see an explosion of blackness rolling over the island. A roar split through the air, but it was not a dragon.

Kealin's eyes widened, and he smiled. This was Taslun's friend.

The shadow beast, crafted by his sister, a fusion of bones and magic known as a Dagarok, now entered the realm of the Glacial Seas. Taslun took position atop its shoulders, and the creature roared as his brother's large staff burned a bright blue.

The dragon had reached the *Truest Bliss* and smashed into the center of its hull. As quick as Kealin was, the *Aela Sunrise* was already closing in on the *Truest Bliss*, firing streaks of energy at the dragon and forcing it from completely destroying the *Truest Bliss*.

The dragon took to the sky, arcing around and

sending a blast of ice directly at Evurn. Without command, Kealin's narwhal angled its own horn and the crown given by the god of the seas, sending a wave of energy, knocking the creature from its rapid attack and literally pushing his chin up toward the sky as several blasts struck the dragon in the chest. The beast landed in the waters just beside Evurn, but instead of turning and taking a chance on attacking the dragon directly, Kealin continued to the *Truest Bliss*.

As they arrived on the railings of the sinking vessel, the captain was bleeding and pulling points of splintered wood from his arms.

"That bastard dragon took my ship. Why did he go after my ship? I'm not the ship launching the sparkly stuff."

The vessel was lost. As Kealin brought his boat up alongside the nearly sunken ship, there seemed to be some delay in the captain leaving his vessel.

"I . . . I have always heard the myths of never abandoning the vessel you captain. A captain must remain with a sinking ship. It seems death quickly finds you afterward if you do not."

"I care little of that myth," Kealin said. "You're not meeting your death this day. Get on the boat so we can go to the island. You're injured."

As he jumped from the shattered railings onto Kealin's boat, Kealin directed them away and back toward the island.

"No, head toward that beast. I want my sword in his skull."

Kealin had never seen the captain as angry as this.

Even in his time before when they took on another ship back before he was captured as a gladiator, he did not seem this ferocious.

The dragon was still tossing in the waters just beside Evurn. Though alone, Evurn was using his staff to attempt to entangle the creature before firing more volleys from the Dwemhar vessel into its form. The water would be their greatest enemy right now. Having an enraged captain on his boat was not helping things at this point.

"Here's the deal, my friend, we will make one pass. I will leap aboard the beast and then to the *Aela Sunrise*. After I strike it, you will stay with the narwhal and get back to shore. If this creature goes down with just one single strike from my blade, I will be very surprised. I will attempt to wound it on top of everything Evurn has already done."

"So, were my bolts just sugary treats for it?"

"You know what I mean."

The captain shook his head and then nodded. "Evidently, my bolts are made of sugar and are simply a treat."

Kealin laughed at the captain's sarcastic tone and then drew the large sword upon his back. Their greatest fear was the dragon sinking, but as it was right now, if the dragon had its way, it would absolutely take out the realm ship of the Dwemhar.

He knelt, making his profile as small as possible and motioning for the captain to do the same. The dragon was already tearing apart the vines, wrapping around it even as Evurn tried to encase it in a fiery prism surrounding its head. Even with that, it was still slowly breaking free.

The narwhal increased its speed, its thunderous tail propelling them faster toward the dragon. At the last moment, the dragon got its head fully free and blasted the deck where Evurn was.

They were close enough. In one motion, Kealin was upon it. He jumped from his own boat and landed upon the dragon's back. He went for its head but caught it directly in the top of its mouth, piercing teeth and gum and sending bits of flesh in a flash of white blood into the cold icy waters.

The dragon swung his head, nearly ripping Kealin straight off him, but instead, his sword went through the tough dragon skin, and he was able to land one more strike, cracking into the creature's wing and breaking a portion of it. The dragon rolled, throwing Kealin into the ocean underneath the monster.

It spun in the water. Its spikes cut into Kealin's back. He couldn't orientate himself, and as the sky above became clear looking up through the waters above him, he could tell the dragon was moving away from the surface of the water. He kicked and pulled with his cupped hands, attempting to drag him and his sword up to the surface, when he felt several vines grab on to him and was rushed up to the top.

It was Evurn. As he was laid on the deck of the realm ship, Evurn did not take a moment to check on them but was at the helm again.

"It seems he is taking revenge on our friends. He goes to the island and to his death, I am sure."

Kealin was freezing cold as his back burned from the icy cold upon his torn skin. He reached at his back, feeling the wounds and noticing the gashes in his armor. He looked to see the massive dragon attempting to fly but falling back into the water, clawing and kicking as he struggled to get to the island. If he could get to land, the dragon could still possibly fly again.

Kealin scanned the island but could not see his brother, when in a sudden explosion of water directly behind the dragon, he saw the enraged Dagarok and Taslun with his blue spear burning bright smash into the dragon. They made repeated strikes against its hide, and the dragon clawed up the island, the Dagarok just behind him. The dragon turned, grabbing hold of the Dagarok, and thus a battle of titans began. As the dragon attempted to bite Taslun from atop his mount, the Dagarok brought his twin blades down, striking the dragon in his shoulder and what remained of its right wing.

But Taslun and the Dagarok were not the dragon's only problem. As it struggled to get away from multiple blasts of magic from Aeveam, it took two white spears of Dwemhar magic and several bolts of lightning. It dodged another blast and then took two slashes from the Dagarok.

It finally backed itself to where its tail dangled off the edge of the island, and did not notice the *Aela Sunrise* hastily approaching from behind it. Kealin made his way to the front of the ship as the dragon began speaking.

"I am the master of the skies ever since the coming

ice and the shifting of the mountains. I have served my master faithfully, attacking that which was the realm of the god Dimn for the Itsu Priest, commanding the swarms of Vankou's cursed creatures to swarm what towns the one of death did not want iced over. Why now shall I have enemies sent against me? Have I been but a pawn? Is the great dragon of old, the near god form that I have obtained, truly meant to fall upon the ice in defeat by his master's own hand?"

The *Aela Sunrise* was now just beneath the dragon's tail. Evurn dropped the anchors, and both him and Kealin ran for the dragon, leaping up onto its massive tail and running up its spine. The two elves sprinted with their weapons out. *Vrikralok* began to glow red as Evurn's staff shined with a burning brilliance, sending waves of blue sparks out even as the dragon turned to spot them upon its back.

It was too late. Evurn cast his spell, striking the creature on the side of the face just as Kealin jumped, angling his sword beneath him as he drove *Vrikralok* into the scales of the dragon. Its blood sprayed out in an arc of red and glimmering white, the power of the sword striking the near-immortal soul of the creature.

The dragon arched up, immediately throwing both Kealin and Evurn high into the air. Taslun rushed forward with his Dagarok. The undead beast stabbed both of its swords into the underbelly of the beast as Taslun leapt into the air, his spear growing as he lifted it above his head before dropping onto the head of the dragon.

It was done.

The dragon flopped madly, spraying blood across the beach as Aeveam lowered her hands, having caught both Evurn and Kealin with her powers. Master Rukes ran forward, striking the creature's head again, adding to the multiple mortal wounds already upon the creature of the ice.

"Perhaps," the dragon quaked in a final attempt to speak, its voice crackling and its tone sputtering with the increased blood running out of its mouth, "I am not the only one led astray. I know you two, elves of Urlas. Beware your paths, for it has always been forsaken. I just did not know that mine was as well."

There was another sound upon the wind, and in a spectral form, the bone dragon from before appeared. It ran into its own bleeding form, and wisps of fog wrapped itself into the body of the dragon.

The creature burst into blue flames that crackled like ice as the winds of the North blew upon the island, sending specs of ice into the sky. The creature turned into a bright white before a gust blew over them, sending the creature to become one with the sky around them.

"We have defeated the beast," Aeveam said. "The path ahead is secure."

"What did that beast speak of?" Evurn asked. "Who is its master?"

"Vankou," said Taslun.

"What does a god of death have with a creature such as this?"

"Does it matter?" Aeveam asked. "It is dead. It cannot harm us."

Evurn pulled his coat around him and walked back to the edge of the cliffs. The *Aela Sunrise* was moving around the edge of the island, Captain Eurna at the helm.

"It cannot, but we cannot ignore all signs. This creature did not know we were coming to kill it. It has a false sense of hope."

"Perhaps there is more evil at work," Master Rukes suggested. "Another player upon this game, a piece not yet discovered."

"The Itsu Priest worked with this beast once," Kealin said, "but even that agreement seemed strange. We released this creature from the island and destroyed it for the threat it was to future events. We are reversing what we set into motion."

Taslun nodded. "The creature is dead. We move forward into what fate would have us do."

"I know this prophecy," Evurn said. "It was mentioned to me by dear Valrin. I do feel he wondered of the true purpose of such things. The purpose of the Stormborn and your kind was always tied to the Dwemhar and the sea peoples. The Dwemhar having ascended and the sea peoples the ones left behind. A path was prepared, but to what end?"

There was a flash of lightning, and in a brilliant white flash appeared the shaman. "That which is done completes the tasks needed for us to move upon the destination we must seek. I have made a mark upon the map of the *Aela Sunrise*. I will await you there. Come, brothers. We must embrace the tower of old."

As quickly as he had come, Iouir vanished.

"Come, let us finish what has begun," Taslun said.

They went back toward the ancient docks, noticing the *Aela Sunrise* was now locked into the dock itself. The ship's scratches and scuffs, the wood that was splintered, was restored. As Evurn moved toward the back of the ship, he twisted several crystals.

"That which powers the ship has been restored, and"—he quickly stood up and looked at the others—"we have more crystals, like the spots that were bare before are now alive. The ship could possibly do much more than before, or at least, the energy contained before it would need to recharge under moonlight has been greatly increased."

Kealin looked down to where Evurn was looking. "So we could take flight for much longer?"

"You know of this power?"

"There was a storm on the first voyage I took on this ship. We ascended into the clouds, though it was only for a short time."

Evurn smiled. "Valrin always looked for places like this, places where augmentations were possible. He once found a place of a Master Shipwright, where such ships like this were made. He always wished to find an ancient port that still had energy. In that place, he only found the corpse of an ancient man. The strangest of stories, and one only he could tell. He claimed the man did not die until Valrin was upon him. A curse of some kind. Not too much unlike the hermit you mentioned before."

"A man not able to die until allowed," Kealin said.

Taslun nodded, "An uncomfortable encounter."

Evurn looked up at the volcanic mountain. "Though fire burns within it, I have now laid eyes on an ancient city and seen the ship of my friend empowered by the old magic of the Dwemhar. In a way, with this simple act, I have seen Valrin's wish fulfilled."

The shadow elf wiped a tear from his eye and motioned for Captain Eurna to move from the helm. "Come now, Captain, you lost your ship. I can't have you losing this one."

Evurn moved them from the island and brought up the image of the map. "There is a place to the north of this island. It is not an island recognized by the map, but we shall go there."

"I guess there is a portal from Urlas to this place?" Rukes asked.

"Unless he has a ship." Aeveam laughed.

The *Aela Sunrise* turned north as Kealin looked to Marr and her father emerging from below deck.

"My father has had another vision," she announced. "The Dwemhar are upon our world. They stir at the doorway to our realm. But a great shroud is upon them. A darkness envelops their light."

10

ASCENSION

KEALIN HAD JOINED Evurn at the helm. The others had not said much to each other following Marr's announcement, and any amount of small talk seemed forced at this moment. Aeveam was meditating on the bow of the ship, attempting to connect with the Shaman.

"I do wonder what this all means," Evurn said.

Kealin looked at the shadow elf and then back toward the open expanse before them.

"Those of Dwemhar blood are gathered now. This shaman made a point to protect you and Valrin but only as long as needed for our friend to serve his purpose. Then you went on your own quest to save your siblings, an act alone, an act away from this path he chose for you. Eventually, after you failed, you returned, and the very Glacial Seas are tearing themselves apart. The world is not in balance. You and your siblings released a dragon upon the region on your quest to protect the god of winds, and now we have struck the beast down. I struggle to find the sense in our actions. Why do we do this?"

"The return of the Dwemhar?" Kealin suggested.

"But would they not return without us? What purpose do we serve to be gathered together? To protect them? For ascended beings, they are truly weak in the form in which they return to this world. I have seen no power that suggests they are at risk."

Kealin looked over to his brother lying on the bow of the ship in a strange sleep-like trance, and then to Evurn.

"The spirit we met on the island where the *Aela Sunrise* was spoke something of a divide in the Dwemhar, beyond simply the sea peoples and the others. There was a schism of some kind. I have to believe that if there was a schism, perhaps we move to protect them from powers still within the world that may threaten them."

"So subservient?"

"What?"

"Oh, the half-elf who burned down half a world is going from place to place at the will of another. It surprises me."

Kealin looked down at the keel of the ship. "I made my own path, and I failed. Perhaps seeing this one until the end will result in a different end."

"Or the same."

Evurn's lack of optimism was strangely comforting to him.

"You do not feel we can be successful?"

"No, we could be, or we could not be. The world does not have to form as our hands try to mold it. We could stand against whatever we are to face in the coming days with absolute victory, or we could all die. I have seen much death, and I ran from that life. I took up magic and have excelled in many ways with that.

As a young shadow elf training on the far eastern coasts of my lands, there was a period of the year with terrible ocean storms that would ravage our coasts. It was during this time that new warriors were given a form of final test. We were left alone on pillars of rock above the ocean. The pillars were small, only able to have a single foot at a time in which to balance, which did not give room for mistake. We were given a series of choices. We could hold our position, we could jump into the sea, or we could wait for the storms to strike and either lightning would strike the pillars or the ocean would drown you.

"Keep in mind, every bit of our training was on survival and delivering the killing blows to our foe. We were not taught to back down. Using the powers of our magic, we could shift through the air with ease, but isolated above the ocean, those powers were useless."

"You were given an impossible task, then. A task that was meant to push our mortal limits. It was still a mere test. Your teachers were there."

"They were. They watched many of us die. The sect of my people did not believe in weakness. The test was not of perseverance or determining how to survive. The key was to see death and embrace it, not giving up, no surrendering, but jumping and choosing our path versus waiting for some miracle. We who jumped learned of a hidden cave just beneath us. It was a narrow window of time from jumping and striking the water to seeing this hidden cave with our mind's eye and shifting our form toward it."

"You used powers like a Dwemhar, then?"

Evurn laughed. "Do not kid yourself, elf. Our magic was nothing like the mystics of the Dwemhar, but our powers were shaped within us from training, and I bring this up so that you understand my stance on the coming days. Whatever it is we are to face as the last few living Dwemhar or whatever Marr wants to call it, death is a path that calls to all. We must not be afraid of that.

"I fear a poor death, that of a coward. One should fear missing the proper death meant for your soul. My people were taught to seek out the perfect opponent, the one who would defeat you. Some referred to it as our *perfect darkness*. That was our purpose. In seeking that purpose, we continually improved, yet were let down by those we faced. I tell you, Kealin, I am old. When I at last find that which I feel my many years on these seas have led me to, I do not fear that death. I came here to be left alone. To die. I put down my blades. Took up magic like some wizard and mastered many parts of it but putting down my blades… that was the coward's way. I see that beyond anything else now. I have lost many I cared for. Those who were once crew on this ship. Then, losing Valrin hurt more than I expected it. He was like my child. I saw him grow up from a young boy to some 'promised Stormborn' hero, and he took that role, but the will of Vankou had him brutally murdered."

Evurn leaned over the wheel of the ship and stared at Kealin. "I wonder if that was the path meant for him. It is why I question what your purpose is, what is all our purpose. The world is curving its energies toward us. I can feel the shifts in the fabric of the energies. All will reveal itself soon. I can feel it."

"I have connected with Iouir," Aeveam announced. "He comes to us soon."

Ahead of them was a small island. It came about suddenly, and as they approached, they saw two glowing basins of green fire on either side of a large shimmering pool. A wisp of green energies circled above the pool, and standing on the edge of the pool was a figure.

As Evurn guided the *Aela Sunrise* near the island, the figure vanished and then reappeared on the deck of the ship. It was the shaman.

But he did not look as he did before. Now, he wore armor much like Kealin's but with crystals along his shoulders, and he held a silver staff with a broken crystal at its head. On his back was not one but three large bladed swords.

Kealin approached him. "You never revealed to me that you had such weapons and armor."

He smiled. "My child, I could not. The Urlas elves would not have approved, and they didn't need to. I was a simple bumbling hermit to them, and that purpose served them and I as it should have."

Master Rukes came from below deck, and upon

seeing the shaman, he gave a slight bow. "Truly, our path comes to a final ascension. I am honored to be with a true Dwemhar warrior."

The shaman bowed back. "I was not of the warrior class of my time. I was not as the hero Riakar and his companions, who so many speak of. Yes, he has many forms of his story, but he was a true Dwemhar. I fought beside him near the end of his life within this realm. I only hope I can be beyond that warrior in the coming hour. Evurn, place this crystal in the power reserves of this ship."

Iouir handed Evurn a red crystal just larger than his hand.

"North no longer means what it once did. The seas shall fall away as our living realm gives way to the ascended realms. There is a point where the two converge, and we must secure the bridge between. Keep a northern heading, Evurn, and trust the ship. It will take us where we must go. This is not a place you can find with a map."

As Evurn placed the crystal in the ship's energy compartment, the many runes of the ship came to life, and new ones spread out upon the deck. Kealin felt a sudden increase in the energy flowing through him. As Evurn shifted the ship to a full northern trek, the ship began to increase in speed.

Marr, Captain Eurna, and their father were now on the deck. Taslun stood with his back against the railing of the ship. Kealin joined his brother.

"You stare him down."

"He has three swords. What, did he take all he

witnessed at Urlas and just go with one more sword than my insane brother?"

Kealin stared at Taslun and then chuckled. "Perhaps he knows beyond us."

"Evidently."

"So, does your Dagarok follow us?"

"It has returned to the realm of Mortua, but it is prepared to return. If I can summon it. I do not know where we go, so I do not know how much my powers and ties to death magic will avail us. But, my Dwemhar energies feel more alive than they ever have."

The ship was beginning to move so fast through the water that the winds shifted over the deck in such a way that ice began to form along the railings.

The shaman went to an area along the side of the ship and moved his hands along the deck. A new, smaller pillar rose up. He moved several crystals, and a blue ward covered the ship, shielding them from the wind before solidifying as crystal and then fading away so that Evurn could safely guide the ship.

"That's a new trick," Evurn said.

"A master shipwright was one of my good friends at one time. He taught me much about the realm ships. I was fortunate near the end of the Dwemhar to have many friends who were quite wise. Riakar as one, but so was the shipwright, and then there was the other warrior, one almost as Master Rukes here but far supreme and wielding a massive white blade. Then, we had a true seer, beyond my powers. At least, as it was then. Being the last upon the living realm, I have focused all I have to assure the return of my people. We must not fail them."

A ripple of energy flowed over the deck of the ship. Kealin looked out and could see swirling clouds in the distance and the appearance of a curvature in the night sky. A grand mountain, narrow but reaching into the heavens, rose out of the sea with a peak beyond sight.

The *Aela Sunrise* began to lift out of the water, moving at a curvature around the base of the towering mountain before them and orbiting around.

Iouir looked at those directly near him. "Dwemhar, we must concentrate our energies on this vessel so we may make a smooth transition. Join me in meditation."

Aeveam, Marr, Eurna, and their father all sat beside the Iouir, closing their eyes. Kealin and Taslun then joined them.

Kealin looked back to Evurn, who was leaning into the next turn of the realm ship as it continued to move upward.

He closed his eyes. He could sense each of those around him. Marr, Eurna, the old man, Taslun, Aeveam. He could feel their energies. As he concentrated on the crystals' moving power through the ship, he could fell a greater presence and looked toward it. The shaman appeared as a great golden light, a beacon of their concentration. Kealin could see their energies flowing toward his greater form, and the *Aela Sunrise* seemed to glow around them.

The deck of the ship shuddered. Kealin kept his

concentration and then heard Evurn shouting. He tried to open his eyes but could not.

You must all hold your concentrations. I will protect us. Your friend at the helm will be protected as well. Keep your focus. Our test comes.

Kealin felt a wave of energy coming toward them. He looked beyond the life forms of the *Aela Sunrise* and saw a great wall of white, a breach of the actual energy of the realm, or so it seemed.

They were about to be enveloped in it. He focused hard on the others and then—nothing.

He was worried this would happen. He was thrown into another vision. He stood with the heads of his siblings in his hands, but they rotted before him, turning to dust.

"Such fallacy!" a loud voice boomed in his mind.

Kealin forced his focus upward. Though he could not make out where he was, he saw the tormentor before him. He saw the blackness. His surroundings were like that of a golden temple. Beyond the temple were red skies with fast swirling black clouds.

"That which has been sought has faded. That which will be sought will fade. All must be given. All must be sacrificed. You cannot escape that which you have fought."

The blackness before him solidified into a dark crystalline figure. He looked at the figure's face.

"Who are you? Who are you who torments me? Vankou, show yourself."

A sudden laughing surrounded him. That which

was crystal turned to flesh but for a moment. Kealin saw his tormentor. His own image looked upon him.

"Such fallacy," he heard spoken by his own voice.

He was shaken from the vision by another rocking and a loud crashing sound. He then heard screaming.

His eyes sprung open, and Taslun was holding him.

"He has come to!"

Kealin looked up to see the dark clouds swirling above them and a large mountainous structure to their right. Aeveam was at his feet, with her staff out and glowing white. Evurn and the shaman were at his head. He looked toward the shaman.

"Your focus waned," he said.

"I am sorry. It was my fault," said Kealin. "I am okay."

Kealin could hear sobbing again. He sat up, looking over to Marr, who was collapsed over her father. Eurna looked at him and just slowly shook his head as he bowed over their father.

"His path led us together, but his energies were too weak to go beyond the void of the realms. Know, dear Marr and Eurna, he has joined the ascended, and take comfort that his spirit will return to these lands. He was strong in life, so you must be strong, and we must prepare ourselves."

Kealin noticed Iouir glancing behind them as he said this. Kealin and Taslun looked to see a massive flock of the strange gargoyle creatures swarming around the edges of the ruins before them.

Evurn and Rasi were the first on the edge of the

deck, looking out to the rocky port the ship had docked at.

"So strange, a port so high in the air. Was there once water this high?"

"No," Iouir said. "This was one of the many ports of the sky, a place for realm ships and the larger temple vessels of old."

"My friend Amhe had such a vessel."

"I remember," said Taslun. "I did not know what to make of such a thing."

"Then your friend had much wisdom," Iouir said. "To make one take flight without one of our race is particularly difficult." He looked around the icy cliffs and the sheer stonework of the clearly constructed materials. "This place is sleeping. We must awaken it. At its peak, there are several large crystals that shall act as anchors for the portal from the ascended realms. It is there we Dwemhar can further focus our energies."

Master Rukes pointed up to the sky and the obvious flocks of creatures circling above.

"What do you suggest we do about those? I doubt they'll let us just move upward and do what we wish."

"No," Iouir replied, "we must open the energy nodules along the sides of the tower. Our people were smart. We only need to activate three to four of them for them to begin activating and moving up the tower. Also, there are constructs locked away, meant to protect this place. They will help us in our greater task of thinning the flock. The nodules are lined up in a criss-cross pattern along the lower footprint of the tower. Within the core of the tower is a stairwell that leads up to the mid-level, and from there, we can advance to the pinnacle."

Iouir moved forward, drawing one of his three swords and holding up his staff. Leaving the docking area, he went to an area of stone that his staff seemed to be pulling energy from. As he scraped off the snow, he revealed a single large dim-blue crystal. He placed his hands on the crystal and bowed his head.

There were several sparks of energy in the rocks near him and all along the pathway, and moving up the side of the mountain, lines of a blue fluid-like substance began to melt the snow and activate small crystals spread out over the area.

"You see? This is simple."

But Kealin and Evurn looked up to the gargoyles circling high above. They had noticed the awakening of the temple grounds.

"They're coming for us," Master Rukes shouted.

Eurna pulled Marr from the body of their father and drew his sword.

"We must find cover," he shouted.

"No cover to be found here," Taslun said. "It is time."

Aeveam pointed up to the sky. "More of the creatures are moving into a group and staring at us."

Taslun pulled out his blade and swung it around himself. The blue fire of its blade shot out, growing in length.

Kealin drew his dual blades. They were lighter than his swords; the balance felt off to him. But as he gripped the hilts, he felt his energy flowing into the blades.

"We must make our way up the side of the temple. This is the first crystal. There is one on the far side of these grounds. Come now, warriors!"

Iouir led from the front, and Master Rukes was just behind him. Kealin followed next, looking to Taslun as he went to Marr.

"You are a Dwemhar woman," he said plainly. "You need a weapon."

Taslun pulled a small black metallic shard from his own body. He moved his hands over the end of it, and a blue fire erupted from the hilt. "This blade is sustained by the energy of our people. Honor your father and do not join him until your time is decreed."

Marr took the blade as her brother pushed her forward. Taslun smiled at Kealin and nodded.

The path toward the other nodule was unguarded, but as the group hugged the bare rocks following the now-lit path, they passed over a small bridge. While the others did not immediately stop, Kealin looked down and could see nothing but a swirling fiery ring beneath them.

"Do not wait, Kealin of Urlas. Move with haste," the shaman shouted out.

He hurried across, looking back to see Taslun running backward as several gargoyles landed just above him. A screech then tore his attention back to his front as multiple creatures swooped down. Aeveam's hands exploded in white fire as she cast her magic at the closest ones. Master Rukes and Iouir had made it to what Kealin believed was the next nodule.

The area they were coming to was large and open. There were pillars like trees, and the gargoyles struggled to attack them from above and instead landed on all fours, running at them at random.

Kealin spun his blades, slashing across the face of the creature. Its face ran black like an orc as it screeched and clawed toward him. Evurn sent a blast of fire at it, striking both the creature and two other gargoyles behind it.

Another flash shot out from the side of the tower, and the ground began to burn with blue energies, surging to the far edges of the greater platform and around the many columns.

Kealin and Evurn moved forward and through the columns. The gargoyles dropped from above, wailing before they charged, just to be cut down by Kealin or blasted with a barrage of fire from Evurn. This was the first time Kealin had used his reforged blades crafted by Rukes. He felt as if they were weightless in his hands, flowing from one neck to the next in near seamless fashion. He carried Alri with him now, as he fought with Taslun in the memory of Calak. All of his paths indeed converged on these moments.

Aeveam floated high above them, sending out her magic in undulating waves to force back their foes that were attempting to land.

Iouir shouted out, "We must move on around. We have two nodules activated."

The shaman moved with Master Rukes, Eurna,

and Marr. Taslun was back near the bridge they had crossed, spinning his scythe in a repeated swathe as more gargoyles were gathering on the surface of the tower.

Kealin ran to where the second nodule was as Evurn worked with Eurna to deter the ever-increasing numbers of enemies moving atop the columns.

As Taslun fell back near Kealin, the two brothers fought back to back as waves of the creatures advanced on them. Taslun would arc his swing high, sending blood and stony flesh flying away from them just for more of them to jump within arm's reach. Kealin twisted his blades in small swathes around him, spinning and clipping multiple foes at once before focusing his energies and sending out a shock wave of power that would clear the grounds around them and send their adversaries flying.

Aeveam and Evurn moved around and up a slight incline where now they could all hear the shouts of Blademaster Rukes.

Taslun and Kealin sprinted to catch up. The gargoyles had nearly completely covered this side of the tower. Aeveam now ran with a ward up at the fore of the group.

"Kealin! Give me your hand!"

He ran toward Aeveam and sheathed one of his swords as they interlocked hands.

"Focus, Kealin. Give me control for a moment."

He did so, sending all his energies to enter her form. The ward she summoned began to ripple with spikes of energy before she shouted, pushing the ward out in an undulating wave of electrified air, catching the mass of gargoyles at once and sending them into a state of paralytic shaking.

"My turn," Evurn said.

The shadow elf lifted his staff before sending multiple small spells all over the ground. His form burned green as he slammed the end of his staff in the ground, sending multiple large vines up into the sky before moving his staff down and causing the vines to slap the stunned creatures repeatedly, crushing their forms.

Near the third nodule, Kealin saw Rukes take a guarded stance with his blade before making several acrobatic jumping spins, severing the heads of the enemies near him.

The two groups met back up. As the third nodule roared to life, this one causing a greater surge of energy that moved up the surface of the tower like strings of lightning, a great fire took the lower levels they were just fighting upon.

"The creatures of the void seek to halt us. We are so close to the ascended realm now; the guardians of the realm will seek to destroy our life forms. The true test is coming, warriors."

As he said that, the edge of the tower was breached by multiple fiery demons unlike Kealin had ever seen. But like the rhyming stanzas of a song, the tower itself answered as multiple large crystals began to emerge along the upper portion of the towers. The rocks of the inner tower shifted as doors opened and massive metallic constructs staggered out. These machines were nothing like Kealin had ever seen, and as the demonic beasts crawled over the edge of the lower grounds of the tower, the constructs hummed to life, moving to purge the impurity near the Dwemhar tower.

These constructs were obviously engineered with highly advanced Dwemhar technology akin to the flying ship of Amhe. Like some form of spiders with tall horns at the center of their bodies, the silver machines flashed blue at the point of the two horn-like protrusions. Lightning formed at the pinnacle of the horns. In repeated blasts of energy, the constructs sent burning blue orbs akin to a wizard's spells at the demons. Like his own blade, *Vrikralok*, the damage inflicted by these constructs caused the demons to burn white.

"They but delay the coming tide," Iouir shouted. "We must move up the tower. The stairwell is up this next level."

The shaman pointed to another incline that switched back toward the area with the columns.

Marr and Eurna were at the front, with the shaman just behind them. Kealin and Aeveam worked with Rukes to strike the straggler gargoyles attempting to move in from the opposite side of the tower, and Taslun watched their flank, casting balls of energy at rogue gargoyles fleeing the demons of the lower level.

The constructs were becoming overwhelmed. Many had been cut down by the demons, and Kealin only saw four still on the lower level.

Iouir had stopped again, finding another nodule and seeing that some of the tower was still not awakened. As he went to press the crystals, a demon crested the upper level. Its black form was reminiscent of a Dagarok. It walked on large front legs, and though not obvious at first, the creature had multiple grotesque heads with horns that flashed with black flames that seemed to feed the rest of its burning form.

Marr and Eurna fell back as Kealin ran forward, sheathing his Urlas blade and drawing *Vrikralok*. But he could not strike before the shaman shifted his form to the back of the burning creature. Iouir used his staff and a large white blade to impale the creature through its heads. In a burning white rush of flames, Iouir shot high above the tower and called down a massive thunderbolt that rumbled across the skies and sent large bolts all over the surface of the tower. The demon was struck, and Kealin moved in. But he was still too slow. Iouir shifted his form back down to the demon, and where before he had a staff and a sword, he now held his blades like Kealin, making repeated fast strikes into the form of the demon before sending it flying off the tower.

"You're too slow, my child," he told Kealin with a plain expression.

Though Marr and Eurna had fallen back, Marr had taken the initiative to activate the nodule. Directly next to them, the rocks of the tower shifted, opening the way for more of the constructs. Though several moved down to face the demons, one turned to look at Rukes, Taslun, and Evurn, who were on the other side of it from Kealin and Iouir.

"The stairwell to the upper level is this way!" Marr

shouted, moving around and up from the last nodule with Eurna. The construct paused as if it was staring at Kealin and Iouir. Suddenly, its horn began to glow blue, and Kealin dove out of the way of its blast. He pushed himself up as Iouir summoned a ward and moved the opposite way that Kealin had went. The construct clamored up toward them, looking now right at Kealin, but it did not attack. It turned to Iouir. Its horns flashed blue as it prepared to send a volley of magic at the Dwemhar warrior. Iouir absorbed the blasts with his ward and then sent a series of white blasts at the machine. Its form was splintered.

"These constructs were never a perfected magic. This one has failed in its duties to protect this place and turned on me," the shaman said.

The others joined them as more of the floating crystals came to life, splashing the top of the tower with a blue glow. The sky above them suddenly became as a pool of spinning gold. A humming melody filled the air.

"We must prepare!" Iouir shouted. "The ascended return. There is little time. At the top of the tower will be the anchor crystal. It must be protected at all costs until the Dwemhar have completed their reemergence! I will focus my energies into the portal to guide them. We must not let the evils of the Glacial Seas upon the sacred tower's upper portion.

At that moment, hundreds of the gargoyles clamored their way up to the level that Kealin and the others were.

"The vile creatures of Vankou and his pet dragon,

they seek to devour the souls of my people! Go, Kealin! Join the others and use your energies to shield the upper tower." Iouir drew both of his blades. "Now, warriors. Defend this ground!"

Taslun charged forward first, Evurn following him. Iouir spun in place before shifting his form into the attackers. Master Rukes noticed that Kealin was not moving.

"Kealin, go. Let us do this. It is you I am proudest of in this moment. You always rejected the ways of the elves, but you have grown into a warrior beyond that of this simple Blade." Rukes smiled and brought his sword up before pointing the blade to Kealin in a form of salute. "I will do my blade work. Embrace that which is your fate and let us protect the ascended."

Master Rukes shouted, running to join the others. Kealin rushed up to where Aeveam and the others were.

The upper platform of the tower was barren. Here, the spinning gold above them seemed so low that they could reach out and touch it. The circular grounds seemed to have lines of blue that went to a large dormant crystal at the center of the tower. Aeveam and Marr both placed their hands on it. It seemed to glow but then darken.

"All of us," Aeveam said. "We must place all our thought upon this!"

Eurna, Marr, Aeveam, and Kealin placed their hands on the crystal. It began to surge with energy and rise out of the ground. As its full form began to emerge, they could each feel the energies within themselves growing. Kealin had never felt his Dwemhar powers so strongly.

At a certain point, Kealin knew they did not need to focus on the crystal, and almost simultaneously, the four of them backed away. The crystal rose above them with its own power and hovered high above the tower, sending a blast of energy into the tower itself as well as up into the portal.

Kealin moved away from the crystal, looking back down to where their companions were. It was then that an innumerable swarm of gargoyles flew up to the upper tower. The creatures had been altered. They looked as the demons now. Their burning bodies were ethereal, and with each flap of their wings fell burning ash. The skies around the top of the tower began to glow orange and red from their fire.

A shrill scream and blast of white energies erupted from the lower portion of the tower, and at once, many of the larger demons began to claw their way to the area with Kealin and the others.

Aeveam took to the air. Summoning a ward around herself, she expanded its energies while focusing on the massive crystal at the center of the sky above the tower.

"All of us must assist Aeveam," Kealin said. "Focus your energies to her."

Eurna, Marr, and Kealin closed their eyes, channeling into Aeveam as she constructed a massive ward that covered the entire top of the tower and burned at the demons that tried to come within its protective circle. High above them, wisps of white began to flow from the golden pool.

"The Dwemhar, I feel their energies," Aeveam shouted. "I have altered the ward to inhibit these beasts from passing but still allow those of Dwemhar origin and elven origin to pass through."

But Kealin wondered of the others. That blast of energy was sudden, and now the grounds were overwhelmed by the enemy. The only reason they were not engaged was because of the shield protecting them.

Suddenly, a burning white form erupted from the lower levels and pierced the shield, landing just before Kealin.

It was Iouir. His skin was covered in a white fire, and his eyes burned red. The very aura around his form sizzled with the energy rolling off his body. He was out of breath. He grasped his staff with trembling hands, and it was then Kealin noticed one of his swords was gone.

"The others," shouted Aeveam. "Where are Evurn, Rukes, and Taslun?"

"Fallen," he said, looking at Kealin. "They have fallen."

Kealin felt a shock to his heart, his mind reeling. The shield Aeveam had created began to tremble, nearly shattering until Marr outstretched her hands and closed her eyes, sending her energies to bind with Aeveam's.

The fiery demons swarmed the shield.

Iouir shouted out, "We must hold, Dwemhar.

These beasts seek to destroy us. They are guardians of the void, and now their powers are bound with those of the gargoyles. We must be the light to lead our brethren through the darkness and back into the living realm."

11
AWAKENING

Marr, Eurna, Aeveam, and Kealin focused their energies into the ward. The shaman made markings upon the stone with his staff. At the angle, it was difficult for Kealin to see exactly what it was, but it appeared to be several interlocking circles with a triangular mark that bound them all together. Iouir then stood in the triangle, lifting his staff by its end and holding it above his hand. He began to chant in his own language.

Kealin did not understand the words and looked at Aeveam, confused. It was clear even a student of Dwemhar studies did not understand the language. Kealin felt his energy began to ark toward the shaman, the tip of his staff flashing blue as a blast of energy surged to the top of the ward, piercing it, sending energies into the glowing gold portal.

The grounds of the tower quaked. Kealin heard what sounded like the roar of dragons and then a strange sweet melody-like sound, something he had heard before, but much louder. From the sides of the towers rose three large objects. They were like Amhe's flying machines. Circular objects with spinning crystals on the bottom that spun to life with a loud whirring.

"More of the Dwemhar constructs," Aeveam shouted.

The flying machines circled above the ward, making several explosive blasts, turning the gargoyles to ash in quick work. They began to fire upon the void demons, sending them into a frenzy and forcing them back off the tower. But then, they moved over the ward several times, angling the direction of their crystals and taking up separate positions along the ward.

"They prepare to guard us," said Marr.

Kealin looked at the young woman and saw that the effects of channeling their energies had taken its toll upon both of them. Eurna and Marr were sweating profusely, and blood ran from Marr's nose.

She noticed he was staring. "I am okay, Kealin. I must stay strong," she said to him even as blood poured from her nose.

"Perhaps we can let down the ward," Aeveam shouted. "The creatures have retreated."

But at these words, Iouir's closed eyes opened, and he brought his staff down into the ground. The ward itself reverberated with energy just as the flying ships of the Dwemhar released separate blasts upon the ward in a brilliant and terrifying blast of light that filled the air with the sounds of high-pitched melody.

Marr collapsed and began shaking, and Eurna fell to his knees. Aeveam held her position with Kealin, but it became hard for him to breathe. Iouir lifted his staff again, and the ward expanded outward, striking two of the Dwemhar constructs that were firing upon the ward. The third one moved out of the way and flew out of range of the flickering ward.

The golden pool was now open, with a great white light at its center. Small orbs began to rush down upon the tower, and Iouir held his staff up high. The orbs began to fly down and around the tower, but then several seemed to flow directly into the ward, flowing into the shaman himself.

"The Dwemhar," said Aeveam, "I feel their power. They return as new souls upon the living realm. They are infantile, young, but retain their powers though locked away."

Iouir began to glow white, his body burning with energy as wisps of blue flames flickered upon him.

"We must remain here to guide them upon me. I will assure that the powers of the Dwemhar remain as they should. Keep the ward strong, warriors. We must not let the devices of old break our resolve. The demons of the void have tainted even the constructs. I must lead our peoples to their new salvation."

Kealin felt the ground vibrating beneath him. Though he expected to feel weak, he felt energized. A raw pool of energy fled from the shaman to him, engorging him with energy.

Why do you forsake us?

The voice was sudden, one he had heard before, but not Vankou.

Why are you upon this void?

The voice was dark, fearful even.

Kealin's concentration waned, and his vision returned. He was once again in the strange temple. He held the heads of his siblings, but he could freely look around. It appeared he was in Dimn's temple now. He saw the gateway. The Itsu Priest was beyond it but silent.

He turned, looking at the figure who stood before him. He saw the image of Vankou, and then a flash in its form revealed another covered in bright light.

All paths converge. Time was altered once to enact a true revenge. That which you deemed evil was but a pawn. All is what no longer remains. The purity of old will be realized.

The voice was not familiar at all. *Not* the gods. *Not* Vankou.

So much wasted in trying to save what could not be saved. Your actions took you upon paths that led so many to death. How many might have lived? Remember, who saved your mother when the elves sought to throw her from Urlas? I am who forced them to allow her to remain, not some actions of your father. You were strong then in Dwemhar power. You have grown. I have formed you. Remember, for your test comes. You are not of such simple blood as the others.

A sudden shrill of power pulled him from his vision.

"KEALIN!" Aeveam screamed.

The flying construct returned, sending a blast of energy at the ward. Iouir floated above them, his form wrapped in a burning white fire that reached up into the portal. The orbs that flowed out were much fewer than before, and like light focusing into a crystal, it seemed the Dwemhar were pulled toward Iouir.

Aeveam was now sweating, and blood was running down Kealin's face.

"Something is wrong," Aeveam said. "We must hold our energies or this construct will destroy us, but I feel something else saps our energy. Where have the Dwemhar gone?"

Iouir screamed, sending energy into the final construct, which evaded the blasts, again moving out of range.

Suddenly, a shock struck the ground behind them. Kealin turned to see Taslun and Evurn. Taslun was engorged with his own blue fire, and Evurn's staff rippled with red energies. Both were bleeding and covered in marks. It was then Kealin spotted Master Rukes just behind Evurn.

The Blade Master fell forward. Pushing himself up, he gripped the hilt of a sword, but not his own. A blade ran through the right side of his chest. It was Iouir's sword.

"Vile betrayer! You were our source of wisdom!" Rukes shouted out.

The shaman opened his eyes and spun around. He sent a blast out, striking both Taslun and Evurn and throwing them back.

Kealin went to pull himself from the ward, but he couldn't move. He glanced to Aeveam, and it seemed she could not turn from the ward, either.

"You were welcomed into Urlas! You were broken when the elders found you! We allowed you sanctuary!"

The shaman landed just between Kealin and the others. "Is that what you remember? It is strange; I remember manipulating the minds of the weaker race to make a sanctuary for myself. A place I would wait within, hidden from those who would seek to stop me, forming a prophecy of my own to enact a revenge long awaited. Perhaps I am wrong."

A flash of white erupted out of Iouir. His form grew, and where before he had two arms, another two arms materialized. He was now double his original size. He drew his blades and held his staff into the air. He began to make a circle, his four arms brandishing three swords and his original staff.

"I am ascension," his voice thundered.

Marr and Eurna floated up into the air. Marr was unconscious, but Eurna was not. The captain drew his sword, but with a slight movement of Iouir's finger, both of their necks broke, and his blade fell to the ground with a clang.

"More pawns. More energy," Iouir said, dropping their corpses. "I had summoned all Dwemhar here so to ensure none could assail me again. I let death take those beyond this circle."

Master Rukes drew the sword from his own body. Elven blood poured forth, but the stalwart elf lifted the Dwemhar blade, sprinting toward Iouir. The shaman spun, striking Rukes across the neck. The Blademaster fell headless.

"Master!" Taslun screamed. The undead Taslun was at his feet, bringing his weapon up akin to his elven form before and sprinting like his once master.

Iouir spun again, but Taslun jumped high, bringing his blade down on the crossed blades of Iouir. Evurn ran around the side of them and sent an explosion of red fire from his own staff, striking the shaman, but though three arms engaged Taslun, the fourth arm bearing the staff blocked Evurn's spell and reflected it back.

Kealin heard Aeveam's voice. *We must drop the ward, it holds us. I can do it; I know this spell. It is a stasis spell. My father taught me of this when I was but a few years old. It is an old power, but it draws the energy from those willing to create a shield capable of both accenting and blocking crystal energies. Let go, Kealin. I can form it and focus the power. Protect me once the ward falls.*

Kealin nodded. He ceased his thoughts of sending energy to the ward. He felt suddenly weakened.

Evurn and Taslun were locked with the shaman.

"I have taken that which was ascended. I was bound from this world, attacked like this once, and I survived. I bound those who assaulted me to eternal servitude, but this time, I have taken the very souls of those who cursed me. I have reached god-form. I am beyond any who ascended before, and I will take my place in the living realm as a living god of the people. None, not even death, can stop me. I have destroyed its threat to me through my pawn, the one form of the entity that yet remained in the living realm, and soon, he himself will come. I now can wield that which was obtained for me, and I will strike down the god of death and take my true place."

Kealin felt a pull on his spine, and then in a sudden ripping sound, the sheath of *Vrikralok* was pulled from his body, the god-killing blade flying into the multi-armed shaman's grasp. At that moment, Aeveam spun, Kealin felt the pull on his body broken, and the ward above shattered in a whirlwind of energy and struck the god-form shaman. His form convulsed, and Evurn jumped upon him, jabbing his staff in the god-form, sending a blast of energy into his mouth. Taslun threw his weapon in an arc, the fiery blue blade sticking into his eye. Kealin drew his blades and charged forward, but then he remembered Aeveam in her weakened form and the enemy they had forgotten about.

The flying ship had realigned itself above them and sent a blast of energy upon the top of the tower. Kealin jumped over Aeveam, and in a weakened form, she embraced him, drawing his power into her and creating a small ward to protect them. Fire rolled over them for a moment, but then a thunderbolt came, and the attack stopped. The flying ship burst into flames and went down off the side of the tower.

Through whatever means they had, Taslun and Evurn had shielded themselves. The god-form of Iouir was blackened but began to burn with a white fire, renewing himself. Bolts of lightning like that which had struck the final flying ship, shot up into the portal still spinning above them.

"This thing has the power of a god. It'll take your

blade to kill it, Kealin! We must get that back!" Taslun shouted. "Time to bring my other friends."

Taslun threw down his strange circular portal device. A green fire erupted, and purple energy surged out.

"Undead of Alri, come forth. We need you! Suvasel, send all you can!"

Shadowlings crawled out, snarling and running for the renewing god-form. They jumped upon its body in growing numbers, and soon, a massive form emerged from the portal. Taslun's Dagarok returned, drawing its large blades. It dropped both into the burning white form of Iouir.

Kealin saw *Vrikralok* drop to the ground, but the fire growing before them created a heat, making it impossible to approach. A flicker of light turned into a blinding bright flash, and the god-form took shape again and incinerated the shadowlings, grabbing hold of the Dagarok and gripping *Vrikralok* once again.

Kealin pulled Aeveam up. "Can you fight?"

"A moment," she whimpered. "He took most of my power, and I used what I had left."

Evurn cast an array of spells. Vines erupted from the ground, grabbing hold of Iouir, but the god-form used his many blades to cut himself free. The Dagarok's arm was cut from its form, and Iouir lifted himself up into the creature's face, opening his own mouth and sending a blast of white at the creature. With his burning hand of blue fire, Taslun climbed up the Dagarok's back and jumped upon Iouir. He thrust the fire into the face of Iouir, and the god-form grabbed hold of him, throwing him off.

Kealin heard his brother speak to him. *Go, my brother. Get to the Aela Sunrise.*

I do not think there is a weapon upon it that can strike this beast.

No, go. I will force this creature from the tower. The void demons might kill him. I see no other option, and perhaps there is something else that can stop him. The Dwemhar have returned, after all.

Brother.

No, Kealin.

A sudden cold struck the tower. The golden portal above darkened. A deep blackness surrounded the pinnacle of the tower. Kealin heard a familiar roar come from the portal, and in an explosion of death magic, a necromantic dragon stuck its head through the portal. A blast of purple and blue fire struck Iouir, and he turned his attention to blocking the blast.

"I have called upon Vankou and death magic to deal a final blow. Go, Evurn. Run, my brother. Go!"

Aeveam gripped Kealin. "I can't fight. I must recover. I am sorry."

Evurn ran for Kealin and Aeveam. "The realms of the living, the ascended, the dead, and the gods converge. We must get to the ship. We will come for Taslun. Perhaps the lazy gods will do something about this."

They ran down the stairs. Kealin lifted Aeveam in his arms as Evurn led them around the edge of the tower. There were many places where the road was broken or the bridges shattered. Evurn cast vines to bridge the gaps as they circled down.

Kealin could hear the organ of Vankou. A deep cold, unlike what had been present before, was upon him. His mind wandered. He tried to fathom who had been speaking to him. Was it Vankou, as he so purely felt, or was it always Iouir? The shaman, the friend his family had known. The one who had given them the very prophecy of darkness coming upon his parents that sent them upon the Glacial Seas. He questioned what was true. He was given *Vrikralok*, but perhaps it was not to kill Vankou as he wanted. He didn't know if his actions were part of a contrived plan, his own actions, or the attempt for even the old Itsu god under the sea, who had given him the blade, to prevent what was happening now. It did not matter. He had lost the blade, and there was little to be done to stop what was coming upon the world.

The *Aela Sunrise* was ahead. The dragon roared above them, but its scream was cut short. The bright green fire that had been present in the air before ceased.

Evurn jumped onto the ship and went to the helm. Kealin jumped with Aeveam, falling into a roll and catching the glimpse of Iouir directly above them.

"Do not leave, my friends," his voiced thundered.

"He will destroy the ship, and we will be trapped," Aeveam shouted. Her eyes flashed white, and her hair rippled with energy. Her magics were restored.

But at that moment, she was pulled head first by Iouir, her body thrown from one part of the tower to the next until she was thrown back just beside the *Aela Sunrise*. Evurn went to run for her, when she stood and used her powers to force him to the ground. He sat up as she looked toward him.

"As my father did before for you and the Stormborn, I am prepared."

Aeveam looked up at the god-form.

"Come for me. I am the daughter of Lorlaam, a descendant of Rusis and Dwemhar blood, trained by those of the god of winds at the Temple of Swia!"

Iouir floated down upon the tower between her and the *Aela Sunrise*. Aeveam flew into the air above him, her hair furling as she formed a Dwemhar summoning of a silver-edged blade in front of her.

"Aeveam!" Evurn shouted. The shadow elf jumped off the ship. He had obtained a potion from one of his bags, and his snake, Rasi, followed him out onto the tower. He chugged the potion and gripped his staff, sending a curling red-and-black spell along his staff.

"Rasi," he said, pointing at the snake, "stay at the ship, my friend! This is not a fight for you."

Aeveam sent her energy toward Iouir, who blocked the attack, but it was Evurn's attack that took the attention of the god-form. Evurn sent a summoning of blood magic, the sacred magic of shadow elves, into the back of the god-form. His own hands were bleeding, his body trembling as he held the spell on point, but the attack was enough to cause Iouir to become further distracted. He turned, the blood magic curling over his body, and focused a blast of his own energy into Evurn's staff. With a crackling pop, Evurn's staff exploded, throwing Evurn back up the tower opposite the side they had gone before.

Aeveam came behind Iouir, a massive ball of white energy in her hands. But Iouir turned and thrust two of his blades into her abdomen. She screamed as the blades ran red, and he threw her body against the tower.

A flash of blue from atop the tower rained down with a furious wave of energy. Taslun was still alive. He held his own weapon and the sword of Master Rukes.

"Will you not just die?" Iouir shouted.

Taslun engaged Iouir. Kealin ran to Evurn and pulled the shadow elf up. Taslun was backed toward the *Aela Sunrise*.

Iouir stopped. He held his four arms behind him as Taslun prepared to attack again.

"Away from me, undead!" With an eruption of energy that covered Taslun, Kealin watched as Taslun was blasted from the tower and fell beyond sight.

Iouir began to laugh, spinning *Vrikralok* and stepping between them and the *Aela Sunrise*.

"So many workings. I used the great dragon half-god to destroy most of the Glacial Seas. Upon killing him, I took control of all that was his. I used the gargoyles to make a desperate fight for you brave warriors. But it was all smoke and visions for you types so eager to fulfill prophecies. Those without the full blood of a Dwemhar are weak. Stormborn prophecy? That became my own. To think, that young boy was so ready to belong. Much like another young one who could have listened to his father. All doomed to die in such horrible ways."

Evurn stepped forward. "You speak of Valrin like he is no one. He gave his life for you and your prophecy. Take back your harsh and shallow words."

"And what is a broken old elf to do without his staff? Your words are worse than mine, for you cannot control the minds of others with your words. You speak spells that do nothing more but irritate me. At least I can look forward to facing the Itsu Priest when I am upon the living realm. That shall be a glorious fight, and for that, I thank Alri, good Kealin."

"You ignore me, demon?" Evurn stood firmly between Kealin and Iouir. Kealin went to walk forward, but Evurn raised his hand.

"I come from the East, Iouir. But you knew that. I came here to escape my old life. I met the father of the young girl you murdered this day. Upon that meeting, I went to the realm of a god and fought beasts of old. It was not the same as this.

"As a shadow elf, we wish for that which is considered our *perfect darkness*, in which we can cease life and do so in peace. A perfect end to a life of bloodshed. I walked away from that."

"Now that you stand in front of a true god of the Dwemhar, do you fear death?"

"No, I walked the path of a shadow elf. Alone I embrace the twilight red moon of the East. I, Evurn, enact the powers of my people. I have found my *perfect darkness*. You are the bane of many this day, and invoking the shadows of the past, I need no staff of a wizard. I need your blood upon my blades."

Iouir laughed. "You have no blades, dear elf."

Evurn vanished in a wisp of red smoke. Kealin stared at Iouir, who seemed strangely baffled. Kealin heard a snap behind him, and his blades were pulled from his hands. Evurn appeared before Iouir, brandishing Kealin's blades.

Iouir laughed and lunged forward just for Evurn to vanish again, appearing in an instant above Iouir. His body surged with blood magic, and in repeated flashes, he cut into Iouir in multiple swathes.

Kealin could not even see the shadow elf as he moved above, flashes of red smoke moving up and down the god-form, sending white blood all over the ground. It was not the edges of Kealin's blades, but forms of shadow and blood magic like razor edges moving through the god-form.

In sheer fury, Iouir began to spin about, attempting to strike Evurn, but he could not. At first, his knee gave way, and then one after another, his arms were severed. In pure rage, Evurn's form moved on around Iouir in a show of power Kealin had never seen in his entire life. At last, with a gushing of white blood, Evurn took form on the other side of a crumbling mass of bubbling flesh. He turned, looking at Kealin.

"A worthy adversary, but I am tired."

Evurn collapsed. Kealin ran, jumping over the body of Iouir. He lifted Evurn up, and the shadow elf struggled to direct him.

"Take your weapon. Strike him."

Vrikralok flowed with the blood of Iouir down toward the *Aela Sunrise*.

Kealin pulled Evurn to his feet, and though stumbling, he began to walk. Kealin ran to *Vrikralok* and brandished his sword. He had to kill Iouir completely. The god-form would regenerate again.

He turned to move against his foe one last time, when Evurn smiled at him. A burning white specter rose up behind him. The shadow elf turned to face his foe once again and his blood sprayed in an arc as a blade slashed across his neck.

Iouir had already taken form again.

"I am ascended. I am eternal. Now, I call forth the one who holds my power. The one who was bound to this land who you struck down. Stay with your dead friends, Kealin. You and I have no other work that must be completed, and you can leave."

Iouir vanished from his presence, and black clouds began to snow heavily upon the tower. The sounds of the organ of Vankou played, and high upon the tower once again, Iouir was at work. A massive form appeared above the tower, and it seemed the memories of every death Kealin had witnessed or caused came flooding back to his mind. He looked down beneath the tower and could see the waters of the Glacial Seas. The tower was moving down into the living realm.

Kealin ran to Evurn. The half-elf struggled to breathe, seeing the proud warrior cut down in such a simple move. Not to mention all of the others that had came with him. Everyone else was dead.

His two blades lay on the ground getting covered

with snow, and he thought of his fallen siblings, all he had fought to save, and the prophecy he was told by the liar Iouir. His life until that point had not been as he'd thought.

He was punished with death for trying to save those he loved, and he had been warned that his path was one of darkness. He would not be played and instructed in what to do by anyone. It wasn't him. Though, the entire events of his last few years were a mix of the work of his own hands, those of Iouir, and in turn, the workings of the living realm with the works of the Grand Protectorate, the arrival of the Itsu Priest, and the old magics and worlds of the gods; Iouir was his own evil. Kealin had to attempt to stop him. He would avenge those who had fallen even if he still failed to stop him.

12

BANE

HE SCALED THE TOWER AGAIN. The vines cast by Evurn were still in place, though the tower itself was shaking violently, and he wasn't sure how much longer the structure itself had. The sounds of Vankou were becoming louder. As he reached the site of the second nodule, he turned to begin up the stairs, when he saw the massive form of a titan in the clouds. Reaching the upper level, the god-form of Iouir was waiting for him. His body was completely healed. His four arms brimmed with energy, and his head seemed to shift, revealing he had gained several grotesque faces.

"I wondered how long you would wait before your emotions took over. You have been the easiest of my life to manipulate into doing exactly what I seek. Now, since you did one of the most difficult feats of obtaining the Bane of the Gods, *Vrikralok*, hand it over and head back down to your ship."

Kealin drew the god-blade and took a guarded

stance. His energies furled around him as he focused all his thought on the entity before him. Iouir reached out in an attempt to take *Vrikralok*, Kealin resisted, remembering Aeveam's teachings.

"Kealin Half-Elf, your time wielding the powers of a stature higher than yourself has passed. I saved your mother. I manipulated the minds of elves and Dwemhar. I bound souls upon islands, and I have used you in every manner possible. You have brought ruin to the empire of elves, empowered the Grand Protectorate of the living realm, and released the Itsu Priest, a form who will start a war between the Itsu and the gods of the North that will make my work much easier."

Kealin said nothing. He concentrated on his breathing. He could feel the rumbles of the stone beneath his feet and the brimming of the surge of energy from the core of the tower up into the bottoms of his feet and out through his eyes into his aura.

"You say nothing? No over-confident jeer? No promise for avenging your fallen wasted rabble of companions? Now, having used all I sought to use, igniting a war between the gods, and destroying the bound form of Vankou, I laugh at his own thought of rule. I will kill this god coming now. He opens the portal to his own realm in an attempt to pull me into it. Now, bring me that blade so I may finish my work."

Kealin's eyes flashed to the vision. He was in the temple once again. The red skies outside the temple were at odds, with golden light coming from behind him. The heads of his siblings were no longer in his hands. He looked up and saw the figure before him. He saw Iouir in his shaman form, and then himself. He saw the image of Vankou from the tower, and then in flashes, he saw every foe he'd faced, from the Itsu Priest in the palace of Dimn to the Legionary General of the Grand Protectorate. The figure became as flame, and the temple beyond burned away.

Now, he saw only the god-form. A voice spoke, a voice he didn't recognize at first, but it was familiar.

All footfalls have led to this. Broken prophecies and fulfilled lies matter little. The understanding of the living realm does not matter when facing the brink of destruction. Engage, have faith. You will not be alone. I will finish what I began.

What? Who speaks to you, Kealin?

Kealin's eyes sprang open. Iouir had begun to spin, his god-form summoning energies from the clouds around him, and multiple circles of light had begun to orbit his body. In his hands, his staff had become as a large rod of fire. His swords were now strange angled blades of strange design, unlike any Dwemhar blade he had seen.

Kealin sprinted, lifting *Vrikralok*. Iouir stopped spinning. Kealin leapt, thinking himself to the flank of his adversary. He instantly was there, but so were the parrying blades of the god form. Kealin locked blades, seeing one of the other blades of his enemy moving toward his side. He jumped, flipping into the air and focusing his powers to propel himself up and over.

Iouir's attack missed him, but just barely. As his feet hit the ground, two more blades swung down upon him, sliding off his blade held in a guard over his head.

He ran the edge of his blade down the hilt of his adversary, suddenly seeing the burning rod of fire upon his face. He switched his grip. Holding *Vrikralok* with one hand, he drew one of his blades in a narrow arc, cutting into one of the hands and partially severing it. He was nearly bound. Iouir attempted to grab him. He pushed off and propelled himself backward. He landed out of range of Iouir and forced himself to stand still, holding both weapons.

Iouir's hand dropped to the ground, and with it went one of the swords. He laughed and attempted to grow it back, but it began to glow a bright gold.

"What evil is this?" Iouir questioned in a thunderous voice. "There is more power than I can sense here, but it is no matter."

Iouir stared at the bleeding nub of his arm, white blood pouring forth. Kealin ran at him again. This time, Iouir's blades pointed at him, and he released a ball of fire that struck Kealin's armor, but even as his skin burned from the arcane fire, he still fought through the pain and focused, vanishing from sight for a moment, reappearing above Iouir's head. He thrust *Vrikralok* down, but the blade would not pierce the godform. He landed again, and Iouir brought his own two blades up in a narrow slash, catching Kealin's armor and slashing up his chest, sending him spinning across the ground.

Kealin had dropped *Vrikralok*. Iouir charged him. He sheathed his blade and focused, sending ripples of energy out from himself. He could feel the Dwemhar powers surging through his arms and legs. He formed the energy in his hands and slammed the ground, knocking Iouir back and nearly toppling him.

He drew both of his blades and saw multiple phantoms of Iouir. He spun, twisting his blades in a dance as he attempted to parry each of the specters, not sure whom the enemy was. Their fight had moved from the physical realm. He felt a draw on his mental power beyond that of what he used himself. Darkness formed in the corners of his eyes, and he struggled to see his foe. He committed to one form, seeing it a bit clearer than the rest. He made a cross slash with both of his blades, and another arm of the god-form was severed. He could see clearly again, but he was on his knees. His blades were at his side, and his opponent now was bleeding from two arms.

"Truly, you have formed some mastery of your skill. Surprising." Iouir laughed. "So many great warriors have fallen before you this day and well before. But now, you are weakened, broken. Your impurity of elven blood makes even focusing a thought nearly impossible."

Kealin couldn't fight. He was weakened. Every word that Iouir spoke was true, and Kealin tried not to show his sudden loss of power. The duel had taken its toll, especially the last part.

"I hope you have not forgotten, but your blade cannot truly harm me. I cannot be touched by any but a Dwemhar. Do you not wonder why I sought to stop their return, to bring with me all of Dwemhar blood? I had to destroy them. Yes, they were to protect me while I absorbed as many souls as I could, but none of you were to leave. I have been in your mind since your birth. I watched all of you half-bloods, and you were the one who was destined to be my hand. Your sister was strong and became stronger than I even expected, but you were strong with your mother's blood."

Kealin forced himself to stand. He sheathed his blade.

"If I don't stop you, the gods will. You are something beyond the Itsu or the evils of the Grand Protectorate. I will not give up this day."

Kealin turned all his thoughts to Iouir's head, attempting to destroy him from within his own skull. He could see the many vessels, but as easy as he had used this power before, this adversary met him in like thought.

Kealin, you must know that to break someone, you do not just attack their physical body. You show them this.

His mind suddenly saw the desert sun again. He saw Jesia, and then he saw his infant brother. He saw legionnaires of the Grand Protectorate and his brother's limbs severed one by one. He then saw Jesia, and he cried out to her. She turned, and at that moment, he saw Iouir upon her. She saw the specter, and Kealin knew he could not fall into this again. He could not save Jesia, but he attempted to reach out and grab the form of Iouir. He blocked Jesia, taking the blow from Iouir.

Kealin could no longer feel his Dwemhar power. He was sapped. The power was gone. He was now on his back. He thought of Jesia and his brother, staring up at the swirling black clouds above him. He did not know if what he saw was true or not. He did not know if his brother was dead or if Iouir had attacked Jesia, but he no longer felt the energy of the Dwemhar.

"Now you lay here, among the bodies of your friends, with not even the power of my ancient race to help you, half-blood. It has been fun toying with you through these years, but I have absorbed almost all that I must. None of your friends, the gods, or any of the Dwemhar can assist you in your final breaths."

A sudden shock wave struck the grounds as the clouds became gold above. More of the ascended began to descend. The god-form jerked his gaze up. His arms now bled more, and the extra limbs shrunk away. He shrank in size and where he had many heads before he now had but one. He lifted his staff, attempting to draw in the new souls.

"What travesty is this? The ascended were done. The titan that was Vankou vanished." The one of death was no longer here, and a grander vision had been projected that confused even the god-form Iouir.

"I felt the presence of angered death, the essence of Vankou. Where has the god gone?"

"A last betrayal of your own people, perhaps?" a voice said in the air around them.

Kealin was flat on his back. Standing above him was a glowing gold figure, a warrior wielding two blades of fire. The figure looked down at him, and his face became clear. It was Riakar, the warrior of old, the one who had told him he had forsaken the blades, but now, returned to life, he stood before the shaman and Kealin.

"You were dead," the shaman growled. "I killed you many thousand years ago."

"My sacrifice was deemed worthy of my ascension. You tried then. You tried to steal the power from your own people then, and instead, you were bound here because we stood against you. You took others against their will, taking the guise of a god and hiding your identity to all, but I knew you were not dead as the ascended believed.

"You were a bane then, and this day, you seek to steal the life force away from our culture renewed. It is not so simple. Our race will be divided within the many races of the lands, hidden away from those such as you. In time, the blood of the Dwemhar will awaken, and the world will find balance once again. I have forsaken my own return, bound my spirit to my dead form, as even Vankou sensed your betrayal of the gods. He seeks his own reign of power, but to allow one such as you to stand and defeat that which was set by the Great Poet is outside of even his design. You will not succeed, beast.

"You betrayed my friends. The Shipwright, the great Seer of the North. I sense it now. One died to lead Valrin upon his path. The other you gamed with until Kealin and his brothers worked through your malevolent plan, and then"—Riakar paused—"my brother, you bound him to the magic of the Glacial Seas and destroyed his mind to disrupt the balance of magic in the Glacial Seas!"

Kealin now understood. The bound souls, the ones who could not die. The man in the hut near the icy tornado when their journey first began. That was the seer. Then, Evurn had told him the story of the master shipwright, the one Valrin had seen. Last, the warrior in the mountains. The one who believed that he and Taslun were Dwemhar assassins was Riakar's brother.

"You will not live past this day, Riakar. I destroyed you once. Your powers are infantile. You are sapped returning to this life. Your life is forsaken!"

Riakar backed up, placing his hand on Kealin.

"My life is not my own. Not all of us seek eternal power such as you. I give my life freely so that the one you have harmed, the one who became your own pawn whom you wished to use against the greater ones, can defeat you with my pure blood. You are the old. Those like this half-blood will be the new. By your own malice your power will be stripped! So it is spoken beyond that of all the gods, in the light of the Great Poet of all the realms!"

Riakar became as a great light, covering Kealin. He felt his body stand just as Iouir struck him with his own blade. The blade stopped just short of piercing his skin. There was no transfer of power from Riakar to Kealin but simply Riakar giving his life to protect Kealin in that flash of a moment. But that was not all that happened.

Kealin drew his daggers, slashing the blades forged with the ashes of his sister in a cross in front of him and throwing Iouir back, stumbling as an explosion of power surged in his body. He rushed forward returning his daggers to their sheaths, summoning *Vrikralok*, though it was out of reach. The sword came to his command. He made an upward arching slash, striking through the parrying blade and rod of the shaman . . . but this time, his blade was not halted, and in a crack of white magic, *Vrikralok* tore through Iouir.

An explosion of energy rocked the tower, sending a crack down the center of the structure. Kealin kept a tight grip on his sword, and as the smoke cleared, he saw the body of Iouir.

Kealin exhaled. His enemy was down. He looked around at the dead around him, and his eye caught movement ahead. Iouir floated upward before vanishing.

"Still, you cannot defeat me."

A shock hit his side, and he was thrown to the other side of the tower. *Vrikralok* was knocked from his grasp and Iouir was still very much alive.

Kealin drew his blades again, catching the blades of the last Dwemhar. He parried the strikes and rolled left, slashing at Iouir's knee. Red blood sprayed all over the ground.

Iouir stopped, collapsing to the ground for a moment.

Blood gushed from his leg. He was mortal again. He was stripped of the powers he had obtained from the ascended.

Kealin sprinted, jumping and angling his blades down as he smashed into the shaman. Iouir was able to shift to the right, and Kealin's strike missed. He jerked to block Iouir's blade, and his sword slid against the shaman.

"You are weak. I can still manipulate that which is the living realm. Do you not think I can reach her? Only what power I gained was taken, not what I already had."

His mind flashed to Jesia. He could see her. The desert sun was behind her body, but then he saw Iouir behind her.

Just a quick snap, Iouir whispered in his mind. *So much would be lost. But like everyone else, you have failed. She will die.*

Jesia collapsed in the image.

Kealin focused his thoughts out of the formed image. He saw the open white eyes of the shaman over him with his own blade aimed at his head. Kealin parried up with his red Urlas blades, stopping the strike, but he struggled and trembled to maintain his block, feeling his body pressed into the ruins of the tower as energy flowed from the shaman and his eyes grew brighter. Kealin felt the cracking of the stone beneath him and he was forced into the rock of the tower's summit.

"The heroes of old could not defeat that which is I. I will not be defeated by some wretch of a half-blood, an insult to that which was and what will still be again. All of you have failed."

Kealin saw a movement to the right, a sudden strike to the side of Iouir's neck. The shaman recoiled, jumping off Kealin, screaming and pulling at his neck.

Rasi, Evurn's white serpent, had survived scaling

the tower and taken that moment to avenge its master. Its venom was horrid; flesh began to fall from Iouir's neck, for regardless of what race or powers Iouir might have had, his immortal form had already been broken. Kealin brandished his blades once again. Rasi twisted and snapped again, biting Iouir's eye.

As Iouir grasped the serpent, he tore it in two, but then shrieked as both of Kealin's blades struck him center chest. Kealin ran him against a broken rock, slamming his form into a slouch. Kealin withdrew his blades and then spun, slashing him repeatedly until a layered bleeding form reached out with a trembling hand.

You have but a choice. I can give you more. But now I have killed everyone. Even the one in the desert far away.

He began to laugh.

Kealin thrust his blades into his foe's head burying them to their hilts, and the laughing voice he heard ceased. Iouir was dead.

He withdrew his blades with a crack from his foe's skull, stepping back. He looked up to the spinning gold portal and saw the spirits of the Dwemhar once again returning to the living realm. Their way was now truly safe.

He fell to his knees as the weight of all who had fallen filled his mind. He saw Marr, Eurna, Master Rukes. He then thought of Aeveam and Evurn. There came a crackling sound, and in the distance, a large dark-blue portal spun to life. An icy hand reached out, and suddenly, being so close to the many realms of death, life, and the gods, he saw the spirits of his fallen comrades leave their bodies, flowing toward the realm of death.

He began to shake, thinking of Jesia and his brother too. His resolve to resist the temptation to not act was not there. Not only that, his injuries were severe. He was bleeding profusely, and he felt death approaching both within his own body and literally.

The half-elf sheathed his blades and gripped *Vrikralok*. He did not know the path ahead, but he forced himself to the *Aela Sunrise*.

He began to cry, now reaching the lower level and moving past the bodies of Aeveam and Evurn. He went to the helm of the *Aela Sunrise*. He thought of Valrin, knowing that Iouir had been behind all the pain he had felt from those days upon the Glacial Seas until now. He moved the crystal switches and released the *Aela Sunrise*. Iouir had taken so much, but he now saw Evurn's and Aeveam's spirits moving toward that of the realm of death.

He pushed the *Aela Sunrise* forward, seeing a lonely path ahead. He went for the realm of death. So much he felt was his own fault, used as a pawn by Iouir. He would confront the god Vankou himself. If the gods could create and hold power unimaginable, his friends could have life. If not, he had fought a god before. He would do it again.

13

THE LOST

THE PASSAGE into the realm of death was not as Kealin had imagined. He emerged on the other side to the sight of rolling dark hills with a single burning green flame like a sun directly ahead of him. He looked up and saw only rock. As he progressed this way, fogs rolled over the bow of the *Aela Sunrise*, and though he had always felt cold when thinking of death or even Vankou, he felt neither warm nor cold. He tried to take a breath, but it was as if his body no longer needed to breathe. Those who came this way were dead, but he was not. At least, he didn't think so.

He guided the realm ship over the hills and noted a river glowing a bright white high in the sky above him. As he walked away from the helm, the ship continued forward as if he was in the current of the river above him. He looked over the edge and saw nothing, save the dark hills.

"What are you doing here?"

Kealin jerked to look to his right. It was his brother.

"Calak!"

But Calak's expression was one of confusion.

"Brother, why are you here? You are not dead. You should not be here. This is not a place for the living." Calak looked at the body of Marr and Eurna's father.

"You do not need to bring the dead here, you have not been cursed to take such a task, why are you here, Kealin?"

"I have to save them, Calak. My friends, or more so, those I got killed, those like you." Kealin went to touch him, but Calak vanished and reappeared a distance away.

"Those of the living must not touch those of death or you will suffer the same as I. Brother, please, turn this vessel back toward the light."

Calak pointed, and Kealin looked. The passage he had come through appeared as a bright light spinning and undulating with red, blue, and green swirls.

"Go. I know you seek to stop death, but it cannot be stopped, only delayed, but what life is that?"

"Calak, you do not understand. They died because I was foolish enough to be manipulated by Iouir. The shaman betrayed us!"

Calak stared at him. "I know. I knew upon death. But, there was nothing I could do of it. Those of the dead cannot converse with the living except under circumstance of ascension."

Kealin looked around them. "You are here. Where is Alri? Where are our mother and father?"

"Alri, she . . . never came this way. She died, but death did not take her in the same form as me. Mother and Father are within the City of Souls, beyond the eternal passage. They are well; I am with them. Taslun was along this passage. I spoke with him, but then he was pulled back to life, though of strange circumstance. Necromancy has become strong in the living realm."

"We tried to save our brother. We have a younger brother!"

"That is a concern of the living. While I am elated for you to have another brother, I accept where I am. Mother and Father accept their place. Those who are dead are not truly gone; we simply await the gathering of those we love before the warmth of the Great Poet. He sleeps, his slumbering soul like a sun above the City of Souls, but events have caused him to stir. It is strange. But you head toward the gateway to that place well before your time. Your ship speeds you ahead of the others who came from the place you were. What do you seek, Kealin?"

Kealin reached for *Vrikralok* and saw a deep concern in Calak's eyes.

"You move to strike the guardian of our city. You see Vankou as evil?"

"The gods do. At least in a form. He seeks to-"

"He seeks nothing. You move to strike that which holds a balance. There is a great price in what you do. That blade was never to be wielded by any, save the gods, yet elves and Dwemhar forged it. It is a deadly object, one that should have remained under the sea. I cannot stop you, for that is not my power. I only can warn you. You will take a great injury to save those within the river below. Striking the god will only serve to distance yourself from your fate. Besides, I sense they are but strangers, save Master Rukes."

"I am the reason for their deaths. If I can, I will save them."

"Well, Master Rukes has already passed into the City of Souls. He has accepted his death. You must think carefully of your path."

"I have."

"I sense your mind has broken. Your emotions take command of reason. Your fight with the god-form Iouir has weakened you beyond that of a normal elf, man, or Dwemhar soul. You should turn your ship, return to the living realm, and seek out those who still wake within it."

Kealin thought of Jesia and his brother. "No, be gone, my brother. I do not need your counsel!"

Kealin turned, going to the helm as his brother opened his arms, "In time, you will join me here. Let us both hope it is not sooner than meant. Your friends in the living realm will be your salvation if to strike the god and steal his quarry is your path."

Calak faded away and with him the body of Marr's father vanished. A flash of white was in the spot where the body lay and then the light itself floated off and dissipated below.

Kealin held the wheel of the ship. He looked ahead at a great dark gateway. Black crystals spun atop the towers that formed the edge of the gates. A thunderous storm cloud was beyond the gate. Kealin turned the ship, moving it upward as he left the straight path that led him to the light and went upward toward the stream.

As he neared the stream, he saw the forms of bodies. He did not recognize them at all. Many were older, gray with years. Others were younger but seemed to have suffered grievous injuries. Then, he saw children of all ages, and he tried to take a deep breath but could not. He scanned, looking for his younger brother, but there were so many. He pushed the ship into the stream of souls, and like he was parting a river, the opaque forms bent around the bow of the *Aela Sunrise*. He ran to the front of the ship, the stream flowing behind him toward the dark gateway. He had hoped he would still find them.

"Evurn! Aeveam!" he shouted. "Taslun!" He did not know if his brother was here, but he had to see. "Jesia!"

He fell to the deck of the ship and began to cry. He did not know what actions he was taking, but he truly felt broken in thought, unable to focus. He stood back up, looking over the edge. By chance, he saw her. He saw Aeveam. He reached down into the stream of the soils and grasped her by her arm, pulling her up and out of the stream. Her injuries were still present, the gaping holes left in her abdomen and chest by Iouir's blade. She was aware, looking at him, but seemed to be in a trance. As she made motions of breathing, her wounds seemed to fill with white light.

"I will take you back to the living realm in time.

Your wounds will heal. I only must get you from this place!"

He looked back over the edge. "Jesia! Evurn!" he cried out.

The souls beneath him began to wail, reaching up to grab him, and he recoiled back, drawing *Vrikralok*.

"I can strike you from this realm. Stay away from me!"

He questioned what he was saying but did not think about it for too long. He looked back to Aeveam. She still tried to breathe, but the white wounds had now healed.

"Jesia, come to me—" he shouted, but stopped. He spotted Evurn. The shadow elf passed under the bow of the ship, and Kealin dove over the side, dipping his hand into the stream of souls and feeling a burning sensation take over him. His hair began to grow greatly, and he felt as if his vitality was sucked from him. He was aging rapidly. He grasped the shadow elf by his leg and dragged him on board. His wounds seared with white fire and began to heal.

He was passing up the river in a sense of time. He had to come across Jesia. He had seen her fall. Iouir must have struck her. He feverishly watched the stream, watching for a sight of her.

"Jesia!"

But he did not see her. He kept watching, hoping he would see her spirit to pull her back to life, but he didn't. The *Aela Sunrise* came to the end of the river, running up against a wall of black clouds. He saw a form within it, and he ran back to the helm. Strangely, his hair was longer. He looked at his skin. He looked the same, but his nails had grown greatly in length. He had aged significantly, but due to his elven blood, he was still as strong as before, untouched unlike if he was part of the race of men. He passed over the stream of souls, but he did not see Jesia. Perhaps she had not fallen. If Iouir had only used that image to distract him, Jesia was still alive.

He turned the ship from the stream and began toward the light. He looked at Evurn and Aeveam, taken from the stream. He prayed that they would not die upon leaving this place, but there was another he still had to face.

As he pushed the *Aela Sunrise* toward the portal to the living realm, he noticed the ship was moving faster, as if they were descending back toward the Glacial Seas. A rolling mass of dark clouds passed between them and the light.

"Kealin, elf and Dwemhar of the living realm, you pass from my realm taking that which has been ordered to me. I tried to use you, yes, but it was to stop who was known as Iouir. I knew that evil. All was as you understood it, but I did not haunt you. My power was taken by Iouir, and the gods were mistaken. He channeled the energies of the downfall of his people, those who attempted to ascend to take a place beyond the gods. I worked with his kin at a time well before now, but all that transpired were the workings of the last Dwemhar upon the living realm. The great prophecies of the Stormborn and your own were real by their own regard for purposes that were misconstrued and corrupted in the end. We cannot right these wrongdoings, but your hand is needed in the living realm. A darkness comes for all gods, a threat of imbalance. I must take that which you have stolen from me."

From the dark clouds came a hand wrapped in rolling ice. The embrace of Vankou had come just as death felt to Kealin in the living realm. He felt the cold, the sudden gasping winds from the god. He ran from the helm and brandished *Vrikralok*.

"They are not yours! I have taken them back. I will not allow you to take them."

"Kealin, you threaten a great imbalance, one that will not end here. They should not have died; nothing should have happened as this. But they did. Kealin, you cannot attack a god of the North."

"You are not of the North. You are of lies. I had your hand upon me, the hand of Vankou. You are my enemy."

The god laughed. "Is not death the enemy of all life? You are wise in some form, Kealin. While the voices upon your mind were not me, my hand was upon you. Yes, Iouir was the enemy of all gods, but he would have succeeded in much without your intervention. In some ways, I, the Itsu Priest, and Iouir all used one another for our own ends. But you, your purpose was not to go south for your sister. You were to die much sooner than now, or so as I saw it. You released much upon the lands, Kealin. With Iouir dead, the Itsu Priest will destroy that which you know. The coming war of the gods will wreck the lands, and upon the waking of the Great Poet, the world shall face cataclysms! In the wake of the dead, I will become supreme. I wait for that day."

The *Aela Sunrise* was nearly to the light beyond the billowing clouds of Vankou.

"Now, I will take back what you stole and allow you the madness in which you return to."

The hand of Vankou once again reached for Evurn and Aeveam. For a moment, Kealin felt a release, a closure. He knew the ship was to pass through the realm. He felt all become still, peaceful, but then he focused, seeing the hand of Vankou, and beyond, the face of the god of death. He summoned *Vrikralok*. He shouted and then leapt from the deck of the *Aela Sunrise*, slashing across the hand of the god and driving *Vrikralok* into the black face of Vankou. Light flashed before his eyes. He saw what his life from birth until this moment was, and then blackness . . .

A lone feminine voice spoke. He could not see it nor anything. He felt as if he was floating.

You were betrayed, Kealin. Vankou never was against you, for he is the only god who cannot choose a side by his nature, but it cannot be denied what his nature truly is. Death is not an enemy but yet another path, a way toward the Great Poet. You gave in and struck down a god, and while you pulled those who had been taken from death back toward life, you did not need to kill your enemy, for he was not your enemy to strike. You took the purpose of a god. You gave into that power when peace was near. In those moments, a true terror is upon you. You now will suffer for giving in. Since you defeated death and struck a god, you will be punished. But we cannot keep you here, for you have defeated a god. You will fall from this place, and if your friends remain for you, survive beyond, but you shall take a share of the injuries that were upon those two you saved.

Truly, you will remain after that, but not with tribulation. Your Dwemhar powers have been struck from you for a time. Upon the new awakening of the Dwemhar, you will gain them back but loose your common speech. You will speak as did the shaman, but you will have a great hand in protecting the Saints to come, leading them to their victory against that which was awoken and allowed into the living realms. Many will die, but you will be as a light, forming a path in the darkness for others to act. In time, you will find death, but never will you die if death comes within the realms of the gods. You have sinned in the eyes of the gods, but your acts have bought you favor to some. The grace of the war god shines upon you. You are both cursed and blessed, Kealin of Urlas. In a way, a god and demon alike. Now, embrace what path is before you. It seems one of Meredaas may come to your aid. It is as I, Etha, proclaim in the name of the gods.

Kealin suddenly saw gray clouds above him. The wind whistled around him. He felt a searing pain in his neck, and blood poured from there and his abdomen. He felt through his broken armor and felt gaping holes in his chest. He had taken the injuries of those he had stolen from death. He saw a memory of the deaths of Aeveam and Evurn and then a flash of striking Vankou. He then felt as if he was stone, and his eyes saw no more. He only felt ice, along with the squeal of a familiar companion.

14
ICY SANCTUARY

"So, you return home. After so many years, Brethor."

Brethor stood just outside the Estate of Elinathrond, the house of his family, the Srvivnann. While he had returned a few days ago, his father had refused to speak to him until now. High in the mountains of the North, the city of Elinathrond was a massive fortress built by the snow dwarves, and as recent, had received many fleeing the armies of the Grand Protectorate. They were in the rose garden, a place favored by both Brethor and his father. News of Orolo's passing was an obvious shock to the family, and the realization that his son had been a part of the massive war to the far west was beyond surprising to his father.

"You wanted to speak with me, sir?"

"I did," his father said, snipping a rose and smelling it as he turned to look at Brethor. "You've grown greatly since you left, not in stature but in mind. I can sense you are beyond what you were or would have been had you not left. I talked with your mother. She says you left the life of a treasure hunter and ruffian and took a stalwart stand against the Grand Protectorate."

Brethor nodded, surprised by his father's words. He expected his father would be angry, or at worse, not accept him home.

"We did. All of us. Elves, Rusis, free men and women of Fadabrin. After the fall of Vueric and my brother, I was with a half-elf from the North, Kealin. We sought to free his sister, and in turn, then save his infant brother."

"Half-elf? What's so special about a half-elf?"

"He was Dwemhar, too."

His father paused, looking at him. "Dwemhar?"

Brethor nodded.

"Strange, I knew of very few who remained who still had our blood, and at extreme costs, we've been able to survive. I'm very interested in this Trell character. He could not come with you here?"

Brethor laughed slightly. "No, he had to remain to guard Fadabrin. After the disappearance of the undead, the Grand Protectorate marched on Fadabrin again. They held, but I'm not sure he can do so again."

"And this one you brought with you?"

"Ruak of Fikmark, a Scion of Starfall. A good friend and strong warrior."

"Scion of Starfall? So, he fought against the vampires?"

"He did."

His father stared at him. "I trust he knows of the Srvivnann, then?"

"He knows. He also is thankful he has been provided refuge in the Estate."

His father nodded.

"Your mother has told me much of this, but I would be foolish to not ask this. How are you handling these events?"

Brethor sighed. "I don't know. I lost not only one brother but another who I considered the same. He went north, likely to die."

"You speak of this half-elf?"

"Kealin of Urlas," Brethor said. He took a sip of an herbal tea and exhaled. "It's just, we all went through so much in such a little amount of time."

"Yet you remain, as does Ruak. A sign of events to come, my son. I feel the greater darkness coming. The sickness you told me about has been found in multiple elven and dwarven villages. The Grand Protectorate is starting to isolate those of magic. Wura has spoken. The god claims all will come here as a beacon of hope, a place of the last stand. I'm not sure how I feel of this, but the snow dwarves have refined the furnaces of the mountains. They form a barrier of spells to protect the city. I do feel, in time, you will be who protects them."

His father looked away. "I am old, Brethor. Even as long as I have been alive, I weaken. You will embrace the way of our family in time."

Brethor nodded. "I know. But not for many years,

my father. I still have much to learn under your teachings."

His father nodded and smiled before embracing him.

"Brethor, I'm happy to have you here. Your mother is as well. We will have a ceremony for Orolo, but then we will move on with his memory in our minds and look toward the future. Ruak has nowhere he can go, and in such, he will remain here as long as he wishes."

"I will tell him, Father."

Brethor noticed that several fairies suddenly flew down into the rose garden. While this was not uncommon, seeing as the fairies loved the roses, several of them fluttered about near Brethor and his father.

"What is it?"

Brethor did not know the language of the fairies, but his father's understanding of the Dwemhar arts allowed him to communicate with them.

"They say we are needed at the grove. They say to come with haste."

Brethor and his father made their way back into the Estate and walked quickly through the dining hall and took a corridor that led to the upper rooms. Passing through a bedroom that overlooked the mountains, they went to the balcony and took the route to the Foundry, a place of magic that strengthened the city. It was here, the heart of the mountain, the Furnace of the Dwarven Hand, rhythmically beat like that of a heart, producing magic to protect the city of Elinathrond. It was also here that the portal to The Grove was kept hidden away. The Grove was a place of supreme magic, a growing place for the staves of the elves of the ancient North, and as of recent, it had become the home to Meredaas and his kin.

Brethor and his father stood in the portal. "I hope there isn't another quarrel between the mermaids and the sirens," his father said. "That was quite a mess."

Brethor nodded and agreed but felt a different feeling suddenly upon his mind. He felt a familiarity, and though he was silent about it, he didn't think this had anything to do with their most recent refugees from the Glacial Seas. A nervous fear fell upon him.

Ahead, he saw several fairies fluttering just within the surf. The Glacial Seas came up to this island where in recent days, his father has allowed sirens and mermaids to settle just offshore.

Brethor sprinted ahead of his father, sending the fairies fluttering away just as he reached the form in the water. He gasped and then dropped to his knees. It was Kealin. His body was ice cold. In his chest were two fleshy wounds. His skin was darkening around his eyes.

"Kealin!" Brethor shouted.

His father knelt with him and put his hands on his hands and chest. "Somehow, he still clings to life."

"We must get him back to the Estate!" Brethor said. "The Priors can help him."

Brethor scooped the beaten and battered Kealin in his arms even as more fairies swarmed his dying body.

"The fairies must be keeping him alive," Brethor's father said.

As they ran back through the woods and to the portal, Brethor looked down at his friend, his brother. *What happened to you? What did you find in the North?*

Back at the Estate, Kealin was laid on the bed just up the landing from the Foundry. A young man attending the room moved out of the way as Brethor laid Kealin down.

"Cusis!" shouted Brethor. "Go! Go to the Priory. Get Master Nelkor, now!"

"Yes, Master."

As Cusis went downstairs, Brethor's father went to work. He went to a chest in the room and removed several vials.

"Blood of a Fairy Mother. This should help seal the wounds."

As he began to pour the liquid on Kealin's chest, his body seemed to react. The marks on his chest glowed red, but what little breathing Kealin was doing turned to a gasping attempt. Brethor's father placed his hands on Kealin again. Brethor watched as his father attempted to use his own powers, focusing the Dwemhar energies he was attuned to but had never mastered. The Scrivnann family's connection to such power was limited considering the vampiric blood.

"I can't see within his form. I don't know—"

"Father, he cannot die! We must do everything."

"We will, Brethor. But this is beyond my healing ability."

The door from the lower level slammed, and in came a man in white robes brandishing a large staff.

"Master Nelkor," Brethor said, bowing as he backed away.

"Who is this?" Master Nelkor questioned.

"He is who fought with my son," Brethor's father said. "A half-elf, half-Dwemhar who stood against the Grand Protectorate."

Master Nelkor was already moving forward as Brethor's father spoke. Lifting his staff, he bathed Kealin in a white light.

Ruak suddenly emerged in the room. "Kealin!" he shouted. "Brethor, what happened to him? What is wrong with him?"

The elf went to move forward, when Brethor grabbed him.

"Out of him, beast!" Master Nelkor shouted.

Kealin's body rose off the bed. His back arched, and a glowing blackness rippled from his skin. A voice thundered from within Kealin into the room. "Bane, darkness. I will not be—"

Master Nelkor gripped his staff with both hands. Several orbs of white struck Kealin, and his body surged with energy before dropping back to the bed.

"More of the blood you have already applied," Master Nelkor shouted.

Brethor took more of the vials and dumped them on his chest. Master Nelkor then reached into his robes, pulling out a pouch. He opened the strings and dusted Kealin with a silver powder that ignited. A purple flame overtook Kealin's chest. The wounds began to heal, and Kealin drew in a deeper breath.

"There was darkness within him, something near dead reaching out once more," Master Nelkor said. "That darkness has been defeated, but his body is battered. He took many injuries."

"He washed onto the shore of the grove," Brethor's father said.

"Then he is lucky to have survived the icy seas."

Kealin suddenly stopped breathing. Master Nelkor and Brethor both touched his neck.

"Master, please!" Brethor begged. "This man is like my brother. I already lost one."

The Prior lifted his staff once again, but the light did not grasp his body like before, as if the spell could no longer do anymore.

"Father!"

"Brethor, we have tried."

"We have not tried everything!"

Brethor stared at his father, and his father looked at him directly in the eyes.

"That is a path that not even you yourself have embraced. We cannot force it upon him."

"He must live," said Ruak. "If you can save him, Lord Raktho, do it, please! Few of our kind remain already," Ruak said, gripping Kealin's hand.

Brethor shook his head and looked down. "That is the only path for him now. He will die otherwise. How did our family start upon this path? The love between two? Upon death, the one would not be separated from the other, but the transformation did not complete due to our Dwemhar blood. It will preserve his life. He has no place elsewhere in the world now."

Ruak glanced at Brethor. "But Jesia?"

"We do not know if she even lives. If he wishes, we can go upon that path in time."

"He fades from life," Master Nelkor said.

"Father, now! You must."

Brethor's father looked down at Kealin as his skin darkened and his body became still. He leaned over his head and placed his forehead upon the half-elf.

As a red magic flowed between Kealin and Brethor's father, it wrapped around his throat and then into his mouth and nose. Kealin's body quivered. But then, his hands opened, and his entire body curled. Brethor went to Kealin's other side as Master Nelkor backed away. The red magic wrapping around his body suddenly converged over his forehead, and a white flash of fire covered his entire body for a second. Then, it was dark. Kealin began to breathe again.

"Now, we wait," Brethor said.

Kealin felt himself once more. He reached out and expected the cold embrace of the sea. But he did not feel it. He could feel the warmth of the air and the smells of sweet oils. He opened his eyes and saw a great light. He turned to his side and saw Jesia. She was lying next to him, smiling.

"You have been sleeping for some time."

He could hear the sea. He sat up, and she touched his chest. "Wait, stay here with me."

"We are in Fadabrin?" he asked.

She smiled.

"I miss you. I do. I am happy you are here. I love you, Kealin."

"This is a dream," Kealin said.

She smiled. "One I have had many nights. I will await you."

"But I am here." He nervously laughed. "Why do you have need to wait?"

"Darkness," she said. "You will defeat it. You have much to live for beyond the icy sanctuary you will soon awake in."

"I do not understand."

She kissed his lips.

He felt suddenly tired, feeling as if he was shaken out of a deep sleep. He opened his eyes again and saw out of a window ahead of him. He could see snowy mountains and a green ribbon of the polar lights. He turned to his side and noticed a blurry outline of a figure. The figure stood up.

"Kealin!" the voice said. The figure disappeared for a moment but then returned. By then, Kealin was seeing clearer. It was Ruak and Brethor.

He went to sit up, and surprisingly, he could.

Both Brethor and Ruak embraced him.

"Brother," Brethor said.

"We had thought you dead!" Ruak said.

"I don't understand," he told them. "Where is this? Where am I?"

"Elinathrond. Home of my family, the Srvivnanns," Brethor told him. "This is the Estate and soon to be a refuge to all of magic."

"I don't understand. I was falling. I was going to strike the water. I heard my narwhal."

"Tulasiro is well," Brethor said. "I have checked on the narwhal many nights. The sirens and mermaids care for it."

Kealin went to stand, and he felt slightly weakened. Brethor and Ruak gripped him. He looked across the room and saw his blades.

"You do not need those here, my friend," Ruak said.

Kealin was able to stand without their assistance. He felt his chest and noticed scars.

"Have I been asleep that long?"

"Nearly one full moon cycle," Brethor said.

Brethor directed him to the stairwell, and they went down to the hallway. Brethor motioned left, and they began toward a large library. Kealin could see massive windows ahead, and the smell of burning wood filled his nose. A young man approached them. "Master Brethor, I see he is up. I will get some coffee."

"Ah, Cusis, thank you. Make sure you bring enough cups," Brethor said with a wink.

"Of course, Master."

Kealin stopped, looking at Brethor. "I think I did it. I struck the god of death, and before that, I cannot tell you of the journey, because none will believe it. I saw an evil unlike anything before. Beyond that of the Itsu Priest."

"We know," said Ruak.

Kealin stared at them both.

"Let us go to the library."

Brethor motioned for them to continue walking. Kealin walked ahead. Turning the corner, he saw a massive fireplace and three figures looking out the window. He stopped walking and nearly fell forward.

Evurn, Aeveam, and Taslun stared at him.

"You defeated that which I could not, Brother," Taslun said.

Evurn and Aeveam walked toward him.

"You were both dead. It worked. I was able to, but I . . . I never made it out with the *Aela Sunrise*. Vankou."

Evurn embraced him, and at the same moment, Aeveam did the same.

"We are alive, Kealin," Aeveam said. "I do not know what you did, but I tasted death and I was upon the path to a great light when I saw your face."

Evurn placed his head upon Kealin's. "I, too, was upon the path. But then I saw you, and then we saw the shade of the god of death. You leaped from the ship as it passed out of the realm. Your sword struck the god, and then the next we knew, Taslun was standing on the deck of the *Aela Sunrise*."

Taslun nodded. "When I was knocked from the tower, I returned to the living realm but survived.

Tulasiro found me once you were brought here, and soon after, we found the *Aela Sunrise* upon the Glacial Seas."

Kealin shook his head. "I was not able to save anyone else. Even Master Rukes, he joined our parents, Taslun. I saw Calak. He told me."

Taslun smiled. "I miss him." He nodded, tears in his undead eyes. "But a new life is upon us."

"Evurn," Kealin said, "I wish to tell you of what happened after your fall, of Rasi."

Evurn's eye teared, "I know my dear friend was lost in the realm of the ascended."

"More, Rasi went to the top of the tower and once Iouir was stripped of immortality, avenged you by delivering a strike that saved me."

Evurn smiled, "She took the glory of that death to strike in a way I could not. A true serpent of a shadow elf! I am happy for Rasi!"

Kealin then looked at Brethor as two other strangers came into the room. "What actually happened to me?"

"My father and I found you," Brethor said. "You had many injuries. Your chest was punctured, and your neck was split open. Death took you. This is my father Lord Raktho of the Scrivnann. He and Master Nelkor of the Priors of Kel, the holy people of this city, worked to save your life."

"But shadow has taken you," Evurn said.

"I took the injuries of those I pulled from death," Kealin said.

"More than that," Master Nelkor interrupted.

"Something of the darkness you fought remained within you. I purged an entity of shadow from you, but I do not know what it was or where it came from. By the skills of our hands, we could not save you."

"But I am alive," Kealin pointed out. "I feel . . . renewed. I feel strange, but . . . I was told by the goddess Etha my Dwemhar powers have been taken until a time in the future, a coming of saints, or something of that wording. That is why I feel strange."

The sun was beginning to shine through the windows of the Estate.

"I must travel south," he told them. The shaman Iouir tried to harm Jesia. I must go to her. I have had enough cold." He laughed. As the light of the sun pierced through the room, Brethor and Lord Raktho covered themselves.

"The early sun of the new spring in the world is always the strongest," Brethor said.

"The warmth of new life. I have defeated death and stand with my friends. I am ready for the embrace of the sun upon my skin."

He stepped forward into the light, and a searing pain shot through his arm. He walked forward, and the light struck his face, and he recoiled back. The pain tore through his body, and he fell to his knees. Brethor and Evurn both gripped him from either side and pulled him back and into a chair.

His vision was blurry for a moment, and he struggled to catch his breath.

"What happened to me? What was that?"

Brethor and Evurn stared at him.

"Young elf, you defeated death, but death was to take you. I have spoken with Brethor, and I offer you this ahead of his words—I know much of your new condition. The shadow elves of the East have a way to reverse what has befallen you."

Kealin stared at Brethor. "What does he mean?"

"You have the blood of my kin, those who took the blood of the vampiric race in the old world."

"Vampiric?"

"It was that or your death," Lord Raktho said. "Your Dwemhar blood will protect you from its effects."

"But he said his power was stricken from him," Aeveam said.

Evurn nodded. "Then we have less time, but there is a way in the East. Kealin, you fought bravely, and you literally saved me from death. I will not call your condition death, but I can help you. With the thought before of the power of your blood to protect you, we were prepared to go south to find Jesia, but now, I can say with confidence, I, Aeveam, and you shall go east. We will pull you from the shadows of vampirism."

"And Jesia? She is alive?"

"She was," Ruak said. "Very near death, but she was taken by the healers into the mountains. The undead were guarding her."

"I will go, Brother," Taslun said. "I will guard her until you can return to her arms. That wretch of an ascended being could not kill me, and I will protect her.

The undead are building a necropolis within the Lost Sands region. She will be safe, Kealin. I will also look for our lost brother, if I find him, all of the undead will go with me to rescue him. I need not your assistance brother." Taslun smiled, "Go, and take care of yourself."

"Or you are welcome to stay here," Brethor said.

Kealin shook his head. "This is your home, Brethor. I will go east with Evurn and Aeveam. What of you, Ruak?"

Ruak bowed. "I already offered before you awoke. But the East is not a place friendly to my kind. It sounds a bit rougher even than the worst dwarven holds from what Evurn said."

Cusis brought out a serving of coffee, and they shared the hot drinks.

Kealin felt beyond awkward, looking around at everyone talking around him. He felt like he had been gone from them for longer than a month. He questioned if any of the events had happened. Recalling the past few years, his mind dwelt on those who had fallen, from Calak back at Dimn's temple to Alri and the coming of the gods of the North. Then recalling the events upon the Dwemhar tower and how a trusted friend, someone he had known his entire life, had used him and everyone around him for literally generations to the culmination of events where the ascended returned to the living realm. He had pulled two almost strangers from the river of souls, saving their lives, taking on their injuries, not to mention striking the god of death. He had lost all the power he had built through the years, that which had become like second nature to him, and then was turned into some form of vampiric beast. But he was alive. Around him in this room were some of the friends he had made, and two new friends willing to journey with him to the East.

He looked toward Brethor and then the Lord of the Estate, and then to Ruak laughing with them. Evurn and Aeveam stared out the windows as Taslun came up behind them. His brother was now of the undead, a new race upon the lands, and who now sought to go protect Jesia, knowing little of their relationship but willing and ready to do what was needed to keep her safe while he sought a cure to his affliction. Kealin then noticed the one other person not in conversation, the servant, Cusis. The servant noticed he was staring and then began to walk toward him, when Kealin waved him off and instead went to him.

"Is there something I can do for you, Master Kealin?"

"No, I just feel I need to talk to someone other than everyone else in this room."

"You are not imagining this," Cusis said with a smile.

Kealin stared down and laughed to himself. "How did you know those were my thoughts? Are you some type of seer?"

"No seer, just a servant. To be a servant, you must put others purely before yourself. I intend to be the best servant as were you, as I understand the story."

"I was no servant. I led more to death than—"

"To death? It seems you did quite the opposite, looking at the woman there and the shadow elf."

"Well, I guess those are two."

"It made a difference to those two. I was here when they arrived, of course. They were covered in broken and bloodied clothing. We expected they would need care as you, but they were healed. Brethor and the others figured out that you had taken their injuries, and then with their stories, it all made sense. I am of no proud house or long elven line. I do not even have magic, yet before you I stand, and I believe what is before me. Embrace it. Love those around you. Time is a shifting reality. In different aspects of our lives, it is but slow and seemingly like a frozen lake and other times it is a rushing river in the springtime. Hold on to each type of moment, because at any moment, your time can end."

Kealin looked at the young man, obviously wiser than Kealin had first thought. "A servant?"

Cusis smiled. "Indeed, Master Kealin. Now," he said, looking at Kealin's empty hands, "can I fetch you a chalice of coffee, or perhaps something a bit stronger? We do have the best wine in the northern reaches."

Kealin smiled. "I'd like some fresh air, actually."

"Perfect," Brethor said, joining them. "Let us walk."

Cusis bowed and backed away as Brethor and Kealin began down the hall.

"I know you did not expect to be as you are now. It is shocking, and you will transform in time if Evurn cannot stop it."

"I am sure he can. I doubt it'll be as simple as the words he says, but I have never been east."

Brethor led them around to the left and to a large atrium. Kealin noticed a massive dining hall to their left and then a large glass dome above their heads. The sky was a bit dark for it to be just past dawn. Brethor went to a closet and then returned with two cloaks.

"What sun there is I'd say is best for you to avoid for now."

Kealin covered himself in the cloak as Brethor led them outside. The sky was a dark pale-blue color. The dawn sky was indeed dark, and Brethor led them down into the courtyard.

"Elinathrond, a snow dwarf settlement, soon to be home to any who seek it. Elf, dwarf, Rusis, and all in between.

Kealin noticed immediately two large statues on either side of the door. Each held large spear-like weapons and almost looked alive in how detailed they were carved. He then looked out to rolling rooftops. There was a large stone circle to the right, and further, a city square and snow-covered buildings. Along the mountains that flanked the right side were dwarves moving along the rocks and even a tower built atop the mountain, high in the clouds.

"There isn't too much light up here," Brethor said. "It is good for those like my father who have fully embraced the bloodline of my family."

Kealin nodded, looking around at several random people who stared him up and down as they passed.

"Your story quickly spread. We did little to keep it secret, to be honest, but you are welcome here, Kealin, at any time."

"I thank you, Brethor." Kealin looked back to the Estate. "So that will be yours at some time?"

"I guess. I still must embrace the bloodline of the Scrivnann."

"Will you?"

"I hope the changing world will prevent that. Sensitivity to the sun is one thing, requiring blood, a bit different." Brethor smiled. "Kealin, my father turned you because of my wishing, and now, we are as brothers within my family. We will feel one another's pain at times. There is a connection between us now."

"Never thought something like this would happen to me."

"Small things. I never thought I'd have someone to call brother who slew a god, and about that particular act, is there nothing else to that? What did you fight in the North?" he asked.

"A cursed ascended being. The last Dwemhar attempting to take all the souls of the ascended returning. He was an old evil, an ancient evil. The warriors who fought him in the times before were legends whom I and Taslun were told of when we were very young. But, though he took many, I understand that still many of the Dwemhar will return, half-bloods or something like that, mixing with the races of the world in time. Safe from the evil that tried to devour them."

Brethor nodded. "I wonder what was within you when you came here, what evil that was?"

"I do not know. Iouir was destroyed. I was within the realm of the afterlife. All I can say is that I do feel cleansed, unlike any sensation before."

"That is your new gift . . . as I see it in a form," Brethor muttered. "I wonder of both our futures and how all of this will turn."

"I don't know," Kealin said. "Etha spoke of saints, that my power would be locked away until that time and then would return, and I would talk strange like the shaman I killed, actually. I don't understand it. I assume it is some time far from now."

"And the Dwemhar? The ascended? Will more of them come?"

"Their energies have returned; their souls came upon the living realm. In time, they will awaken, but of that, I really do not know. That is beyond us, my friend."

Brethor embraced him.

"Brother, I know you will not waste too much time here. I already heard Evurn mention to Aeveam you would be leaving very soon. I bid you take care of yourself on your journey east."

Kealin nodded and then looked back to see Evurn and Aeveam. Evurn was holding his blades.

As Kealin approached him, Evurn smiled. "You will be needing these where we go. I hope you still know how to use them without that Dwemhar power."

Kealin took the blades and brought them to his chest.

He had a flash of every event leading to this moment, and tears filled his eyes. He pushed back the tears, strapping his blades around his waist and drawing both of his blades. They had been cleaned and polished.

"A parting gift from the Scrivnann family," Taslun said, joining them outside. "By Evurn's command, the way is ready for you each to return to the Glacial Seas."

Kealin followed the others back through the halls and upstairs to the balcony and the walkway that went to the Foundry. He noticed a brightly burning flame to his right and several dwarves bowing to them as he passed by. They came to a large stone device, and after they had all joined hands within it, Kealin felt himself rushing through the portal and seeing only darkness for a moment. They emerged in a great forest where fairies jumped from place to place. Down a snaking path, they came to a grand display of starlight and the polar lights high above. The cold felt refreshing to him, and as he took a deep breath, he saw the masts of the *Aela Sunrise*.

Then, as if waiting for him alone, Tulasiro began rolling in the waves, much to the surprise of several mermaids who fled away.

Now, Tulasiro was missing the crown. The narwhal squeaked, but Kealin shook his head. "I cannot understand your words, but know I will return."

"And the servants of Meredaas will watch over the

brave Tulasiro, Kealin." The voice was sudden, but emerging from the waters was the mermaid who had saved him before. "Your path is east, or so the fairies have told me. Be on guard. The Shadowlands are not for the faint of heart. I will see you upon the Glacial Seas again, Kealin of Urlas."

"He'll be fine there," Evurn said confidently. He walked away from them and boarded the *Aela Sunrise*. Aeveam followed him.

Kealin turned to Ruak and Brethor, embracing both of them.

"My friends, my brothers, I will return here in time. Perhaps then we can put down our blades."

Ruak pushed him off. "Now, Kealin, warrior elf of legend, do not go getting too soft on me. You put down your blades and I'll be picking mine up and making sure I cut you really good."

Kealin laughed. "We can finish that duel!"

Brethor stared at them. "Good thing you're leaving, Kealin. I'd hate to constantly be patching you two up!"

They each shared a laugh before Kealin took a few steps back. He stared at both of them in the eyes and then smiled again, bowing slightly. He turned his look toward the *Aela Sunrise*.

As he stepped off the shore of the grove and onto the *Aela Sunrise*, Evurn immediately raised the sails of the ship and they were off. He looked back to Brethor and Ruak, and in a few moments, the protected realm of the grove faded from sight, and that was it.

. . .

They were sailing east. Dark clouds rolled over them. He joined Evurn and Aeveam at the helm.

"Shadowlands?" Kealin asked.

"Not only a dark place from the ash, it is not like any other place in the living realm," Evurn said. "But finally, I'll admit I miss it. There is much I left there."

"Well," Aeveam said, "I have only heard stories about it for years. We'll see if such types like Evurn are plentiful there."

Evurn laughed. "Yes, I guess we will."

Kealin saw something at the bow of the ship. He ran up to the front of the vessel, noticing a break in the waters. He leaned over the edge as Tulasiro jumped just within reach of him. He reached down and brushed the narwhal's hide before Evurn turned their course slightly. The narwhal squeaked wildly and then disappeared into the depths.

I will return to you, my friend.

The wind blew upon him, and he heard a slight tune to the sounds. It was a cold wind, frigid upon his skin, but he no longer heard the haunting sounds he had before. The dreary feeling upon him was gone. He looked to the east, seeing a single splinter of light in the clouds, and tucked his cloak around him. His journey was complete. He had fought the darkness that was foretold to him by the darkness itself. The ascended were once again to breathe the breath of life within the living realm, and in time, he would hold Jesia once again. He wondered what awaited him now in the Shadowlands of the East.

. . .

The end...

The Rogue Elf #7 and the continuation of Kealin's epic continues with *'Of Shadows and Blood'*

Join my mailing list to assure you are notified the moment it is available!

AUTHOR'S NOTE

Happy times, right? :)

At one time, this was the end of an older series called *'Half-Elf Chronicles'* but it is a far from the end of Kealin's story.

His new... condition... has quite a few challenges and as of the writing of this in April 2021, I'm nearing completion of *The Rogue Elf #9*.

Vampirism has many not-so-obvious advantages...

Considering that Evurn and Aeveam are becoming much more important characters in the coming books, this is a good time to familiarize yourself with them by reading the *Stormborn Saga*, if you haven't. You can find those books on my website or by simply searching for it on Amazon.

That said, it isn't required reading by any means but if you've read this far into this series, I think you'll enjoy the other books, too! :)

While there have been lots of up and downs in these first few books, you're in for a lot more fun and a growing epic-ness as you journey into the Shadowlands of the East!

I'm thrilled to be sharing these stories with you. I'm so thankful to have you as a reader and I can't wait for our adventures to continue.

Thank you for reading,

Jeremy

**Join my mailing list if you haven't yet:
www.subscribepage.com/therogueelf

For a complete list of titles please go to:
www.authorjtwilliams.com/series-timeline.html

GET YOUR FREE ROGUE ELF SHORT STORY!

Bloodblade is a unique story set in the *Dwemhar Realms* that takes place just before *Seer of Lost Sands*. Beware, it's brutal.

Kealin doesn't put up with kidnappers… in fact, he deals with them quite well.

Of course, there is no charge for this. I'll add you to my mailing list and you'll never miss a new release!

Tap below and you'll get it sent to your inbox soon! www.subscribepage.com/therogueelf

Printed in Great Britain
by Amazon